Praise for the Y

"If you haven't read this series yet, I highly recommend giving it a go. The mystery will delight you, and afterward you'll be itching to start a knitting or crochet project of your own."

—*Cozy Mystery Book Reviews*

"A cozy mystery that you won't want to put down. It combines cooking, knitting and murder in one great book!"

—*Fresh Fiction*

"The California seaside is the backdrop to this captivating cozy that will have readers heading for the yarn store in droves."

—*Debbie's Book Bag*

Praise for Betty Hechtman's National Bestselling Crochet Mysteries

"Will warm the reader like a favorite afghan."

—National bestselling author Earlene Fowler

"Get hooked on this new author . . . Who can resist a sleuth named Pink, a slew of interesting minor characters and a fun fringe-of-Hollywood setting?"

—*Crochet Today!*

"Fans . . . will enjoy unraveling the knots leading to the killer."

—*Publishers Weekly*

"Classic cozy fare . . . Crocheting pattern and recipe are just icing on the cake."

—*Cozy Library*

Praise for the Writer for Hire Mysteries

Books by Betty Hechtman

Yarn Retreat Mysteries

Yarn to Go
Silence of the Lamb's Wool
Wound up in Murder
Gone with the Wool
A Tangled Yarn
Inherit the Wool
Knot on Your Life
But Knot for Me
Knot a Game
Knot Dead Again

Crochet Mysteries

Hooked on Murder
Dead Men Don't Crochet
By Hook or By Crook
A Stitch in Crime
You Better Knot Die
Behind the Seams
If Hooks Could Kill
For Better or Worsted
Knot Guilty
Seams Like Murder
Hooking for Trouble
On the Hook
Hooks Can Be Deceiving
One for the Hooks
Killer Hooks

Writer for Hire Mysteries

Murder Ink
Writing a Wrong
Making It Write
Sentenced to Death

Knot Dead Again

BETTY HECHTMAN

BEYOND THE PAGE
PUBLISHING

Acknowledgments

Thank you to Bill Harris for his editing expertise and everything else. I wouldn't be where I am without my agent, Jessica Faust. Dar Albert keeps coming up with great covers.

Thank you to my loyal blog commenters, Linda Osborn, Patty Jenkins, Sally Morrison, Miss Merry and Chkntza. And top fans Valley Weaver, Melissa Phillips Cook and Catherine Guerin. Thanks to Mirium Lubet for posting pictures of my books on Facebook.

Thank you to Samantha for the story about singing softly to her class to get their attention.

I am eternally grateful to my writers' group of Joan Jones, Jan Gonder, Linda Bruhns and Jack Warford. We have long since gone our separate ways, but without their encouragement and help with my first book, it might never have happened.

When I was writing this book, I was concerned that the storm might seem too extreme. But then everything changed when California got the winter rains. There were floods, cars washed down streets, rockslides covering roadways and houses slipping off of cliffs. What happened at Vista Del Mar seemed completely possible.

My research trip up to the Monterey Peninsula and the town that stands in for Cadbury by the Sea was extra fun because Max and Jakey were there. Lucky for us it was in the summer when there wasn't much worry for storms.

And of course, thanks to Burl for all your support and acting as my taste tester for the recipe.

Chapter 1

"Feldstein, put that cop out of his misery. Stop telling him you have one foot out the door of that town that reminds me of a chocolate bar. Tell him the truth—that you're going to stay there putting on those yarn meetups at that place across the street," Frank said. He took a breath and I heard the rustle of paper, letting me know he was having this phone conversation while he ate one of his usual sub sandwiches. I wasn't sure if it counted as lunch or dinner, but knowing Frank it was probably a snack. It was still afternoon where I was on the edge of the Monterey Peninsula, but early evening in Chicago, where he was.

"You still there?" he asked and I let out an *uh-huh*. "And tell the poor guy exactly what feelings you have for him. You know, that you, you know . . ." He let out a groan.

"Can't say the word, can you?" I teased.

"Okay, Feldstein, then let's hear you say the word," Frank said, adding a chortle.

"I don't have to say the word." I tried not to sound defensive. "He probably knows how I feel. It's not the word that counts anyway. It's about actions," I added. I hardly wanted to talk about my personal life with Frank. He was a PI and my ex-boss—though the temp job had only lasted for a few weeks. It was my favorite of all the temp jobs I'd had, and so when I went to Cadbury by the Sea, California, we kept in touch. He had become my go-to when I got in the middle of a murder investigation. This time he had called me.

"We kind of got off the subject of your call," I said.

"Right. Yeah, I called to thank you for the box of muffins, but figured I'd make it a two-fer and give you some advice. I've been hearing about that guy and how you didn't want to break his heart when you left. He's a cop and I bet he could take it. That is, if you did actually leave."

I started to protest and bring up my history of not sticking with professions and stopped myself. I knew that Frank was right. Not that I told him that exactly, I just ended the call.

Once I'd acknowledged that Frank was right about how I felt about Dane Mangano and that I wasn't really on the verge of leaving, I wanted to do something about it right away. I would be brave and tell him how I felt.

I hadn't seen him for several days and I assumed it was due to his schedule being all over the place. But I was sure where I could find him now. Dane lived down the street from me and had converted his garage into a workout room with mirrors and mats. He used it for his own workouts and to give karate lessons to local teens to keep them out of trouble. No matter how his schedule varied, Tuesday afternoons were set aside for the karate kids.

I tried to make it to the kitchen door, but Julius rushed in front of me and blocked me. The black cat looked up at me with a plaintive meow. It had nothing to do with him being sad at my leaving and everything to do with his needing a snack, immediately. I was still new to living with a cat. But one thing I had figured out was that calling him my cat was incorrect. It was more like I was his human.

"Sorry, buddy, but this time you're going to have to wait," I said as I walked around him. He jumped up on the counter and let out another meow, as if he couldn't believe what I was doing. I left without looking back, afraid his pleading eyes would get to me. I had to do this before I lost my nerve.

I marched down the street imagining what I would say to Dane. I hoped it would come across better than my attempts at flirting. We both agreed they were laughable. But I worried that me being mushy would come across as clumsy and funny. Maybe the best thing to do was to assume that he would laugh. Then I would laugh too and all would be fine.

I could hear the kids shouting out karate noises before I opened the door. They all stopped when I walked in.

I wasn't planning to profess my feelings in front of them and had thought I would quickly pull him aside and then spill my emotions. I was so worked up that I started to say his name and that I wanted to speak to him, only to see that he wasn't there.

"Where's Dane?" I said, looking at the five teenagers all dressed in white pants and kimono tops tied with multicolored sashes. They all looked at each other and then one of them acted as spokesperson.

"He's in the house," the gangly boy said.

I made a move toward the door. "Maybe you should text him," another of the teens said.

For a moment the idea of texting my feelings seemed more appealing—i.e., easier than saying the words directly. I shook my head. No, I was not going to take the easy way out and propelled myself out the door, walking across the backyard, anxious to find him before I lost my nerve.

His house was small like mine. The back door was unlocked and I walked into his kitchen, which smelled of simmering spaghetti sauce. Along with teaching them karate, he fed them. His sauce was the best and the smell temporarily distracted me as I imagined eating a plate of noodles smothered in it. I thought I heard voices coming from the living room and went down the short hall that led to the front room. And then I stopped in my tracks. Dane was sitting on the couch next to a woman. Not exactly next to, as she had her head on his shoulder and he had his arm around her.

All I could think as I turned on my heel and fled was thank heavens I had not texted him.

I went into my house only long enough to give Julius the treat he'd missed, which always took longer than I wanted due to all the unwrapping and rewrapping of the can of stinky cat food. But there was no reason for him to suffer just because I felt like an idiot, even though I had not actually said a word. I grabbed my purse and car keys and drove straight into downtown Cadbury, glad that I had a meeting about the upcoming retreat.

I did not notice the sky or the weather, but then it was almost always cloudy and cool, so it slipped into the background even when my mind wasn't on something else, like wondering who she was and why they seemed so cozy. Maybe I had simply waited too long and Dane had found somebody who seemed a lot less hesitant than I was.

He had been the one to mention living together, but I had held back. I had a lot of excuses, like my parents planned to visit, but maybe the truth was that I had been afraid of commitment. Notice I said *had been* afraid. I had gone to his place ready to spill it all. Clearly, our timing was off. The shock I had felt was already wearing off and it occurred to me that if it was so easy for him to take up with someone else, maybe it was good that I had never told him how I felt. I took a deep breath and let it out as I tried to recover.

I parked my yellow Mini Cooper in front of Cadbury Yarn, barely remembering to curb my wheels on the sloping street, and rushed up the steps of the pale blue bungalow that had been turned into a yarn shop.

The days were short at this time of year and it was hard to tell if it was getting dark or the sky was really that leaden color. This was the season when all those cloudy skies actually could drop rain. Because it happened for such a limited time, it was always a surprise.

I forced myself to push away all my thoughts about Dane and focus on the matter at hand. That was how I dealt with disappointments and flops. Push thoughts of it out of my mind and move on. The meeting was about the upcoming weekend's retreat. I had gotten a late start on making all the arrangements because the holidays had interfered. But now it was January and the remnants of tinsel hanging on the pine tree outside the post office looked tired. It always amazed me how wonderful all the decorations and lights looked before Christmas and then how desolate they appeared after.

The interior of the shop seemed extra cheerful and inviting after the gloom outside. The living room of the converted bungalow was the main sales area and there were cubbies of yarn stacked up against every wall. Several revolving displays offered knitting and crochet tools. A rack of books and magazines sat next to a table covered with scarves and sweaters for sale. Crystal Smith was behind the cashier counter working with a customer. She had her usual colorful attire of layered shirts of assorted colors over black jeans. One of her ears had a large silver hoop earring and the other a dangling teardrop. She was right. Who says you have to wear a matched set? I envied how she did her makeup. She wore a lot, with her eyes outlined in dark eyeliner, but it looked good. When I tried to emulate it, I ended up looking like a raccoon. She glanced up as I came past and smiled, then pointed to the former dining room at the back of the small house.

An oval wooden table dominated the space and had high-backed chairs around it. There was an assortment of knitting needles and crochet hooks in several decorated coffee cans in the middle of the table, ready for any customers who wanted to try out some of the yarn. By now I understood why. There was no way to really tell how a particular yarn was going to be to work with or look when it was knitted or crocheted. It was even harder with all the self-striping and variegated colors that were popular.

I felt my thoughts going back to the image of Dane and that woman. Despite my resolve, I went right back to thinking about how embarrassing it would have been if I had blurted out my feelings and then seen her. I grabbed an errant ball of yarn sitting on the table and a pair of knitting needles. I was not an accomplished enough knitter to be able to think of something else while I knitted, so the image faded as I put all my attention into casting on some stitches and then knitting back across them. There was just a fleeting thought that maybe it was a sign that I should leave Cadbury. There were the offers of my mother for culinary school in Paris or that detective academy in Los Angeles. I shoved the thought away. I had a retreat to prepare for and put on. Then I could think about what I was going to do.

"What are you making?" Madeleine Delacorte said as she approached the table.

"Just a swatch to see what the yarn looks like," I said, not wanting to tell her the real reason I was looking for something to distract myself. We both looked at the swatch, which was a tangle of stitches, and I pushed it away and invited her to sit.

Madeleine and her younger sister Cora were the local royalty in the small California town. The Delacorte family owned all kinds of real estate, including Vista Del Mar, the hotel and conference center where I put on the retreats. It had seemed that the two women were the end of the family line, but it had been uncovered that their late brother had a love child who happened to be Crystal's mother Gwen. It had not exactly just popped up out of nowhere. I had been the one to figure it out and it had stirred things up in the small town for a while.

I was still an outsider as far as the locals were concerned. How long did you have to live there before that changed? My move to Cadbury had been a last resort when the temp job working for Frank at the detective agency had fallen apart and I was faced with moving back in with my parents. They were both doctors and I was a thirty-something drifting from career to career. I couldn't take the worried looks and the reminders that I was basically a disappointment. Not married, no children and fleeting careers.

My father's sister, Joan, another black sheep in the family, had used her earnings as mostly a commercial actress to buy the house in Cadbury and start a new chapter in her life putting on yarn retreats. She had offered me her guest house—well, converted garage. There was not even a moment's pause before I accepted my aunt's offer. My mother called it running away, which it probably was.

I had expected it to be temporary while I put my life back together. Since one of my many past careers had been creating desserts for a bistro, I had used the experience to get a job as a dessert chef for the Blue Door restaurant, and on the side I baked muffins for the various coffee places in town. All those cloudy skies made coffee a big thing. Even when my aunt was killed in a hit-and-run accident and left everything to me, I thought I would just handle the retreat she had already had on the books and sell everything. By then I had made friends and met Dane. I tried to push the thought of him back out of my mind, but it just wouldn't go. If Dane had just been another guy, I might have left it as a fling and then let it go. There was no question there was a lot of chemistry between us. But there was more. I always said that he had character to spare. What else could you say about a guy who had an alcoholic mother, an unknown father and had been the one to take care of his mother and sister. He had put on a front of being a bad boy while he was doing things like helping his sister shop for her first bra. His mother and sister still showed up whenever their lives went south and he took them in without a second thought. All of that could have given him a serious personality, but he was fun and playful— at least with me.

While his cop duties were mostly telling tourists to slow down and reminding people to pick up after their dogs, he tried to stop trouble before it started with the karate lessons. Thinking of the karate lessons reminded me of the spaghetti he made for them and me. My mouth started to water at the thought. I was an expert at dessert but had little interest in preparing what came before it.

I looked down at the abandoned swatch and considered unraveling the lopsided stitches.

"Is anything wrong?" Madeleine asked, bringing me back to the present. I was hardly going to burden her with what had just happened. She was just coming out of her shell after a very sheltered life and I was more conscious of being her support than expecting her to be mine. She accepted my denial easily and turned the subject to the upcoming retreat.

"I've been thinking," she said. "Since I have been helping with the retreats, I should be listed on the staff."

It took me a moment to process her request. It was true that she had participated in the last retreat I put on. It had been her idea to make it a mystery weekend and that she would take the part as Mrs. Maple. She had made a point that part of all the new things she was experiencing included having a job—even if it was pretending to be an imaginary detective. Not only did I like her, but was also indebted to her and her sister for letting me keep the deal on rooms they had forced the manager to give my aunt.

I appreciated how she had taken my uncovering the new branch of her family. Her sister Cora was still struggling with it, but Madeleine seemed happy to find out she had a niece and was developing a relationship with Crystal.

"I think it's a great idea," I said. "How about we call you the Director of Hospitality."

Her face lit up. "That's perfect. I promise to do a good job. I like the idea of being a career woman, even if it is a little late." She had taken a seat and pulled out a crochet hook and was absently making a long chain of stitches. "I think I'll stay at Vista Del Mar during the retreat. You never know when my services might be needed."

"I'll make sure there is a room for you," I said. I looked at her for some sort of acknowledgment, but it seemed like she was thinking about something else.

"You know that Milton is coming for the weekend." Her voice sounded all fluttery.

"Is he coming for the yarn retreat again?" I said, rummaging through the file of papers I had to see if he was on my list.

Milton Carruthers, also known by his pen name of Talulah Barnsdale, was a mystery writer who had come to the yarn retreat mystery weekend. He had been smitten with Madeleine and they spent time together. He seemed nice enough, but I was suspicious of his motives. She was a wealthy heiress and he was a writer who might have his eye on her bank account.

"We've kept in touch," she said with a blush showing in her face. "He was here for a writers' weekend as one of the presenters. He was busy the whole time and we just had a couple of walks together and coffee in the café. He said he was coming to work on his book and to see me."

My trouble antennae went up. I would have to keep an eye on

things. She was a grown woman who should be able to look out for herself, but I still felt protective of her.

"It's going to be wonderful to see him again," she said, fluttering her eyes. "I'd like to invite him to dinner at my home, but I hope Cora won't ruin everything. She thinks everyone is after our money."

I didn't want to say it was my concern too.

I looked toward the cashier area in the yarn shop and saw that Crystal was talking to her teenage daughter. It seemed more like listening. By the body language it appeared Stephanie was upset about something. And whatever she was saying was not pleasing her mother. It was hard to imagine Crystal as the mother of two teenagers. She was about my age, but then she'd gotten an early start. She'd run off with Rixx Smith, self-proclaimed rock god, and stayed with him long enough to have the two kids before it was more than he could deal with and he found a younger replacement. Crystal and the kids had come back to Cadbury and moved in with her mother. Crystal had told me that her mother had been great and there were no *I told you sos*. Gwen had simply made Crystal and her children feel welcome. Crystal was an expert yarn crafter like her mother and helped her run Cadbury Yarn.

Even when Gwen found out that she was a Delacorte, things didn't change too much by her choice. She wasn't fond of the sisters and was accustomed to her life as it was. She probably would have ignored the whole family situation except for Crystal's son Cory. Her grandson had been working at Vista Del Mar and developed a love for the place before he found out who his great-grandfather was. Knowing the place was in his blood only made him feel more attached.

Crystal caught my eye and rolled hers as her daughter continued on. Madeleine was crocheting a row of stitches over the length of chain stitches. Her yarn skills were a little behind mine and it felt like she was more concerned about being part of the group than learning to turn out sweaters.

"That was a lot," Crystal said when she finally joined us. "I should have figured the rough time I gave my mother would come back to haunt me." She let out her breath. "It's just a little funny about the difference. I was on my mother's case for being so stodgy with her clothes." Madeleine and I both looked at Gwen, who was helping a customer fix a dropped stitch. It was hard to connect her with Crystal, who always looked like a kooky rainbow. Gwen wore neutral colors and sensible shoes. Her earrings always matched, as did her socks. There was a feeling of sturdiness about her. "Stephanie went on about how embarrassed she is by how I dress. She actually said I should grow up and stop looking like a goofball," Crystal said.

She looked down at her attire. "How could I have a daughter who is so not fun." She pulled out a chair and sat down with a sigh. "And that's nothing compared to how she and Cory are both reacting to my dating. I kept it on the down-low for a long time, but it got ridiculous. Cory walked in when Eddie and I were kissing. Geez, I'm thirty-seven, not dead," she said.

I was surprised at her kids' reactions, and at her upset. I always assumed that her daughter was glad to have such an interesting mom. As for the dating part, it had never occurred to me her kids would object. Then I imagined seeing my mother cuddling up to some man. Before I really thought about that image, I went off topic and realized that would mean my father was somehow out of the picture, and I got caught up in thinking about how that would happen. My mother wasn't the type to cheat, so they'd have to be divorced or he'd have to be . . . I couldn't say the word even in my head.

Crystal let out a sigh and a chuckle. "But I probably would have been the same if my mother had been all over a boyfriend." She put her hands on the table. "Enough about my issues. How are you two?"

Madeleine fluttered her eyes again and smiled. "Do you remember Milton from the mystery retreat? He's coming for the weekend," she said, blushing again. "He's just going to be a guest of the hotel this time."

Crystal patted her great-aunt's hand warmly. "That's wonderful."

She turned to me and I must have had a sour expression. I hadn't wanted to, but all this talk of romance and dating had made me think about Dane again and that woman. "Is something wrong?" she asked.

I was going to gloss over it, but then decided to get it off my chest. Madeleine and Crystal were like my girlfriends, and wasn't that who you were supposed to tell your troubles to? "I saw Dane with another woman," I blurted out. I wanted to sound like I was cool with it, but somehow it came out that I clearly wasn't.

"Oh," Crystal said, her mouth pursed in discomfort.

"Then you know about it, about her?" I said.

"Not exactly that she was with Dane," Crystal began. "I know who she is. She's his high school girlfriend. He took it pretty hard when she left and now she's back. I certainly know about leaving and coming back. Suddenly Cadbury doesn't look so suffocating after the world outside shows its true colors." Crystal toyed with a pair of knitting needles. I knew that she was referring to her own return when her marriage exploded. "Her name is Stacy Werner. She worked at one of the Pebble Beach resorts and ended up getting a job as a hostess on private flights. I heard she married some rich Silicon Valley type. Since she's back, I guess it didn't work out."

I was a little overwhelmed with the news of who she was and what it meant. She was the girl who got away and who he now had a second chance with. There was no fighting that. I would just have to deal with it as I had when things had not worked out with jobs and such. I was good at pivoting and I would have to do it again. In that moment, even though I didn't say anything, I started to consider that this upcoming retreat might be the final one. I would do what had been in the back of my mind since I'd come to stay with my aunt—make plans to leave for real. All the more reason to make this upcoming retreat the best possible. Go out with a bang.

I pulled myself together and even sat a little taller. "Enough about romance, let's talk about the retreat."

"Hey," Cloris Dunphy said, greeting us as she came up to the table.

She was tall and slender, wearing her blue blazer with her name tag, which was her uniform as assistant manager of Vista Del Mar.

She had worked her way up to the position and then had almost lost it recently. The job meant everything to her. She had always been a help with my retreats and in the process had become a friend. She was there wearing both hats.

Chapter 2

"I'm afraid I can't stay long," Cloris said. "I have to get back to Vista Del Mar and get more instructions from Mr. St. John. He's going to a seminar for hotel managers in San Diego. He's never left me in charge before." I could imagine how that was going. Kevin St. John viewed himself as being more than the manager. He was more like the lord of the place. Leaving anybody but himself in charge would be a problem for him.

We promised to make it quick and I launched into my spiel. "This retreat is going to be a little different than the ones I have put on before. This time it's designed for novice yarn crafters," I said. I went on about the appeal of yarn craft to a new audience who had a different view of it. They were interested in quicker manageable projects they could show off to their friends.

Crystal took out a couple of cloth bags and said the participants would have everything to make the project she had come up with. "And fingers crossed, they'll be able to finish it over the weekend."

Then I showed off a sample of the tote bags each attendee would get. Since the accommodations at Vista Del Mar were rather spare, I liked to give them some luxury touches like fancy chocolate and lavender sachets to tuck under their pillows. The toiletries Vista Del Mar provided were very basic, so I added small bottles of nice shampoo and shower gel along with a small bar of fancy soap.

"My part in all this is to tell you who else is going to be at Vista Del Mar for the weekend. It's a small crowd since January is always a slow time of year. That's why we shut down most of the buildings for maintenance. Actually, there are only two other groups coming. And then there are a few individual guests," Cloris said.

"Like Milton," Madeleine chimed in, and Cloris acknowledged her comment with a nod before going back to talking about the other groups.

Trent Nicholson is putting on his Getting Unstuck program again.

13

I'd describe him as a charismatic psychologist. I can't imagine that any of his workshops will interfere with yours," she said, looking at me. "The other one is a diet group. Dorothy Spenser has a group coming for a program she calls something like the Last Diet. There are some logistics to deal with because her group has a special menu and is getting their own food delivered. I have to work it out with the kitchen staff so that their meals and eating times will not interfere with the preparation of the rest of the guests' meals."

"Madeleine is officially part of the staff for my retreats," I said. "She's going to be listed as the Director of Hospitality." Madeleine beamed with pride and the other two gave her a little applause. I asked her if she wanted to say anything and Madeleine stood up.

At first, the other two complimented her on her denim outfit. Part of Madeleine's making up for lost time was discovering the wonders of the blue fabric. I had to admit that it shaved years off her appearance and made her look cute compared to the way she used to dress in stodgy suits. Today's outfit was a pair of straight-leg jeans and tucked-in white shirt, topped with a jean jacket.

"I intend to take my job seriously," she said. "I can help out when people check in and at meals." Then she sat down.

Cloris looked at her watch. "I have to go. Final instructions and all." Her expression dipped. "If you want to know the truth, I am a little nervous. What happens if something goes wrong?" We all promised to help her and she smiled with relief. "You have no idea how much it means."

The meeting broke up with Cloris's departure. When I walked outside, a damp breeze blew off the ocean with some raindrops, which surprised me. I was from Chicago, where it rained year-round, but here on the edge of the continent, it only rained in the winter and usually not that much. And somehow it always got me off guard. My fleece jacket was hardly rainwear, but I pulled it tighter and walked up the slope to Grand Street, the main drag in the small town.

I had successfully kept Dane out of my mind until a police cruiser passed me and I automatically squinted trying to see if it was him driving. The car was gone before I could tell. It was hard to believe that he would drive by without stopping, but then maybe he had no idea what to say. Would he just disappear from my life? It all felt strange and unsettling. All this time, I had been so busy ruminating about my life and fighting acknowledging how I really felt about him, it had never occurred to me that he would suddenly have somebody else.

I rushed up the steps to the porch that ran along the side of the Blue Door restaurant. The white wood-frame structure had been a residence at one time and there had been only small changes to make it into an eatery. The inside felt warm and inviting compared to drizzle. Lucinda Thornkill was standing at the front counter taking a reservation on the phone. I felt a little sloppy in my jeans and T-shirt with my hair pulled into a scrunchie when I saw her sunny yellow dress, which I knew had a designer label. Her blondish hair was in a short easy-care style. I instinctively pressed my lips together, realizing they probably needed a little color as I looked at hers coated in a bright shade of coral.

She smiled and gave me a look to let me know the people on the other end were being difficult. She gestured toward the empty dining area to let me pick the table of my choice. I went through the main space, which was the former living room, and on through an adjacent area that had probably been the house's real dining room, to the small sunporch that looked over the back and down to the ocean.

I'd barely picked a table when Tag Thornkill came over to the table with a glass of iced tea. It was hard to notice anything beyond his thick head of brown hair, which seemed off for a man in his fifties. When we'd first met, I was sure it was a wig. But Lucinda had confirmed that it was all real. He put the glass on the table with a slice of lemon exactly in the middle of the toothpick lying across the top of the glass. I saw him eyeing the knife that was a little out of line with the rest of the place setting. Though he greeted me, his eye kept going back to the knife. I smiled at him and held out my hands, inviting him to do the adjusting he felt compelled to do.

He let out his breath when the knife was straight. "Don't tell Lucinda, she thinks I annoy the customers. I want everything to be just right," he said. It seemed to go beyond wanting everything to be just right to the point of being obsessive about it. He waited while I sipped the iced tea and appeared relieved when I assured him that it was just the way I liked it.

A copy of the menu was on the table and I turned it over and reread the story of Lucinda and Tag. The menu rendition seemed a little too precious about how they had dated in high school and then gone their separate ways, only to meet up again years and years later. They were both single at the time, he a widower and she divorced, and the menu said something like it seemed as if time had stopped and they picked up where they had left off, married and moved to Cadbury. Having a restaurant in a small town had been both of their dream.

Reading about a couple made me think about Dane again. Was this his and Stacy's story? I thought back to the quick look I had gotten of her. She was nothing like me. She seemed more put together than I was. I bet Dane didn't laugh when she batted her eyelashes. Hers were probably perfectly shaped thanks to an eyelash curler. I cringed thinking back to my attempt to use one.

Just then Lucinda came over to the table. She had a smile and was about to say something when she caught sight of my expression and the smile faded.

"What's wrong?" she said.

"Have you ever used an eyelash curler?" I asked.

"That's it? You want to curl your eyelashes?" she said with a chuckle.

"Not exactly," I began, and then told her about Dane. She pulled out a chair and gave me a sympathetic pat. Despite the differences in our ages and life situations, Lucinda had become my best friend in the small town. She was also my boss of sorts since I was the dessert chef for the restaurant and was there most nights after they closed, working my magic.

"Her name is Stacy," I said and Lucinda nodded.

"I know, she's his high school girlfriend." When I seemed surprised, she shrugged. "Life in a small town. Just like everybody knows about his mother and what he does for the local kids. He's kind of a hometown hero." She gave my arm a squeeze. "I didn't want to say anything. I hoped that she was just passing through."

"It doesn't look like it," I said. "Thank heavens I didn't say anything." I told her about Frank's advice and how I'd been about to tell Dane how I felt.

Lucinda smiled. "The way you describe your ex-boss, he sounds like someone more likely to recommend his favorite sub sandwich than give you advice on your love life." She looked at me. "There's that word *love*." She watched me squirm in my seat.

"I know," I said, letting my shoulders sag. "I have a hard time with words like that. It leaves me feeling too vulnerable. I'd rather have him laugh at my attempts at flirting. After my conversation with Frank, I had considered using *that word* in a text to Dane. Easier than saying it out loud. I am so glad that I didn't."

"What are you going to do?" she asked.

I looked at her, mystified. "Do? What can I do besides let it be. I've always made it seem like I just wanted a casual relationship. She's his old girlfriend who left and came back. He's probably thrilled about getting another chance with her." Lucinda insisted on getting me dinner. She knew that while I loved making desserts and muffins, I lived off of frozen meals and plates of spaghetti from Dane.

When she returned from putting in the order, I changed the subject to the upcoming retreat and told her about the meeting.

"It's going to be a different kind of group this time. I expect most of them are beginners who may have bought a kit online at most. They're not interested in making an afghan that takes forever. Crystal has come up with kits that have everything so they can complete the project over the weekend." Lucinda liked the idea.

"Madeleine is part of the staff now," I said, explaining her request.

"You have no idea what you have done for Madeleine," my friend said. "She went from being practically mute, letting Cora boss her around even though Madeleine is the older sister, to having a life. She must be thrilled with her title. I know how much she likes being included in the retreats."

"I was glad to do it. It has been fun helping her join the world and getting herself out there. But," I said, letting out a sigh, "I feel responsible for her."

"Is there a problem?" Lucinda asked. I told her about Milton Carruthers coming for the weekend. Lucinda remembered him from the mystery weekend and I filled her in that they'd kept in touch.

"She didn't say it, but I think she wants to impress him. I still have my doubts about his intentions. I can't help but feel protective of her." I could feel my expression dim. "What if she's imagining there's more there than there is? It's taken him a long time to come back here. She said he's coming to work on a book and in her words, to see her. Assuming that he is coming to see her, is he really into her or the fact that she and her sister are so wealthy? I just don't want her to get hurt."

"Or worse," Lucinda said. "I read one of his books and the plot was about a man who plots to kill his rich wife. What if he is coming here to see her with plans to sweep her off her feet then whisk her off to elope. And then . . ." Lucinda's voice trailed off. "Think about it. He probably sits around all day thinking about ways to kill people."

I had been worried about his intentions, but until she brought it up I never thought it might include murder. I was worried about her ending up with a broken heart, not one that stopped beating. "Do you think he would be so transparent? He'd have to know that the cops would recognize the plot in his book if he married Madeleine and she died suddenly," I said.

"Maybe he'd change things up," Lucinda offered. "Instead of the woman eating a kabob cooked on oleander twigs, he'd take her whale watching on a private boat and she'd somehow slip overboard."

"And maybe he is just smitten with her," I said hopefully.

"Or, he really is just coming to work on a book," Lucinda said. "Vista Del Mar is a great spot for that. No electronic distractions. Meals included. He can work in his room or sit in the social hall. And if he needs to clear his head and get a little exercise, there are plenty of places to walk. I agree that she's probably not good at interpreting signals. It could be wishful thinking on her end and she could have read more into what he said." She looked toward Tag going through the dining room and adjusting the place settings. "He's really out of control now. An online review said that his attention to detail was what set this restaurant above the others. It's only encouraged him to be even more fussy. Maybe the reviewer was right, but it drives me buggy anyway. Whatever the theme of the retreat is, sounds good to me. With the short days and the dip after the holiday festivities, I need a change. It will be so nice to hang out and work on the project Crystal came up with in front of a cozy fireplace with a glass of wine." She had a dreamy look. "I can't wait."

Just then a server brought my food. Lucinda saw that I was pleased with what she had chosen for me and excused herself to deal with a group of people who were coming in the door.

The window was open on the sunporch and the breeze smelled of the ocean and carried a few drops of rain, hinting that it might not be over. I was going to have to remember to grab an umbrella. But for now, I was going to feast on my dinner.

Chapter 3

I was still thinking of the delicious meal when I returned to the Blue Door that night. This time I had plastic shopping bags with the ingredients for the apple cinnamon muffins I was going to bake for the town's coffee spots. The restaurant had a different feel now. The dining room was empty and the tables set up for the next day. Tag must have checked every setting because there was not one knife that didn't resemble a soldier standing at attention. Lucinda had presented me with the priciest entrée on the menu. The grilled salmon was perfection with sides of mashed potatoes and a mélange of roasted vegetables. I might not have an interest in cooking meals, but I enjoyed eating them and had savored every morsel. The chef came out of the kitchen with his knives safely packed in his backpack. I wanted to tell him how delicious the dinner was, but he barely nodded at me before looking away. We did not have the best relationship since we both viewed the other as being an intruder in the kitchen, which actually did not belong to either one of us.

I heard Lucinda call out to tell me that she and Tag were leaving as I set the bags down in the restaurant's kitchen. I gave it a minute and then went back to the dining room, turning on some soft jazz and letting peace settle in the place.

I always worked on the desserts for the restaurant first and had the apple pies in the oven before I got everything out for the muffins. Mixing them only added to the scent of apples and cinnamon in the air. The apple pies were cooling and pans of muffins baking when I heard a knock at the door.

When I had first started baking at night, I had felt threatened when someone came to the door and had armed myself with a frying pan or rolling pin before answering. But I had reminded myself that I was not in a big city anymore and everybody in town knew I baked there every night but Saturday and felt free to stop by. Mostly it had been Dane taking his break when he worked a night shift.

All things considered, I doubted that it was him this time. I didn't even know what his current work schedule was since I had not heard from him for a few days. I had chalked it up to him being wrapped up in the disaster training they were doing, but now I realized he might have been busy with something else.

I felt nervous anticipation as soon as I saw his face through the window of the door. I tried to be cool but still felt a reaction to seeing him. Along with all that character, Dane was incredibly hot-looking in a cute sort of way. Before I even opened the door, I had already decided that I would get right to it and confront him. "Is there something you have to tell me?" I said. He seemed more serious than usual and there was no joking around to see if I still was armed with a frying pan.

He seemed surprised at my comment and a little uncomfortable. "We do have to talk," he said. "But not now." He gestured with his head and for the first time I saw that he was not alone. There was another uniformed officer and Lieutenant Borgnine.

"We're doing a check on emergency kits in case of disaster. We stopped at the all-night pharmacy and came here since the lights were on," the other officer said. Out of the corner of my eye, I could see Lieutenant Borgnine sniffing the air.

"Is that the muffins I smell?" Lieutenant Borgnine asked. He was dressed in his usual rumpled sport jacket. His salt-and-pepper hair was cut into a long crew cut and made me think of a lawn that needed to be mowed. His neck was almost invisible and his gruff expression was only slightly softened by the smell of the baked goods. A bell went off and I excused myself to go to the kitchen and take the muffins out. The three men followed me as I set the pans out to cool. With the muffins out in the open, the wonderful smell only intensified.

"Muffins made with fruit," the lieutenant said, noting the pieces of an apple showing through the top. "That has to be healthful, right?"

I knew where this was headed. While the lieutenant wasn't exactly a fan of mine, particularly when it came to solving crimes, he was definitely a fan of my baking. His wife was always on him about his diet, urging him to eat fruits and vegetables instead of the cop staple of doughnuts.

"They'll be cool enough to eat in a few minutes," I said. "They have lots of apples, and cinnamon, which is supposed to be good for all sorts of things. I'm sure Mrs. Borgnine would approve."

"Okay, but that's not why we're here," he said, giving the cooling muffins a longing look. "We're here to check for the restaurant's disaster preparedness." I showed him the backpack with the first aid kits, some protective gloves, a battery-operated lantern and a radio. Then I showed him the shut-off for the gas and electricity.

"Any particular disaster you're thinking of?" I said.

"Just general preparedness," Dane said. When the other two were busy with the muffins, he mouthed that it was their idea to come there and added an apology. Somehow when he said *I'm sorry,* it seemed like it was about more than the interruption.

I fed them all muffins, giving the lieutenant some to go, and they finally left. Seeing Dane made me realize how hard it would be for me to stay in Cadbury. There was no way I could avoid seeing him. It would be even worse seeing him and Stacy together. In my imagination, I saw them coming out of a church with rice being thrown and then it moved on to them walking with a stroller. And then there was me, the dessert-baking old maid.

I was still feeling desolate when I gathered up the containers of muffins. The air was filled with a fine mist as I went down the empty streets of Cadbury, leaving the muffins at the assorted coffee spots for the morning. Maybe it was wishful thinking, but I half expected Dane to pop out of somewhere. But the street stayed empty. He was probably home and in bed by now. I did not want to complete the picture.

• • •

I was looking forward to sleeping in the next day. It was the kind of morning that made me want to wrap myself in the covers and stay in bed. Waking to a cloud-covered sky was normal, but it was usually a bright white. This was real gloom, a gray sky made even darker by the lower position of the sun in January. The white clouds weren't a precursor to rain, just the effect of the moisture of the Pacific Ocean meeting the Monterey Peninsula. The clouds this morning looked like they had something planned. I turned on my side and was drifting off when a sandpaper tongue ran over my cheek, whipping me back to present. When I didn't make a move, the black cat draped himself on my shoulder and let out a loud grunt of displeasure.

I rolled on my back and he fell off, landing on the bed. "Julius, there's food in the kitchen. You can help yourself." To deal with situations like this, I'd gotten a dry cat food dispenser that made sure he always had a full bowl. He let out a little impatient meow to let me know that did not fit the bill.

It was my fault that I had spoiled him. I had seen Julius wandering on the grounds of Vista Del Mar and even felt a little kinship with him when I saw that Kevin St. John seemed to be as annoyed with the cat as he was with me. I didn't think about the cat's housing situation or who was feeding him until he showed up at my door and walked inside when I opened it.

When I really thought about it, I realized he had most likely been abandoned. Maybe somebody had rented a house for a while and had the cat, and when they left, left him to fend for himself. I melted at the thought, and even though I had never had a pet and was not sure how long I'd be staying in Cadbury by the Sea, I had invited him in. I hadn't thought about our future together then, but times had changed. If I went, he was coming with me.

I named him Julius, and to make up for time on the mean streets of Cadbury had offered him a selection of wet cat foods. Big mistake. He passed over all of the ones that smelled like prime rib or a chicken dish before choosing what I'd come to call stink fish. It was actually mackerel and a sickly pink color with an awful stench—to me at least. To him it was nirvana. Since Julius was my first cat, I had not realized that they are the ones in charge. Before I knew it, he had trained me to feed him the smelly fish dish on command. My only win was giving him only a dab each time. I had made the mistake of thinking if I gave him more, it would keep him satisfied longer. It didn't. He just gobbled it all up and then threw it up. The smell was worse the second time around.

I threw back the covers and shivered at the chill air. There was a heater but I barely used it, though this morning I was going to need it to take the edge off.

The cat led the way with his tail proudly swishing. Was he gloating that he had won?

I took out the open can stuck inside a sealed plastic bag. Then I began unwrapping the layers of aluminum foil, wax paper and plastic wrap. It felt like I was unwrapping a mummy, but they probably smelled better. I'd done this enough times that I went into hold-your-nose mode the minute I unsealed the bag.

He was on it before I could tap it all off the spoon. Then I had to rewrap it again. I let myself return to breathing through my nose when I slipped it back in the refrigerator.

I needed coffee. I glanced at the jar of instant left from before Dane had convinced me to brew my own in a coffee maker. I felt a twinge at the thought of him. He'd been so different last night. Not just because he was with another officer and the lieutenant. Instead of a teasing smile in his eyes when our eyes met, he'd looked uncomfortable.

I had an even stronger reaction when I saw the plate in my dish drainer. It was from the last dish of spaghetti he had left me. I thought about how I would get it back to him. That led me to thinking about him and Stacy and what they might be doing on this sleep-in sort of morning.

"I can't do this," I said out loud to myself. "It is what it is and I have to stop tormenting myself." Making a pot of coffee was only going to make me think of him again. The special blend had been a gift from him. He had made it his mission to get me to expand my baking skills into everyday meal prep without much luck so far.

I left Julius to finish off the stink fish and went to shower and get ready. A change of scenes would lead to a change of my thoughts.

When I was dressed, I pulled on my green fleece jacket and left. The feeling of gloom was even stronger outside and the air felt overburdened with moisture. As I walked across the street and past the stone pillars that marked the beginning of the Vista Del Mar driveway, I was already thinking about my coffee order. This was a double cappuccino morning. I had walked up and down this driveway so many times that it faded to the background. I took it for granted that I was going into a much more rustic area than my street. I lived on the edge of town, where the front yards were hardly orderly and had either ivy or native plants, also known as weeds.

There were no shadows falling across the pavement from the lanky Monterey pines towering over both sides of the road. And the brush and bushes around them seemed to blend in with the background. I did notice the corpse of one of the pines lying parallel to the road. There was no tidy cleanup of a fallen tree, but instead a dead tree was left in place to decompose. It was rumored the same was true with any wildlife.

Vista Del Mar had started out as a girls' camp over a hundred years ago, and while it functioned as a hotel and conference center, it still had a camp feel. No plush towels or high-thread-count sheets, and no lawns or even patches of flowers like the fancy resorts in nearby Pebble Beach. Even without really paying attention, I sensed that I had crossed over into a timeless wild atmosphere.

The guest room buildings were covered in weather-beaten shingles that once had been a dark brown. The buildings had names like Sand and Sea, Tides and Gulls and were spread over about one hundred acres of rolling slopes that made it so that most of the rooms had nice views.

All the guest room buildings had cozy lobby areas with fireplaces that were always glowing. I could smell the woodsmoke in the air along with the tang of the ocean, which was just beyond the sand dunes that marked the edge of the property.

It was more quiet than usual. I noted the small parking lot was almost empty as I passed it. It was Wednesday, which was always the slowest day of the week. People who'd come the previous weekend were gone and those for the upcoming one hadn't arrived. This time of year was slow, too. The holidays had recently wrapped up and a new year started. Not the time when people thought of coming to a moody resort. As Cloris had said, most of the buildings were closed off for maintenance.

Luckily, the shutdown didn't include the Sand and Sea building, as it was the one I always used for my people. I glanced up at it on the hill above me. It dated back from the days of being a camp and I had heard it was where the counselors stayed. All the buildings were in the Arts and Crafts style so they looked similar, but each one had its own differences. The Tides building had a number of comfortable rooms with fireplaces on the ground floor, while the Sand and Sea had just one room that functioned as a lobby at the foot of the stairs. The furniture in all the communal rooms in both buildings was designed to make them a nice place to curl up and read or gather for an impromptu yarn craft gathering.

I always used the small, single-story Cypress building for my workshops. It was the same style as the original structures but had been added when Vista Del Mar became a conference center. It had two meeting rooms and was tucked in between the guest room buildings. I caught a glimpse of it surrounded by trees and thought about what preparations were needed.

The brisk air had snapped me out of sleepiness, but I still wanted that double cappuccino. There would be company, too, which would help keep my mind off of the situation with Dane.

I was not a weepy, *he did me wrong* type who got drunk and listened to sad songs. I had always been good at picking myself up and moving on when things went south. I had figured out after one semester that law school was not for me and dropped out. I had stuck with the teaching job for a year before moving on. I'd had some regrets when the bistro I was baking for went out of business, but I accepted the situation and did temp work. My last temp job was working for Frank. I loved being an assistant detective, even though he insisted I was a detective's assistant. But whatever my title, I excelled at it. If only he had not run out of money everything might have been different. My aunt's offer of her guest house had come at the right time and I had relocated from Chicago to Cadbury. I had learned to be ready for change. I could do it again, if need be. There were the details to figure out, which at the moment seemed overwhelming. I decided to do a Scarlett O'Hara and put off thinking about it for now.

All I wanted to think about was how good the double cappuccino was going to be. I imagined drinking it in front of the fireplace in the Lodge.

The exterior of the Lodge appeared dark and forbidding and didn't hint at how inviting the inside was. It was the real center of Vista Del Mar. It was where people went to check in and where the business of the place was conducted. It also functioned like a lobby or gathering spot for the guests.

The interior was cavernous, displaying the framework overhead and the very high ceiling well above that. A huge stone fireplace dominated the main area and had leather couches and mission-style chairs around it. High-backed chairs and small wood tables were scattered around the rest of the large open space. Shelves with board games took up the back wall. A table tennis setup was next to a pool table. It also featured a gift shop and café in mirror-image rooms that were at either end of the building.

It was more quiet than usual, even for a Wednesday. In busier times, there would have been clumps of people lingering over a second cup of coffee before their morning activity—whether it was a weeklong retreat group waiting for a yoga workshop, guests gathered for a morning nature walk, or a group waiting for the van to take them to an off-site excursion like whale watching.

The gift shop was just opening and the clerk put out racks of T-shirts in the main area to entice customers. The table tennis setup and pool table were deserted and all the board games were neatly stacked on a shelf behind them.

Cloris looked up from her post behind the massive wood counter that designated the check-in area. "Good morning, Casey," she said in a friendly voice. She appeared crisp in her blue blazer and badge that said *Cloris Dunphy, Assistant Manager.* "You're here early."

"It's all about the coffee." I pointed at the open door to the Cora and Madeleine Delacorte Café. I could already smell the pungent fragrance of freshly brewed coffee and moved toward it like a magnet was pulling me.

"I thought so," she said.

"Is it that obvious?" I said, suddenly self-conscious of how wrung-out I must look.

"You look fine," she said in a reassuring tone. "I just know when you come here in the morning, it's for a coffee fix."

I was about to add that the company was part of the appeal too. Cloris was always a cheerful face in the morning. I suspected she didn't always feel that upbeat but did a good job of acting as if. Her position meant everything to her and she wanted to keep it. Cloris had started as the host in the dining hall and then filled in everywhere before becoming assistant manager. Even with her new title, she was continuing her studies for a degree in hospitality at the local community college. I admired her dedication to the place and how intent she was on doing the best job possible.

I was surprised when there was a dip in her smile and asked her if something was wrong.

"Mr. St. John is getting ready to leave," she said.

I was careful with my words. If I were her, I would be looking forward to him leaving. But I was not about to say it. I knew she was worried about being in charge because of how he would react if anything went wrong.

Instead, I gave her a pep talk. "I don't think you have anything to worry about. You said he's only going to be gone for the weekend and the place is practically empty." I offered her a hopeful smile. "To quote the current favorite slang term, *you got this.*" I looked ahead to the café door and inhaled the scent. "And now for that coffee."

Chapter 4

I was anxious for that jolt of caffeine and a hot drink on the chill morning, but there was a delay. I had barely taken a step toward the café when the door on the driveway side opened with an impatient whoosh. A woman marched in with a younger woman lagging behind her. The older woman was rail-thin with sharp features and seemed agitated.

"I'm Nancy Limpkin," she said in a sharp tone. She pointed to the woman behind her. "She's checking in. Her name is Mindy Limpkin and she's here for the diet retreat. I wanted to make sure she was here early." She looked back at the girl, who seemed embarrassed by the whole thing. "I know it doesn't start until tomorrow, but in the meantime she must be on a no-carb plan with whatever food you serve here. If she doesn't lose five pounds over the weekend, I'm going to expect a refund."

Cloris put on her customer service smile. "I would be glad to check her in now, but the leader of the retreat hasn't arrived yet, and whatever meals she has arranged don't begin until tomorrow. As for the meals before then—Mindy can choose what she wants from what the dining hall offers. I'd love to accommodate your request, but any special meals have to be ordered in advance."

The woman huffed and puffed as she looked around the room. "There's no way that she can order a pizza, is there? I was assured there was no cell service." Then she saw the line of old-fashioned phone booths and let out an annoyed sigh. "How can I make sure she doesn't use one of those to order a pizza? She has no self-control, unlike me."

"Mother," Mindy said, dragging out the word and seeming like she wanted to disappear. Compared to her slender mother she seemed curvy, though it was hidden under a voluminous apricot-colored sweatshirt. I guessed she was in her early twenties. Her mother went on that finding out about the retreat that promised to be the last diet anyone would need was her last hope to put her daughter on the right path. It was more information than we wanted or needed as Nancy Limpkin described how she ate the same meals every day and was in complete control of her intake, down to telling us her lunch was always a salad with a sliver of chicken—no dressing, just lemon juice—and six grapes sliced in half.

The same door opened and a tall woman came in pulling a suitcase. She had a fluff of wiry graying hair and a self-assured manner. She glanced over the group of us and stopped.

"I don't mean to interrupt. Finish whatever you have going on and then you can check me in. "I'm Dorothy Spenser, the retreat leader for the Final Diet."

The other woman's eyes lit up. "It's the program that is the last diet anyone will ever need?"

"That's what I hope," Dorothy said, eyeing the woman with a little concern

"Wonderful," Nancy said in a relieved tone. "This woman wasn't helping me at all with Mindy's situation. I'm Nancy Limpkin and this is my daughter. I was trying to arrange for her to have no carbs today, but this woman—" She looked at Cloris's name tag. "Ms. Dunphy was giving me no satisfaction. Maybe you can do something." She repeated the expectation that her daughter would lose five pounds over the weekend and be changed forever. She added her concern about Mindy lapsing and ordering pizzas. "She has no self-control. I've tried to get her to see the light and not be a slave to her appetite."

When Nancy finally took a breath, Dorothy gave her a friendly smile and suggested they go into the café, where they could talk in a more private manner. They left all their suitcases, and Dorothy led the way.

Cloris tilted her head and gestured for me to follow. "Weren't you on the way for your coffee?" I knew what she was doing. She wanted me to keep tabs on what was going on with the three women. With Kevin St. John leaving, it was going to be all on her, and she wanted as much information as possible about potential trouble. I was glad to oblige.

They were already at a table when I walked into the small café. The rest of it was empty except for the barista, who was leaning against the wooden bar, reading. I had given up on the idea of a double cappuccino and took a paper cup to pour myself the brew of the day. I tried to be nonchalant and selected a table close to them but not next to them. It was near the wall of windows and I could appear to be gazing out at the scenery while I listened to their conversation.

Dorothy got up and went to the bar. She came back with cups of coffee for each of them. Mindy looked at the brown liquid. "I need cream," she said and Dorothy pointed at a stand with vacuum pitchers of milk and cream, along with sweeteners and napkins.

Nancy Limpkin shook her head with distress. "You see what I mean. She's hopeless."

"I think you might have misunderstood what the retreat is about," Dorothy said, measuring her words.

"Oh, no, I understand. You call it the last diet, that means you know that it's going to work."

Dorothy seemed hesitant. "I will say this—All of the past retreaters did leave the weekend with a new relationship with food."

"And they all lost five pounds, right?" the mother said.

"We don't really focus on numbers. But there was a testimonial in my brochure from a woman who did lose five pounds," Dorothy said. "If you noticed, my title is food therapist. I'm sure your daughter will get a lot out of the weekend." The barista had set aside his book and moved the basket of muffins I'd delivered the night before to a prominent spot on the wooden bar. The smell of apples and cinnamon rose above the fragrance of the coffee. The mother's head swiveled in the direction the scent was coming from and she appeared captivated by it, then she straightened and turned back to the others. "It's not going to be like that all weekend. You can't tease us, I mean them, with that sweet smell."

Dorothy still seemed to be watching her words. "I can only control what my people have at mealtimes. We have a special menu arranged that will be served separately from the other food in the dining hall. Everything is being delivered tomorrow morning so all the fruits and veggies will be super fresh."

Nancy seemed unconvinced. "Maybe I should stay until your program starts to make sure everything goes right." She looked at her daughter.

Dorothy used her therapy skills and in a soothing voice assured the mother that her daughter would be fine on her own. "Maybe I should talk to the kitchen staff," Nancy said. "Where is this dining hall? I'm sure if I explained the situation, they could accommodate her need for no carbs for today. Maybe I should just stay for the weekend."

Dorothy was staying calm, but Nancy's badgering was getting to her. "The retreat doesn't start until tomorrow, but I understand your concern and I will bend my own rules and help your daughter get started today. And I'm sure you don't really want to stay for the weekend."

"You're right. I do have plans. I was just going to drop her off and then go off to meet a friend in Santa Cruz for the weekend. Then you will see to it that she has no carbs and no pizzas?"

"As I said, I will let her start the program today." I noticed that Dorothy was not answering the mother's specific question. I think the mother realized it too, but she really wanted to leave.

As soon as she was gone Mindy let her breath out and leaned back in the chair. "I'm sorry for everything she said and did. She has my best interests at heart, but she simply won't accept that I am not her." She glanced toward the counter with the muffins. "She would die rather than eat one of those. Her idea of breakfast is a tiny bit of bran cereal and a half a cup of skim milk. Have you ever noticed that skim milk looks almost blue."

"And how do you feel about the muffins?" Dorothy asked.

"That one of them has my name on it," the younger woman said.

Dorothy nodded. "Personally, I like half-and-half on my cereal."

The girl's head shot up in surprise.

"I see. This is going to be one of those weekends where it's do as I say, not as I do. At least my mother does live by her own rules."

"Maybe, but I think she was salivating at the scent of the muffins. And no, I don't expect my retreaters to do anything different than I would do. This weekend is not about starving yourself. It's the last diet because the point is to make friends with food. There are no devil foods or angel foods. The goal is to get back to eating without all the emotional issues. It's about learning how to deal with physical hunger, and learning to enjoy what you eat. No guilt. And then the magic happens." She saw Mindy eyeing the muffins. "How about this. We share it and each have half." Mindy's eyes widened in surprise and she nodded in agreement.

I was relieved to go back to Cloris and report that it seemed everything was okay.

As we were talking, Kevin St. John came out from the business office and stopped next to Cloris. As always, he was dressed in a dark suit and white shirt that seemed too formal for the rustic look of Vista Del Mar. His moon-shaped face seemed agitated as he surveyed the area behind the counter and off into the communal space on the other side of it.

"If you have any questions or problems, call me," he said.

"I'm sure everything will be fine," she said in her professional voice. "I won't need to bother you." He still wasn't sold on her being assistant manager and had only agreed to giving her the position when the Delacortes had prevailed on him with my help. It was second nature to her to go the extra mile for the guests or people like me who put on events at the hotel and conference center. I think it bothered Kevin St. John that she was so good at what she did, afraid that it would make him look bad.

"We just have the three retreats and a few scattered guests. Go on and enjoy your seminar."

Kevin looked around the room, giving it a last inspection. Then he turned to me with a glare. "One of the topics is on adding revenue by arranging programs for retreats instead of simply renting space to people like you."

Here we go again, I thought. Ever since I'd done the first retreat, Kevin had been trying to push me out. He had already succeeded in putting on some retreats directly and he was anxious to add mine to his repertoire. I wondered if the meeting he was going to would give him the tools to oust me for good.

It had gotten tenser between us now that I was friends with Madeleine since she and her sister were the main owners of Vista Del Mar. They were the ones who offered me the same special deal on rooms they had given my aunt. It was the difference between me making a profit and not, but was also a threat to Kevin's power. I could only imagine how he would feel if he knew that Madeleine was now going to be on the staff.

"I'll be in San Diego," he said. "If there's anything you can't handle, I can always come back." He straightened his jacket. I think we were all wondering if he was ever going to leave.

"You don't want to miss your plane." She said it in a pleasant voice.

"Well, then," he said at last. With a final glance around the place, he went out the door. The moment the door closed behind him, it seemed like the whole vibe of the place got better.

Chapter 5

At last I got to follow my original plan, and instead of going back to the café I took my coffee to a chair near the fireplace. It had the advantage of the warmth and cheer of the fire and I could watch what was going on.

Now that it was later, there was more activity in the large room. A couple came in from breakfast in the dining hall and went to the counter to check out. Cloris addressed them by name and they told her how much they had enjoyed the extra peace that came with the emptiness of the hotel.

As they were leaving, a man dressed in jeans and a hoodie came in and stopped at the registration counter. Cloris was much more relaxed with Kevin St. John gone and took time to chat with the man in a friendly manner. I was impressed at how she was so familiar with the guests.

"I hope you got what you wanted out of your stay, James," Cloris said.

"I needed this time of solitude to deal with something that was keeping me from moving on. It's back to the real world tomorrow," he said. He gestured to his shaggy brown hair and untrimmed beard. "All of this will be gone."

"You had good timing. It's not going to be as quiet," Cloris said. "We have three retreat groups coming for the weekend. Some of the people have already arrived. I expect some more today. The retreat leaders always come a day early."

He surveyed the cavernous room and his gaze stopped on me. I glanced away quickly, so he wouldn't think I was eavesdropping. "That's Casey Feldstein," Cloris said. "She's local and putting on a yarn retreat." All of Cloris's conversation seemed wasted on him. He didn't seem interested in hearing about who was arriving or in meeting me. He only reacted when she mentioned the evening meal.

"Since it's your last night do you want to eat in the dining hall with everyone?" she said in a friendly voice.

"No, thank you," he said, shaking his head for emphasis. "This trip was about me being alone. That's why I chose to stay in that cottage this time instead of in one of the guest rooms with all the racket of people around me. I'd like my dinner packed to go as usual. I'm going to eat on the beach, where the only sound is the rhythm of the waves."

It hardly seemed like weather for a picnic to me, but different strokes for different folks.

Cloris made a call to the dining hall and assured him it was taken care of. He left saying he was going to do a meditation walk around the property.

I got a refill on my coffee and took one of the muffins. They would usually be gone by now, but with the place so empty, they weren't moving. The strong coffee mixed nicely with the apple and cinnamon flavor of the muffin. It was delicious, if I said so myself. There was no reason to rush off and I was enjoying the coziness of the fire and the warm glow given off by the amber-colored glass shades on the table lamps. I decided to just stay there until Crystal arrived with the yarn supplies for my retreat. The plan was that we would put together the kits for the group.

The door opened again and I felt the cool damp air cut through the heat coming off the fireplace. A tall man with a solid build came in. He had wavy brown hair that was longish but without looking unkempt. It was hard to see his features as he wore large black-framed glasses. There was something determined in the way he moved as he headed to the counter. The woman with him was checking out the rest of the room as if she was taking it all in. The man nudged her and she turned her attention forward. I was glad my position was close enough that I could hear without being obvious.

"Welcome, Trent," Cloris said. She turned to the woman and stared at her for a moment, as if she was confused.

"It's Dr. Nicholson," the woman corrected. "And I'm Mrs. Nicholson." Whatever confusion Cloris had felt seemed to have cleared up.

"I'm sorry for being informal," Cloris said.

"That's okay," he said. "Just as before, you can call me Trent." He looked at the woman. "Audrey is acting as my assistant and she's very serious about her job." She had dark brown hair and was dressed in a red sweater over dark wash jeans. Her lips were a perfect bow, but her eyes were narrowed, which made me think she was either very tired or bothered about something.

As the conversation continued, I realized he was the other retreat leader. By process of elimination, he had to be the therapist whose program was called Getting Unstuck. I listened in on their conversation as he described what a perfect time of year it was for the subject of his retreat. "The holidays are over, the new year's resolutions have already gotten tossed to the wayside," Trent said and Cloris nodded. "But then last summer worked for it too."

I was surprised that I had never seen him before since he had done at least one other retreat at Vista Del Mar. But then, when I wasn't putting on a retreat at the hotel and conference center I didn't hang out there all the time. He had an engaging manner as he asked Cloris how things were going.

She surprised me by telling him about the manager leaving and that it was her first time being in charge. But then I got it. She was reacting to the fact he was a therapist and thought he would understand. It was obviously not the first time a non-client had shared their feelings, expecting some insight. It was the same as doctors at a dinner party who were faced with people telling them about a mysterious ache. She seemed about to go into more detail, but Trent stopped her and offered a reassuring nod.

"I'm sure you will do a splendid job," he said. He might have said more, but his wife shot Cloris an annoyed look and intruded, asking about their accommodations.

"We are to have two adjoining rooms," she said in a sharp tone. "I was very specific about which ones." Cloris had gone back to her professional mode and went to get the keys.

"We only have one set of rooms that are adjoining," Cloris said, putting the keys on the counter.

Audrey grabbed them quickly and looked back at Cloris, as if she needed to explain the need for separate rooms for the couple. "These weekend programs are very draining for Dr. Nicholson and he needs to have a space to be alone and regroup his energies." Despite the explanation, I had the feeling that Mrs. Nicholson was not really pleased with the arrangement.

"Of course," Cloris said with her professional smile. The rest of the discussion was on the rooms set up for his program. She had arranged for the same meeting rooms he had used in the past. One of the lobby rooms in the Tides building had been closed off for his group sessions and a smaller room set aside for his one-on-one meetings.

I watched the whole exchange with interest since our paths were likely to cross during the weekend, as were the people for our retreats. I always felt the jitters before the beginning of one of my retreats. Would the people get along and would they be happy with the yarn project and other activities? He seemed the opposite—completely calm and self-assured. Was it real or just a cover?

On the other hand, his wife seemed nervous and possessive of him.

They had slipped into chatting about what else was going on that weekend at Vista Del Mar. "You'll get a chance to meet the other group leaders at dinner," Cloris said. She glanced in my direction and waved me over.

"Casey is putting on a yarn retreat," the assistant manager said.

"A yarn retreat?" Trent said. "What exactly is that?" Now that I was close up, I got a dose of what Cloris had reacted to. He looked at me directly and seemed completely interested in what I had to say.

"It's not yarn as in a story," I said. "It's yarn as in knitting and crocheting." I went on to explain that the group got to socialize and learn how to make something. I was cut off as his wife put her arm in his.

"That sounds very nice," Audrey said, giving him a look. Her tone made it obvious what she really thought. That I had a group of old ladies coming for a trivial weekend compared to the importance of what they were doing. I forced myself not to react and tell them that yarn craft was actually appealing to a whole new group of younger people, and add how therapeutic it was.

A van pulled up in the driveway next to the building. A moment later, two women walked in. At first, I thought they were twins. They were both tall, slender with short dark hair, and dressed in the jean style of the moment topped with jean jackets. They had scarves wound around their necks and gave off an aura of trendiness. They were laughing and talking as they came in, trying to take in their surroundings at the same time.

One of them let go of the handle of her suitcase and it went gliding across the room on its own. Trent stepped away from the counter and caught it.

"Thank you," the woman said, reaching for the handle. Her hand brushed his and she glanced up at him and smiled.

"Are you here for my retreat?" he asked. The two women looked at each other and chuckled.

"Not unless your name is Casey and you're into yarn," the woman with the runaway suitcase said. I studied the naturalness in her flirty manner, wishing it would rub off on me. Trent definitely reacted to it and gave her a warm smile before he gestured to me.

"What's yours on?" the woman said, keeping her attention on him.

"I call it Getting Unstuck. You know how it is. You make all those new year's resolutions and two weeks later you haven't made a move."

"I like that," the other woman said, mostly ignoring me. "Maybe we should switch." She turned to her friend. Audrey put herself in the middle of it before it could go further.

"All the slots are taken," she said firmly.

"I'm afraid she's right. I keep the number small so I get a chance to work with each attendee personally." He glanced back at me. "I'm sure you'll be very happy with your yarn thing."

"It's therapeutic too," I said, annoyed at his tone. "Everyone talks, and working with yarn is good for reducing stress."

"I'm sure you're right," he said. His gaze went to the open door to the café. "If you'll excuse me, I need a cup of coffee after the drive from San Jose." His wife nodded in agreement and led the way, seeming glad to get him away from us.

I introduced myself to the two women and explained I was the one in charge of their upcoming retreat. And they gave their names as Lexie and Bella. They resembled each other so much, I looked for something to differentiate them. Then I noticed that Lexie had a tattoo of a heart on her hand and Bella had a rose tattooed on her wrist. "The program doesn't start until tomorrow," I said.

"We know," Lexie said, sounding defensive and maybe a little hostile, as if I had implied that they had made a mistake. I waited to see if she was going to offer a reason for their early arrival, but she said nothing.

"As long as I'm here, let me help you get checked in," I said. They both looked at me as if I'd just offered the most absurd thing.

"I think we can handle it," Bella said in a dismissive tone. It was a different attitude than I was used to. Most of my attendees had always been mellower. But then these two were part of the younger crowd who had become interested in yarn craft now that it had become a trendy pursuit. It was all about making something small that they could show off to their friends. Beanies were popular, as were small toys and objects like baskets made of yarn. There were social media groups formed around these new versions of the old crafts of knitting and crochet. Though crochet seemed to be the more popular since it was better for the baskets and such. I had no doubt that they had pictures on their phones of what they had made, which they would be showing off soon.

Thinking of their phones, I wondered if they had paid attention to my very clear mention on the registration form that there was no cell service or Internet or even TV. They looked like the type that slept with their phones in their hands ready to text at a moment's notice.

I considered bringing it up, but with the way they had treated me, I thought they would take it wrong and decided to let them find out on their own that it was going to be a text-free weekend.

Cloris took over checking them in and I had to choke back a laugh at their expression when they saw actual keys for their rooms, since they were used to the plastic cards most hotels used for unlocking the door. I could only imagine how they would react when they saw their room. The beds were more like cots and the décor spare. The bathroom served its purpose in a tiny space.

I went into the café to get a refill of coffee. The last cup had helped, but with the extra gloom in the air and the surprise at dealing with the early arrivals, another cup was definitely in order. As I went to the air pot and took in the surroundings, Dorothy and Trent were standing near a window that had a view of the entrance to the boardwalk that led to the beach. They appeared to be in the midst of a discussion. There wasn't any flirting involved as when he talked to Lexie, and they seemed to be on equal footing. His wife was a few steps away but excluded from their conversation, which did not seem to please her. Mindy was at the table she'd shared with Dorothy. She had cut her half of the muffin into a number of pieces and was forcing herself to eat slowly.

I was curious about the conversation between the diet leader and the psychologist, so I lingered by the drink accessory station to see what I could hear. It took me a moment to figure out what they were talking about. As soon as I understood they were talking about a seminar they both had gone to that had information about putting on successful programs, I got myself in the conversation.

"I couldn't help but overhear," I said with a friendly smile. "I didn't know there were seminars about putting on seminars and retreats." I introduced myself again and reminded them that I put on yarn retreats and explained that I had inherited it from my aunt. "I've just followed what she was doing, but I'd sure like some pointers on how to grow the business."

Neither of them seemed impressed by the kind of retreats I put on. "I believe the seminar was really aimed at therapeutic programs," Trent said. "I don't know that we have any tips to pass on for what you do." I couldn't tell if he was being condescending, but his comment made me feel uncomfortable and I quickly excused myself and took my fresh cup of coffee back into the main room.

I chided myself for how easily I had gone to feeling lesser than. It reminded me of the conversations I had with my mother during her frequent phone calls. She always reminded me that by my age she had been a doctor, a wife and a mother. She was so hung up on diplomas or certificates that the fact that I was a professional baker, if that meant being paid to do it, did not seem to count. She had continued with tempting me to leave Cadbury and all that went with it to go to Paris for cooking school that would lead to a certificate. When she understood my passion for investigating, she added an offer of going to a detective school in LA, which would lead to me getting a PI license.

I had continually turned her down. But now that the whole Dane situation had blown up, I was thinking about her offers with a fresh eye.

I went back to a spot on the couch and glanced around the seating area, imagining how it would feel to leave this all behind. I felt a gush of sadness, but then pushed myself to think about the excitement of doing something new in a new location to sweep away the feelings of loss. I was giving myself a mental speech about the need to be resilient when I noticed Cloris waving me over.

"She's here for you," the assistant manager said when I reached the counter. She nodded to the woman holding the handle of a suitcase. She was petite with dark chin-length hair and an angular face. She put on a big smile as Cloris introduced me.

"JoJo Westerly," she said. She seemed a little awkward, like her timing was off, and when she reached out her hand to shake mine, ended up grabbing my arm instead. "I'm sorry," she said, retracting her hand. "Let's try again." This time our hands connected and she let out her breath. "I always like to get everywhere early. Be situated before the program starts." She suddenly looked worried. "You don't have to know how to knit or crochet for this retreat, right?" I nodded and she continued. "I'm a complete novice and I really need an activity that will iron out the kinks. I am always so busy with my handmade soap business." She didn't wait for me to even give her a nod before going on in a choppy voice. "It's all done in small batches. I try to hire people who need a second chance." She brought out her card attached to a cellophane-wrapped piece of the soap. Even with the wrapping the wonderful scent came through.

I looked at it and smiled. "I'm familiar with your soap," I said. "In fact, you'll be getting some in the tote bags I give out." I explained adding little luxury items like nice-smelling toiletries and fancy chocolate since the accommodations were so sparse.

She seemed pleased and then glanced around the cavernous room to take in her surroundings. She stopped when she saw the psychologist coming out of the café.

She ducked as if she didn't want him to see her and moved closer to me, arranging herself so that her back faced him. "I didn't realize he was doing a retreat here this weekend. I bet it is the one he calls Getting Unstuck." She had dropped her voice. "Been there, done that. There was no staying power. I'm still looking for a program that makes a real difference. You know, changes your life and gives you a big aha moment—enlightenment—when all the scattered pieces of your life fall in place." She took a breath. "And stay there." She looked up at me. "Who knows. Your retreat could be the one."

She waited until Trent and his wife had gone out the door before arranging to leave her suitcase and going to the café. I traded looks with Cloris as we watched her go. "That's a tall order," I said, shaking my head. People came to my retreats with assorted expectations. Most of their wishes seemed connected to getting away to spend extended time with needles, hooks and yarn. She was the first one who hoped my program would change her life. I went back to my spot by the fireplace to think about it.

But not for long.

Chapter 6

People arrived at Vista Del Mar in different ways. Those who came from places nearby like San Jose or San Francisco drove. If they came from farther, most flew into the tiny airport and were brought by the Vista Del Mar van or a cab or a ride-share service. The people who drove trickled in, but there was usually a group arrival from the flights. Lexie and Bella had arrived in the van, which meant they'd flown here, and when no one else had come in with them, I thought they were the only ones. But I noticed that the van was still parked in the driveway. A moment later, the door opened and a woman poked her head in. She wore a floppy hat and large dark glasses, which seemed out of place on the dimly lit day. The glasses blocked her eyes, but the way her head was moving, it seemed like she was scanning the interior of the Lodge for trouble, or maybe someone.

Apparently, neither Cloris nor I concerned her, because after a moment she came inside pulling her bag. She wore a paisley print dress with leggings underneath and a long cream-colored sweater over it all.

Once she was inside, she plastered herself against the wall as if she was trying to make herself invisible, and checked the room again. She finally proceeded to the registration counter and sidled up next to Cloris. She had definitely piqued my curiosity and I scooted to a closer couch, anxious to hear what her story was.

"Evie Delano," the woman said in a low voice. She checked the area around her again. "You're sure there's no cell or Internet."

Cloris assumed she was one of the people who freaked out when they realized they were going to be cut off from their electronics and tried to reassure Evie that there were landlines. Instead of being reassured, the young woman gazed at the row of phone booths as if they were doorways to hell. "But they're only for calls out, right?" Evie said in a nervous voice. "Has anyone called looking for me?" She seemed to tense her whole body in worried anticipation.

Cloris looked down at a log and shook her head. "No. But if anyone calls for you, we will post a message." She pointed to the large board at the back of the room.

"Nooo," the recent arrival said, elongating the word. "You can't tell anyone that I'm here."

"We usually just take a message without confirming if someone is a guest, but I'll make sure that no information is given out about you." She waited for a nod from Evie before looking for her reservation. "Are you here for one of the retreats?"

"Yes," she said quickly. "I know I'm early, but I had to cut the cord."

"As long as you understand that the program you came for won't start until tomorrow," Cloris said, waiting to see the woman's reaction.

"That's fine." While Cloris pulled up her information, Evie pulled out her cell phone and looked at the screen. I expected her to appear even more agitated when she saw that there was no service, but instead she let out her breath in a gush. She took the key and listened as Cloris instructed her where her room was located. And then she took off in a rush.

"What was that about?" I said to Cloris. I had waited until the woman cleared the room before approaching the counter. Cloris looked at the computer screen in front of her and shrugged.

"I don't know. But I was relieved that she was glad we are cut off, electronically speaking. She's here for the therapy retreat, and from the looks of it, she really needs it."

"She did seem like a rubber band pulled too tight and like anything could make her explode." I was going to continue that it seemed as if that could describe a lot of the people who came to the weekend retreats at Vista Del Mar. They were at wits' end and needed the space and time to clear their minds from the harassment of electronics. Or they needed to retreat from their everyday world for a while. I felt the whoosh of damp air as the door opened again. I was concerned that Evie had come back for something and I certainly didn't want her to hear us talking about her. Cloris and I both watched as a man walked in. Cloris put on her welcoming smile, but I tensed up as I recognized Milton Carruthers.

I doubted she recognized his face other than he looked familiar. She had a good memory, but who could possibly remember all the names and details that went with past guests. As soon as I gave her his name and said he'd been at my murder weekend retreat, she nodded as the pieces came together. "He's the one Madeleine keeps talking about."

"She said he's here to work on his book, but she thinks he really came to see her," I said. I watched him approach us, and while I put on a friendly smile, I was already thinking of how I could cross-examine him to find out what his intentions were and if it was her fortune he was after. I was in fierce mode and realized I needed to be calmer and more benign before I grilled him.

"Nice to see you again, Casey," he said to me. "No yarn for me this time." Then he chuckled and pointed at the computer bag on his shoulder. "At least not your kind of yarn. I'm here to work on a book."

"And to see Madeleine," I said. I studied his reaction and he appeared uncomfortable.

"Right. That, too." He turned and took in the rest of the room. "Is Madeleine around anywhere?"

For a moment, I thought of asking directly what his intentions were beyond that, but it sounded a little old-fashioned and too intrusive. "She's not here now, but I expect her later. She's part of the staff of my retreats now and she'll be staying on-site. Her title is Director of Hospitality."

"Impressive," he said with a nod. "She is certainly having new experiences. I suppose she had to battle her sister about her position with your retreat. I gather she is used to running the show even though Madeleine is the older of the two." He looked to me for confirmation.

"Madeleine is her own woman now," I said. "She doesn't want to be viewed for who her family is or what they have."

It seemed like he swallowed hard and I wondered if I had touched a sensitive spot. He had a pleasant face with crinkles around his eyes from a lifetime of smiling, or maybe it was from squinting at the sun. But was the pleasant exterior a real indication of who he was? I had barely gotten to know him when he had come for the yarn retreat.

There were all those old sayings about looks being deceiving and not judging a book by its cover. I stopped on the last thought and considered whether it was true. It seemed to me that book covers did hint at what was inside. I had looked at one of Milton's covers. It was considered a cozy mystery and the cover had a friendly look with the sleuth's cat Samantha striking a pose on a red stool that looked like a throne. The plot had gone along with the amusing look of the cover. Just as I was convincing myself that he might be as he appeared, I remembered another something else. He spent a lot of time plotting ways to kill someone. They might not be gory deaths, but the end result was the same. Someone's heart stopped beating. I tried to push away the bad thoughts.

While Cloris checked him in, he noted how empty the social hall was and I explained that most of the place was shut down for maintenance and there were just the three retreats and a few other guests.

"There should be plenty of peace for you to get your work done," I said. Instead of being pleased, he seemed concerned.

"I guess that's good, but it will be harder to stay in the background then," he said. Cloris handed him a key to a room in the Tides building.

"Stay in the background? That sounds like he wants to hide from something," I said to Cloris after he had walked away. "That doesn't sound good."

Cloris seemed ready to shrug it off. "As long as it's nothing illegal, it's none of my business," she said. "You have to be discreet in the hotel business. It's a touchy situation. Guests like to think you remember their needs, but also don't like to feel as if you're watching them. The man who was in here before is a perfect example. I didn't know whether to let him be or if I should make any suggestions about his eating with the others tonight. He said he wanted to be alone, but I thought he seemed a little lonely." She glanced in the direction that Milton had gone. "Maybe he's here to hang out with Ms. Delacorte and he's trying to be discreet."

Her choice of calling it *hanging out* amused me. It had struck me that whatever was between Madeleine and Milton was something more formal. It seemed that it had been strictly talking so far. Her comment about him wanting to be discreet made me wonder what their plans really were for the weekend. What if he had something else in mind? I was being ridiculous. They were both adults and what they did was not my business. Except I didn't want Madeleine to get hurt. She hadn't gone through the ups and downs of romantic relationships to toughen her up. If things turned out badly with them, I worried she would be crushed.

I considered talking to Crystal about it. Madeleine was her great-aunt, after all, even though they were still getting used to the idea. There was nothing to do about it now. The light coming in the window didn't hint at how late it had become, but my watch did. Any time now, the bell outside the Sea Foam Dining Hall would ring to call everyone to lunch.

I needed to go home to gather up everything for the tote bags before my afternoon meeting with Crystal. I gave Cloris a goodbye salute and went outside.

I rushed down the driveway making a mental list of what I needed to do before I returned. When I got to the street, I automatically glanced down it to Dane's house. The driveway was empty, as was the street in front of his house. I assumed that meant he was on duty and Stacy was somewhere else. Probably out shopping for new curtains or something, I thought in a glum mood.

I ordered myself to snap out of it and to remember that I was supposed to be accepting the situation with my usual resilience.

Julius was parading in front of the door when I walked in. His food bowl was full. The automatic feeder kept it that way so there was no telling if he'd eaten any, though I had a pretty good idea that he hadn't. "When you get hungry enough," I said, looking into his yellow eyes.

But in the meantime, I gave him his snack of the stink fish. While I was doing the rewrapping I went back to thinking about my upcoming retreat.

I always made cookies to go along with the coffee and tea that was available during the workshops, and decided to bake them before I went back to meet Crystal so I would not have to worry about remembering them the next day.

The rolls of cookie dough were already well chilled in the refrigerator. I let the oven preheat while I sliced them into perfect little circles. They were like blank canvases after that. I had the choice to add sprinkles of colored sugar, press in some chocolate chips or some nuts. I decided to go fancy this time. I didn't add anything before they were baked, but when they were cooled, I spread a dab of butter cream icing on them and put another on top to make sandwich cookies. The fragrance of vanilla wafted my way as I packed them in a tin with a doily between the layers. I was pleased with the presentation and half wanted to take a picture and send it to my mother. I don't think she had ever baked one cookie and seemed to believe they only came in pink boxes from a bakery.

I started to make up a plate of the cookies to leave at Dane's as I'd always done. But as I put down the doily, I reconsidered. No cookies for Dane anymore. Even I wasn't that resilient.

51

Chapter 7

"Over here," I called out to Crystal. I was situated on the couch in the Lodge with the bin of tote bags and the tin of cookies. She seemed to brighten up the whole interior of the Lodge with her colorful outfit. Her kelly green T-shirt was layered over a purple one with an orange one underneath. Her black curls bounced as she walked in pulling a large bin. The mismatched earrings of the day were a teardrop on one side and lightning bolt on the other. I was surprised to see her massaging her temple and letting out a sigh as she joined me.

"All the gloom is giving me a headache," she said, glancing back toward the window. "I'm used to cloudy, but the sky is usually a lot brighter. It's practically taupe out there. You know it's going to rain. I wish it would do it and get it over with." I followed her gaze to the window and nodded in agreement.

"At least it's nice and cozy in here." She sat down and reached out her hands to feel the warmth coming off the fireplace. "I brought everything for the kits."

"And I have the tote bags to put them in when we finish." I flipped off the lid of my wheeled bin, displaying the array of blood-red tote bags with *Yarn2Go* emblazoned on the front.

"Where shall we do it? Here or in our room in the Cypress building?" She glanced around the large room. "It seems pretty quiet in here."

"For now," I said. "There were a bunch of early arrivals for the programs that start tomorrow. And then there was Milton Carruthers."

"You say that like he's a problem." She shrugged. "He's not here for our retreat, so we don't have to be concerned."

"Yes, but Madeleine thinks he's here to see her and I feel responsible. She met him during my retreat. What if whatever happens between them turns out badly?"

"Madeleine is a grown woman. True, she's been overprotected until recently, but don't you think that it's better she have a relationship, even if it doesn't work out, rather than not having the experience."

"I'm sure you're right. But I'm staying here for dinner to see how things go with them and to keep track of the three here already for our retreat."

Crystal chuckled. "I think I'll join you. It's better than having another lecture from my daughter about how inappropriate my clothes are." Crystal let out a heavy sigh. "She even ordered some clothes for me, on my credit card, of course. They're in the car ready to be dropped off at the UPS store to return them. No way am I going to wear anything so drab." She looked at the tin on top of my bin. "Any cookies in there?"

I flipped off the top and her eyes widened as she saw the sandwich cookies. She announced she was getting a cup of coffee to go with them and I took out a few of the red tote bags and put them on the table.

"Let's see what goodies you have for our group," she said when she returned and had polished off two of the cookies followed by a sip of the coffee. She pulled out a cellophane-wrapped bar of pink soap.

"It turns out that the soap maker is one of our people. She's already arrived. She seems to be a veteran of wellness weekends that haven't worked out and now she's hoping yarn craft will solve things for her."

Crystal put the wrapped bar of soap to her nose. "Her life might not be going as she wishes, but she makes lovely-smelling soap." I handed her an extra bar I had in the bin and told her to keep it. She thanked me and tucked it in her bag.

"Your turn. Show me what you've got," I said.

Crystal finished off another cookie before she put her things on display. She brought out two samples of the completed projects. Because we were expecting newbies, she had come up with something simple that required only the most basic of stitches and would work up quickly even if our attendees were novices. She held up a long strand of stitches with red hearts dangling from it. She took the garland and showed how it could be hung on a fireplace, a window or a door. I imagined it could be hung on a wall as well. "There is a knit version, too," she said.

Cloris had come out from behind the counter and was arranging three easels with posters for the upcoming retreats and looked over at the garland in Crystal's hands. "That's really nice. I wouldn't mind having one of those myself."

Crystal took the crocheted version and was demonstrating how it could be hung on the registration counter as I explained how our people would have a souvenir from the weekend they could show off to their friends. "It's the new thing," I said and told her about Lexie and Bella. "Just a warning," I added. "I think they consider me old."

Crystal made a face. "Then they'll see me as being ancient, too," my yarn specialist said. "Particularly if they find out I have teenage kids." She laid the garland on the counter. "How old are the trendy twins?"

"I'm guessing early twenties," I said.

"We're only in our thirties," she wailed.

I felt a gush of the heavy damp air and turned to see who had come in. Madeleine had stopped just inside the door and seemed hesitant, as if she was intruding, which was crazy. She had every reason to be there since the place belonged to the Delacorte family and the café was even named after her and her sister, but she was easily intimidated by Kevin St. John. As soon as Cloris explained that the manager had gone to his seminar, Madeleine seemed more at ease.

After missing out on wearing denim, Madeleine was making up for it now. Today's outfit consisted of a denim skirt made out of an old pair of jeans she had put over black leggings. She topped it with a loose black sweater. Her blondish bob finished the look. She looked cute and stylish and tens of years younger than when she had dressed like her sister.

Her face lit in a bright smile. "Is he here yet?" she said, bubbling with excitement, which was a change too from the time when she let Cora do all the talking. I had actually wondered if Madeleine wasn't able to speak. There was no doubt about that now.

"Yes. He checked in a while ago. I think he went to his room,"

Cloris said.

She suddenly got flustered and seemed to be blushing. "I don't know what I should do. It's the first time I've seen him in person since he came for that writers' weekend. He was one of the presenters, so I barely saw him. Since then, it's just been Facetime. Maybe I should just wait until dinner. You'll be there then," she said, looking at me. "I'm anxious to see him, but a little nervous too."

"I'll be there too," Crystal said. "Don't worry, you'll have your posse for backup."

"I know you said that you would arrange a room for me," Madeleine said. "But I was thinking I could stay in the cottage." She looked down at the ground and lowered her voice as she continued. "I thought it would be nice to have a place where Milton and I could be just the two of us."

The cottage was a small structure away from the other buildings. It was surrounded by trees and underbrush and felt cozy and private.

Cloris heard her and her expression dimmed. "Of course, I understand. There's someone staying in it, but he's leaving tomorrow. We can have it all ready for you then."

Madeleine seemed a little disappointed. "Then I'll just leave my suitcase and go home after dinner," Madeleine said. She looked at the bins and stuff on the table. "Can I help with anything?"

"That would be great. We need to get the kits ready," Crystal said. "Since we're dealing with inexperienced crafters this time, we want to have the first heart already started."

"That's a splendid plan," Madeleine said, picking up the sample of the garland and admiring it. We each took a bunch of the drawstring bags that held the supplies for the project and began doing the beginning stitches for each of them. We were talking among ourselves when a woman's voice cut into our conversation.

"Oh, no," she said. "This can't be." Her white-blond hair was slicked back in a short style and she wore bright red lipstick. The color worked on her, but I had tried wearing it once and I thought it made me look like a vampire. I could not even look at myself in the mirror.

She was standing near the three signs for upcoming retreats and seemed distressed. My first thought was it was mine that was giving her a problem, but then she said something that made me realize it wasn't. "He can't be here. He never does it this weekend. I made sure to pick a time when he wouldn't be here." She seemed angry and frustrated. "He ruined my life. Get Unstuck, my foot. He ought to get stuck on one of those glue traps they leave out for vermin. And one for her too." She smacked something on the sign with such vehemence, it fell off the tripod and hit the floor with a thud.

"I guess she's not a fan," I said, and Crystal rolled her eyes.

• • •

With the short days at this time of year, it was totally dark when the dinner bell began to ring announcing the meal in the Sea Foam Dining Hall. Normally, there would be a line of people waiting to go in, but this time only a small clump waited outside. The air felt heavy with moisture, like a sponge that was swollen with too much water. It was a relief to get inside. The dining hall was one large space lined with tall windows. The stone fireplace glowed and added a feeling of cheer. More than half the room had been roped off and only a few of the large round tables were set up for the meal due to the small crowd.

The smell of hot food was intoxicating and I realized that I hadn't had anything besides the muffin and a lot of coffee. I dropped my things at one of the tables and went directly to the cafeteria-like setup at the back of the room. As soon as I saw the array of food I chuckled, thinking of how Mindy's mother would have reacted. The food was always tasty and carb-heavy. They had mashed potatoes and macaroni and cheese, along with corn bread, as sides to the fried chicken. In fairness there was salad and broccoli as well. Dessert was white cake with frosting I was sure came out of a can. I passed on it, but filled my plate with a little of everything else, glad to have dinner made for me and not having to eat alone, which I was sure would lead to thinking about Dane.

The tables were beginning to fill up. The psychologist and his wife had chosen seats at the next table. Their seats were close enough to mine that I could hear them commenting on the food. The wife, whose name I know knew was Audrey, was a vegetarian and not happy there wasn't an alternative to fried chicken. "I let them know that wasn't acceptable and they're making something for me." She got up and went back to the food line.

The trendy twins, as I'd come to think of Bella and Lexie, took spots at my table. Madeleine hung by the door for a moment before claiming two seats at the table. "Maybe I should wait for Milton before I get my food," she said with her eyes still glued to the door.

Crystal came in with an unfamiliar man. She pointed out the food line, but he was searching the room. His gaze stopped on Trent Nicholson's back and he cut through the room. He had dark hair and a wiry build and seemed angry about something as he started to lay into the therapist. "It all fell apart when I left," the man said. "I did what you told me and I'm not any happier than I was. I need to know how to fix it. You said we could repeat the retreat for a discount. Ha! I want it free."

Trent stood up and put an arm around the man's shoulder and moved him off near the windows in an effort for privacy as he tried to calm the man.

Even so, everyone had their eyes on the pair. The man seemed very agitated and I hoped it wouldn't escalate into violence. It was a relief when the man finally went to the food line and Trent returned to his table. He had a self-satisfied expression, as if he had settled things with the man.

Crystal took the chair next to me. "What was that about?"

"Judging from what the man said, he must have gone to an earlier retreat and not been happy with the results." Crystal checked my plate of food and got up to get her own. She glanced toward the door.

"Uh-oh. It looks like more trouble for him," she said, staring at the latest arrival. It only took a moment for it to register who the woman with the white-blond hair and bright lipstick was. She was the one who had punched the poster with details of Trent Nicholson's retreat. She had already picked him out of the crowd and was glaring at him. It seemed as if he could feel her eyes on him, because he turned and looked in her direction as she crossed the room. He appeared to be about to dismiss her but then she said, "You don't recognize me, do you?" He scrutinized her more closely as she did a model twirl. "I made a few changes."

He clearly did recognize her now and seemed mesmerized by her for a moment before his expression changed. "What are you doing here?" he demanded.

"Don't worry. I'm not here for you," she said as she perused the rest of the room. "I came for a craft weekend. It's something for the new me."

Just as it was sinking in that she was one of my people, her gaze stopped on me. She totally missed Audrey's harsh glare at her as they crossed paths. Audrey dropped her plate of the vegetarian alternative with a clatter and began fussing at her psychologist husband.

"Are you the yarn person," the woman asked, giving me the once-over. "The person behind the registration counter said you were here."

"Casey Feldstein, at your service," I said with a friendly smile while trying not to stare at the bright lipstick. "You do know that our program doesn't start till tomorrow."

"No problem. Lisa Montez." She stuck out her hand to shake mine. "But just to let you know, I'm expecting a lot out of this weekend."

When Lisa had gone to get her dinner, Crystal gave my back a supportive pat. "I wonder what that means."

"There he is," Madeleine said, waving her hand at Milton, who was standing at the empty host stand. Her face was lit up with anticipation as she called his name. I hoped there would be a big romantic moment when their eyes met for the first time. Except that wasn't what happened. She looked all dewy-eyed and dreamy, but he hesitated, taking a deep breath as if readying himself for something difficult.

Chapter 8

It had started to drizzle while everyone was eating and Cloris came in to announce that the campfire in the outdoor area was canceled due to the weather. Instead, everyone was invited to the Lodge for complimentary wine, and she reminded them about the available activities. Crystal and I stayed behind while the rest of them went to the Lodge.

The drizzle had turned to light rain by the time we walked outside. "We can leave now," Crystal said as we neared the Lodge. "You still have desserts to bake tonight. With this weather, the coffee places will be mobbed tomorrow. You should consider making extra muffins."

"You're right. Just the hint of rain brings out the coffee drinkers," I said. "But first I want to check on everybody. There are already four people here for the yarn retreat and there's Madeleine and Milton."

Crystal nodded in agreement. "Count me in. I'm not in a hurry to go home and have my daughter give me a disapproving glare."

We stopped by the registration counter to check out what everybody was doing.

There was a wild table tennis game going on at the back of the room. Cloris saw me watching as Mindy rushed around on one side of the table, while the diet guru stood at the other side and hit the ball back with little fanfare. "Mindy was going on and on about all the carbs at dinner and what her mother would say. She said she had to get some exercise." Cloris shrugged. "I guess it helps that she's not a very good table tennis player."

Trent Nicholson was sitting at one of the tables that were spread around the room. A box with a jigsaw puzzle was open and his wife was poking through the pieces, giving the evil eye to Bella and Lexie, who were leaning in close to the psychologist.

"As soon as they realized he was a therapist, they moved in on him and started telling him their troubles. His wife doesn't look pleased."

"What about him? What's his story?" I asked, noting that the man who had made the fuss in the dining hall still had an agitated expression and was sitting nearby.

"His name is Leon Rissel. He checked in and said he was here for the Getting Unstuck retreat. When his name wasn't on the list, he insisted that it was okay and that Dr. Nicholson would take care of his bill. I told him that I needed authorization before I could do that. But he made such a fuss, I finally agreed to check him in and get the authorization about the billing later." She blew out her breath as she looked at the short, dark-haired man. "Now I'm wondering if I made a mistake."

Lisa Montez and JoJo Westerly were hanging around the bottles of sherry and port that Cloris had set up at the front. "They seem to be happy with the wine," Crystal said. "I don't think we have to worry about them."

"Too bad I can't say the same about those two," I said. All three of our gazes were on Madeleine and Milton in the seating area near the fireplace. She was on the couch and he had taken one of the mission-style chairs. There was no conversation going on between them. She kept cycling her glance around the room and letting her breath heave in and out, as though she was trying to think of something to say. Milton didn't seem to notice as all his attention was on Trent and the people around him.

"What should we do?" I said.

"Do we have to do anything? We aren't matchmakers," Crystal said.

"Now I'm wondering how this weekend came about." I looked to Cloris for an answer.

"He made his own reservation, but she is comping the charge," the assistant manager said.

"They don't have wine," I said. "I'll bring them some and see if I can ease the situation."

Before I left, Evie Delano came to the desk complaining that she'd missed dinner and could she still get a meal she could have in her room. She had taken off the dark glasses but still wore the floppy hat. There was a touch of paranoia about her as she checked out the crowd, while Cloris called the kitchen and managed to get a meal packed for her.

"I brought you some wine," I said as I approached Madeleine and Milton. They both seemed relieved at my arrival. When I had handed them each a glass of port, I attempted to start a conversation between them by reminding Milton that Madeleine was now part of my staff. "She's a working woman."

"That's right. Congratulations on your position," the writer said and turned to Madeleine. "What exactly are your responsibilities?" Madeleine had a deer-in-the-headlights moment and I stepped in.

"As I think I mentioned, her title is Director of Hospitality. She'll be helping make everyone feel welcome and step in where needed."

"I'm taking it very seriously," Madeleine said. "I probably should get some business cards made. Maybe after this weekend."

Lexie and Bella were making their way to the seats next to the fire. My best guess was that Audrey had somehow shooed them away from Trent. Leon Rissel seemed to have taken advantage of their leaving and was deep in conversation with the therapist. I hoped it was about dealing with Cloris regarding who was going to pay for his room. I brought Bella and Lexie into the conversation, hoping it would ease things up. I introduced everyone and turned the attention on the new arrivals.

"Why don't you tell us about what you've crocheted before," I said.

"I can show you," Lexie said. She opened her large bag and started to unload a bunch of small creatures.

"How darling," Crystal said, picking up a little penguin. "The style is called amigurumi, which is a Japanese word that means knit or crocheted small stuffed dolls, though now it seems to cover any kind of small creature, toy, or even things like birthday cakes."

"Making them has gotten me over some rough spots," Lexie said. "I call the penguin My Breakup with Jac, the bunny with a basket is called Long, Long Flight to Hawaii to Get Over the Breakup with Jac." She plucked a small unicorn with a pink horn and multicolored mane.

"She is called Sitting Home on Saturday Night." Then she pulled out what looked like a work in progress. "I'm going to call this one No Internet."

"Yeah," Bella said. "What gives with the phone service and no Internet. When's it supposed to be fixed?"

I wanted to say *never* but it seemed a little harsh. Even though I had mentioned the lack of phone service and Internet numerous times on the registration form, they had clearly missed it. I tried to smooth it over while mentioning that it was on the form they had filled out.

"It's okay, electronic detox is a hot thing now. We can post about it when we get back," Bella said in a cheerful voice. She turned to her friend. "This is going to be such an experience."

Milton had stood up. "I'll leave you all to talk about your yarn craft." He turned to Madeleine and smiled. "See you tomorrow." I watched him go and almost bump into Lisa Montez, who was eyeing Lexie's creations.

I was glad for all the conversation as it seemed to smooth over Milton's departure. I gave the room another survey. It took a moment to place the shaggy-haired man playing pool by himself. I saw some dishes on a nearby chair and remembered his name was James and he'd wanted to have a picnic on his last night. I gathered by seeing the dishes that the weather had altered his plans.

After that the room emptied pretty quickly, leaving Crystal, Madeleine and me. I got us all glasses of the port. When I returned Madeleine was complaining about Milton's behavior.

"I'm not sure how a beau is supposed to act," she said, looking off in the distance. "But it doesn't seem like that."

Crystal and I traded glances, knowing she was right, but neither of us wanted to say it. "He just got here. Give him a little time and I'm sure he will be different," Crystal said, patting her hand. She had left her bin in the corner, and when she went to check the kits realized we had missed a few and they still needed to be started.

Madeleine seemed to want our company and offered to help. "I am on the staff now," she said.

We were intent on our work and it was only when I looked up that I saw Sammy Glickner playing solitaire at one of the tables.

I got up to say hello. As I passed the window, I saw slashes of rain across the wood-framed windows.

It was actually Dr. Sammy Glickner. He was my ex-boyfriend from Chicago who had followed me to Cadbury. He'd insisted it wasn't in an effort to win me back, but instead was his chance to work on his magic career away from the endless criticism of his parents. He was a urologist by day and did magic shows in the evening. I often worked as his assistant and we had become like a comedy team. No matter what he had said, I still felt that he thought we might get back together. At least until recently.

I went over to greet him. There was something reassuring about his tall teddy bear build and the way he always had a warm smile for me.

"I didn't want to bother you. You seemed pretty intent on your yarn work." He set down the cards. "I just stopped by to see when I'm scheduled to do table magic this weekend in the dining hall." He looked toward the counter. Cloris was on the phone. "I'm waiting for her to be free," he added quickly.

I knew there was more to it than that. Most likely, he was waiting for her overnight replacement to show and then they would go off somewhere. "That's okay. I know about you and Cloris," I said. He looked stricken.

"We were trying to keep it quiet. I thought we succeeded," he said.

"I won't tell anybody," I said with a laugh. "I'm happy for you."

"Really?" he said, and I nodded. He seemed almost disappointed. "I guess I thought after what happened with Dane . . ."

I hung my head as my worst concern was confirmed. Everybody knew about Dane and his old girlfriend and that I was the odd man out. He seemed ill at ease after that and said he was going into the café to practice some new card tricks.

"Port wine, I could use a glass of that," a familiar voice said.

Lucinda Thornkill had just come in, pulling a suitcase. She opened her raincoat, Burberry of course, and water dripped off it and made a puddle around her.

"Tag gets so distraught when he sees me leaving with a suitcase. I thought it would be less upsetting if I brought it here tonight and then came back tomorrow for the retreat." She went on that she had everything arranged for her absence at the restaurant. The mention of the Blue Door reminded me that I still had to do my baking.

"I have to go," I said. Madeleine and Crystal announced they were ready to go as well. The four of us decided to walk out together. At least until we opened the door and looked out. In the time that Lucinda had been there, the light rain had turned into a downpour. "You can't drive the golf cart home in this weather," Crystal said and offered to give her great-aunt a lift. "We just have to get to my car. I'm parked on the street. Kevin St John's order," she said with distaste.

The hotel and conference center was over a hundred years old and had never made accommodations for a lot of cars. The manager had given an edict that the small parking lot was for guests and everyone else had to park outside the grounds.

As we were standing there, the downpour turned into a torrent and we shut the door. It sounded like an army of drummers as it hit the roof of the Lodge. With the open construction, there was nothing to absorb the sound. I checked the window and big drops of rain were splashing in the massive puddles that were already forming.

"Let's give it a few minutes," I said. I kept thinking about Chicago and how this kind of heavy rain never lasted very long. We all went back to a cozy spot by the fire. But when a few minutes became an hour and it was still pouring, I announced I was going to make a run for it to my place.

They were anxious to go, too, and we considered what to do. The only one with rain gear was Lucinda. "We need something to protect us," Madeleine said. "Maybe there are some umbrellas behind the counter."

"Sorry, ladies. No umbrellas. This is the best I could do," Cloris said, holding up three large-size black trash bags. She did a little work with some scissors and called Crystal over. Cloris slipped the trash bag over my yarn helper's head. "Voilà, a rain poncho. It's not Burberry, but it should keep you dry.

Crystal eyed the shiny plastic covering and shrugged. "It's better than getting soaked." We all slipped them on and got ready to face the rain.

The ponchos kept me dryish from the shoulders down, but before we got to the driveway my hair and face were soaked. The black pavement seemed to disappear in the darkness and we found out the hard way it was flooded, with water flowing down toward the street. A strong gust of wind blew more rain in my face and sent all the tree branches shaking. Crystal and I each grabbed one of Madeleine's hands to keep her steady. More wind made the trash bags flatten against our bodies and then begin to flap and billow. My feet and pants were drenched and we had not made it halfway to the street. The grounds were on a slope raised up from the street and the current of flowing water down the driveway grew stronger as we continued downhill. We went from holding hands to grabbing on to each other as the swift-moving water threatened to carry us with it. The wind gusts grew stronger and whistled through the trees on either side of the driveway. There was a swishing sound and then several loud thuds as two of the tall lanky Monterey pines fell across the driveway, blocking us from going farther.

Grateful that the trees had not hit us, there was nothing to do but retreat. We were walking into the wind and against the current of water swirling toward lower ground, trying to keep from being pulled backward. We pushed toward the beckoning lights of the Lodge and finally pulled the door open and almost fell inside.

Cloris and Sammy looked in shock as the four of us came inside dripping all over the floor. "I think we have a problem," I said.

Chapter 9

The four of us stripped off the trash bags as we told Cloris and Sammy about the situation. She was on the phone before we got the last words out. But her confidence seemed shaken by the time she hung up.

"The dispatcher said they're getting reports of problems all over this part of Cadbury. They are telling everyone to stay where they are. She specifically said not to try to get through flowing water." Cloris swallowed hard. "She said that six inches of flowing water can knock a person off their feet, and if they fall face-first it's enough to drown them. Water flowing at seven miles per hour is equivalent to an EF5 tornado wind. And driving isn't an answer. Six inches of water will reach the bottom of most cars and could cause them to stall. And that doesn't take into account what else might be floating in the water or the trees that fell."

She let out her breath. "I guess I know now why the overnight guy hasn't shown." And then as an afterthought she added, "Hopefully the rain will have stopped by morning, and once the damage is evaluated, help will be on the way. I have to check on the guests."

I reminded her that the two guest buildings were on a hill, and told her we had seen the water flowing away from Vista Del Mar. "They should be okay," I said.

"I need to be sure," Cloris said. She went to get her rain gear.

"You can't go alone," Sammy said. He asked for one of the trash bags.

"I'll come too," I said. I left Madeleine in front of the fire with Crystal and Lucinda next to her. Then Cloris, Sammy and I went outside with flashlights to see the situation around the two buildings our guests were staying in.

The lights in the rooms were all off and the only lighted areas were the entrances and the lobbies. It was a relief to see that there were no other downed trees and that there was no danger of the buildings flooding.

We stopped in the Sand and Sea building first. The fire had almost gone out in the fireplace and the easy chairs around it were all empty.

"Should we knock on doors and tell them what's going on?" Sammy asked, and Cloris shook her head.

"Why wake them to tell them that there's nothing to worry about."

We moved on to the building next to it. The lobby of Tides had a different layout. The couches and chairs were all empty. It was deadly quiet and we assumed the guests were all asleep. "There's nothing leaking or seeping in, so let's let them be," I said and the other two concurred.

The trash bag ponchos only went down so far and Sammy joined me in having wet feet and pants legs when we returned to the Lodge.

"This counts as an emergency," Cloris said, holding up a key before going to the closed gift shop. She returned with a pile of souvenir fleece travel blankets, socks and the few umbrellas the store had stocked.

We all found spots around the fireplace, and I passed around the tin of cookies before we all huddled under the forest green blankets with *Vista Del Mar* emblazoned on them and tried to sleep.

• • •

I awoke at first light. The rain had lightened from the downpour into more of a shower. Not wanting to disturb the others, I put the trash bag rain poncho on and took one of the umbrellas from the gift shop. Everything felt wet and the world seemed in monochrome. There was less water flowing down the driveway now that the rain was not as heavy. I'd had a fantasy that I might be able to climb over the fallen trees and get to my house, but that dream was shattered when I saw several more trees had fallen and then what lay beyond them. The street had a layer of muddy water littered with tree limbs and other debris. Stuck in the middle were several cars that must have been carried by the flood and were bobbing in the water and bumping against each other.

I knew there was a service entrance to Vista Del Mar and went to see what the situation was. The street outside was a mucky mess with tree limbs, debris and a layer of mud. I backtracked to the main area and took the boardwalk that led through the sand dunes to the street, hoping it might be better. My hopes were dashed when I reached the end of the Vista Del Mar grounds. The combination of high tide and the storm had brought the waves all the way up to the street. I could not even see the pavement for all the lapping water, sand and boulders.

It took a moment for it all to sink in. For all intents and purposes, Vista Del Mar had become an island. I backtracked through the grounds to report what I had seen to Cloris. I was surprised to see a figure coming up the driveway pulling a suitcase. It took me a moment to process who he was and where he was coming from.

"You're James," I said, realizing that when we checked on the guests we had forgotten about him. "You're the one staying in the cottage." I remembered he was supposed to be going home that morning. "You won't be able to leave," I said. "Everything is a mess." The rain was slicking down his shaggy hair and droplets were glistening in his untamed beard. I bet he was sorry he had not shed all that excess hair.

"What?" he said, sounding annoyed. I assumed his expression matched his voice, but the beard made it hard to tell. I told him about what the dispatcher said and my findings. He joined me as I went inside the Lodge. I went looking for Cloris and he went into one of the phone booths.

Cloris was awake when I returned and I told her about the situation. She wanted to see for herself and I took her on a tour. On the way back, she opened the door to the dining hall and shook her head with dismay. It was dark and silent instead of being abuzz with activity as the crew worked on breakfast.

"We have to call somebody for help," Cloris said as soon as we got back to the Lodge. I was with her when she went behind the counter and called 911. "I got a busy signal," she said, hanging the landline up. With no TV, radio, or Internet there was no way to get any news, but it seemed like a good guess that there were problems all over.

"Forget it for now," I said. "The guests are going to be expecting breakfast."

Cloris got a stricken look. "You saw—the kitchen staff didn't show up. What are we going to do?"

Lucinda had awakened and joined us. "We could use the café. I can put on coffee and tea." The three of us went into the space off the main room and looked around inside. Baskets of snacks sat by the end of the counter. The refrigerated display case had a pan of bread pudding I had made as a test to see if I could expand my baking business. Crystal peeked in, stretching with a yawn.

"We can't deal with the guests looking like this," Cloris said.

We all did look pretty bedraggled after the night we'd just spent and trooped to the restroom to repair what we could. We had given Madeleine the prime spot to sleep, letting her have the whole couch so she could stretch out. The noise of us coming back across the social area woke her up. She sat up and joined us. Only Sammy slept on.

We finger-combed our hair, washed our faces and made minor adjustments to straighten our clothes. Except Lucinda, who added lipstick.

Lucinda took over making the hot drinks. Crystal went through the snacks and pulled out granola bars and bags of cheese crackers. I dealt with the bread pudding, cutting it into small squares, and added the tin of sandwich cookies I had made. Madeleine volunteered to set up the tea bags, cream and sugar, along with cups and such.

When she was done, Madeleine announced she would go to the main room and send the guests our way. "As a representative of the Delacorte family and Director of Hospitality, it's my job to act as host." Her expression dimmed a little. "One of you will have to explain the situation, though. I wouldn't know what to say."

It was nice to see that Madeleine wanted to do something useful, even if she opted out of telling everyone we were stranded.

Cloris and I took up positions at the front of the small café. We had already decided to wait to tell the guests about the situation until after they'd had some hot drinks and food. Though It didn't take long for there to be problems with the plan.

"This isn't the breakfast promised," Dorothy said. "Why is it being served in here?" Mindy was right behind her and mumbled something about all the carbs. There was more grumbling from others who had come in. Cloris seemed overwhelmed by it all and I knew we had to say something.

"Life always throws curveballs," I said, trying to sound cheerful. I was about to ease into the situation when Madeleine came in with Audrey in tow. The Delacorte sister pushed through the crowd and stopped in front of me.

"She says there's something wrong with her husband," Madeleine said. "She wants us to call the emergency number." That seemed to be all that Madeleine could handle and she left the woman with me.

"What's wrong?" I asked, not wanting to tell her that we were having trouble getting through to 911.

"I can't get him to wake up," she said in a panicky voice.

Chapter 10

Cloris was surrounded by angry people expecting her to fix things and there was no way I could give her something else to deal with. I offered Audrey a reassuring pat on the shoulder. "We have something even better than emergency services. We have a doctor right here, right now." I led the way back into the main room, where Sammy was still sprawled on one of the sofas.

He awoke with a start when I stopped next to the couch. With barely a yawn, he sat up and appeared alert. He had learned how to do that when he was a resident on call overnight and grabbed sleep when he could.

I gave Sammy a quick rundown and we joined Audrey, grabbing an umbrella before we went out the door. Light rain was falling as we rushed to the Tides building. She seemed nervous and started to ramble about why they had adjoining rooms rather than sharing one. "He has to have his own space during a retreat," she said. She rushed inside her room and a moment later opened the door to his room from inside. "I heard his alarm on his phone, and when he didn't turn it off I came in to check." Her voice sounded shaky. "He won't wake up." Trent was laying on his side facing the wall. Instinctively, I looked for some rhythmic movement, but there was none.

Sammy pushed closer and I was surprised by his manner. There was none of the goofy "making coins appear from my ear." He had morphed from the Amazing Sammy the magician to Dr. Glickner the efficient doctor. His specialty was urology but obviously he knew about the rest of the body too. He went right to checking his pulse and a second later had moved Trent on his back and started doing CPR. He told me to call for help.

I leaned in close and told Sammy the situation and he heaved a sigh and continued pressing on Trent's chest, starting to hum the Bee Gees song "Stayin' Alive." Audrey gave him a dark look and I explained that Sammy was not being flippant and that the rhythm of the song was the correct tempo for CPR. Sammy gave it his all, but when minutes went by and he could not get a heartbeat, he stood upright and turned to Audrey. "I'm sorry."

"What?" she shrieked. "He can't be dead. Do something."

Sammy explained there was nothing more he could do and then began to ask her questions about Trent's health. "We've only been married a short time and he kept a lot to himself. All I know is that he had high blood pressure and took a pill for it every night." The amber plastic container was sitting on the night table next to the bed with a glass of water.

Sammy picked up the pill bottle and read the label and turned back to her. "It looks like he was ready for a refill." He held the bottle up and there were just a few white pills on the bottom. "He might have had a heart attack. If it's any consolation, it appears that he died peacefully in his sleep."

She seemed wobbly, as if she might faint. "This is horrible. What am I supposed to do now?" She reached out and grabbed on to Sammy for support.

"You need to sit," Sammy said and offered to help her to the lobby.

I was pretty shaken by the whole situation and didn't know what to do, but then I heard Frank's voice in my head telling me to pull myself together and act like an investigator. I took a couple of deep breaths to steady myself and think it through. I had been around enough death scenes to know that there would be an investigation—when the police could finally get there. Frank's voice continued in my head. "Feldstein, take advantage of the moment. If you want to ever win points with that lieutenant, this is your chance to do him a favor."

"Right," I said out loud to myself. There might be no cell service, but the camera on my phone didn't need cell service to be functional. I pulled it out and began taking pictures of everything. Less was not more in this case. I got shots of Trent and the area around him from all different angles. I took pictures of everything in the room down to the pillow under his head and the gray feathery fluff stuck to the pillowcase. I captured the doorway between his and Audrey's room.

When I joined them in the building's lobby, Sammy said we couldn't leave her there. "She may be numb and the reality hasn't kicked in. She should be with the others," Sammy said.

She seemed relieved to let us take over and huddled under the umbrella with us and went back to the Lodge. People had spilled out of the café and were spread around the Lodge, but I was able to find a spot for Audrey by the fireplace where she could have her own space.

Sammy and I went to find Cloris. This was different than when she had tried to call the emergency number before. Now that someone had died, the authorities had to be reached.

Cloris had gone back behind into the business area as though the massive wooden counter gave her separation from the guests and all their demands. She was looking off into the distance at the rain spattering against a window.

I dreaded adding one more problem, but there wasn't any choice. I was glad when Sammy offered to be the one to tell her. He did a good job of keeping an even tone and told her in a matter-of-fact doctor sort of way. He did not even say *died*, but used *deceased*. Her eyes widened and she started shaking her head. "No. Just no," she said in an overwhelmed voice. "The food delivery isn't going to happen, the kitchen staff isn't going to show, nor are the housekeepers or the maintenance guy. My relief counter guy isn't coming. And now this. A dead guest." She slumped against the counter as if she was being crushed by it all.

The phone on the counter began to ring and she looked at it with horror. I thought she would recover and answer it, but she just let it ring until it finally stopped. I mentioned that she needed to try the emergency number again and tell them about Trent, but she put up her hands and shook her head. "I can't. I just can't."

Since Trent was past the point where paramedics could make a difference even if they could get there, there was no reason to rush. I tried to get her to take some deep breaths and assured her that she was not alone in dealing with everything.

It didn't seem to help and she kept muttering that the hospitality classes she was taking never covered a situation like this. Sammy stood by seeming to want to help, but not knowing what to do.

The phone in one of the phone booths rang just then and Cloris kept looking away as if ignoring it would make it disappear. She had always come through for me when it came to helping with my retreat people, and it seemed I ought to pay her back by coming through for her. She was frozen in place, muttering about only being the assistant manager and saying that this was all beyond her.

I liked to pride myself on my ability to rise to the occasion. I had always found a way to deal with whatever happened. How many times as a substitute teacher had I walked into a mess. Obviously, it had never been quite like this, with someone lying dead in bed, but a class of entitled kids who knew every trick to trip me up was always a challenge. They would lie about what they were supposed to do and play dumb games with fake names, but I always managed to work it out and by the end of the day we were all on the same side. "I can do this," I said half to Cloris, but mostly to myself.

I went to the phone booth and picked up the handset. "Vista Del Mar," I said in a business-like tone.

"Who is this?" spewed an angry voice I recognized as Kevin St. John's. Without missing a beat or giving me time to answer, he continued. "What's going on? Why didn't someone answer the main phone?"

I finally got a chance to identify myself, which hardly pacified him. "Where's Cloris?" he demanded. I was not about to tell him that she had freaked out because of the storm, no food, no help and a dead guest. Instead, I said she was helping with a problem in the café. It was sort of true and enough to get him to calm down a little, but not enough to keep him from saying that he was cutting his conference short and coming back.

"Have you already left?" I asked, trying to keep my voice neutral.

"I was just going to arrange for a flight."

"Don't do it," I said.

"Since when do I have to listen to you?" He sounded annoyed. "Is Cloris back yet?"

"I think it's a problem with the espresso machine," I said before turning back to why he shouldn't try to return. "You don't understand. Vista Del Mar is surrounded by a mote of mud, rocks, water and cars that got washed down the street."

He was even more upset to hear that Madeleine was stranded with the rest of us. "Has she said anything about me not being there?" he asked. Then he demanded to talk to Cloris again. I leaned out of the booth and looked toward the registration counter. She seemed to be trying to pull herself together but wasn't ready to deal with the irate manager, and I made another excuse. "I know you're covering for her. I knew there was something wrong when she didn't answer the Vista Del Mar phone." He sounded frustrated.

"There's something else," I said. I hated to add the latest problem, but it would only be worse if I didn't tell him. "One of the guests seems to have died in his sleep."

"Get Cloris on the phone this instant," he demanded. I was desperate and resorted to something childish, the only thing I could think of.

"Here she is," I said, then made a bunch of fake staticky noise to add to the crackling that was already on the phone line. In frustration, he yelled that he couldn't hear me and hung up.

Cloris had come out from behind the counter and sunk into one of the chairs. She looked up when I exited the phone booth. "Thank you for dealing with that." She had already figured out who it was and seemed concerned when I said he wanted to come back.

"Except there's no way he can until the rain stops and the roads get cleared," I said.

"But when he does, he'll probably fire me." She looked toward the door to the café as Madeleine came out. "And she'll probably tell him to do it."

"I don't think she blames you for the circumstances."

"But she will blame me for not dealing with them," Cloris said.

"I'm sure if we put our heads together, we can figure out how to manage."

She grabbed my hand like it was a life preserver. "Thank you."

"And the first thing to do is get through to the emergency number and report Trent's death," I said. She was relieved when I offered to do it. The phone rang and rang, and when it was finally answered by a harried dispatcher and I told her the situation, she said she would put me through to the police department.

The phone seemed to ring forever and I wondered if the phone line was out, but then someone answered in the usual impersonal tone and I asked for the lieutenant. The officer started to give me the runaround. "It's about a death at Vista Del Mar," I said and gave him my name, and then everything changed.

"Muffin girl," he said, losing the official cop tone, and apparently ignoring the part about me wanting to report a death. "We could sure have used some more of those apple cinnamon ones this morning." His change in manner surprised me, but then I suppose cops dealt with so many messes even in a small town that they could brush off clogged roads and a stranded hotel and think about muffins.

"It's muffin lady, if you don't mind," I said in a mock offended tone. I realized he was the officer who had stopped by the Blue Door the other night with Dane and the lieutenant. Now it seemed like it was light-years ago. "I left my days of being a girl a long time ago."

"Okay, sorry about that. It's hard to keep up with what's considered insensitive these days." His voice dropped. "Sorry too about, you know." He let out his breath. "I'm not usually into gossip, but I guess it's a big deal when you get another chance with someone." Was there anybody who didn't know? He abruptly went back to official mode, and I guessed someone must have walked by. "You said someone died."

As soon as I said yes, he put me on hold while he found Lieutenant

Borgnine.

The lieutenant answered in a gruff impatient tone. "What happened? Did they drown, a tree fall on them? Are you sure they're deceased?" Lieutenant Borgnine said in a harried voice.

"Dr. Glickner is here," I said, "and he is the one who called it. It's one of the guests, not someone for my retreat. He was the leader of his own program for the weekend. It seems like he died in his sleep." I heard the cop let out his breath.

"If that's true, then it isn't homicide. It's up to the ME to rule on that. But in the meantime, everything is on the table. Don't touch anything." He asked for more details about who the deceased was and if he was there alone. I mentioned his wife was the one who found him. "I'll do a video and get a statement from her," he said. He let out a displeased grunt as I reminded him there was no cell service or Internet. "It's like the dark ages there. Then it will have to just be a call. Tell Kevin St. John to bring her to the phone." The lieutenant's displeasure grew when he heard that Kevin wasn't there. "Then have the assistant manager bring the woman to the phone."

"I'm helping her out under the circumstances," I said. "She's pretty upset. I think it would be better if you could do the interview in one of the phone booths."

He considered it for a moment. "You're probably right about that." We arranged for him to call back.

"The main part of Cadbury is wet but okay," he said, going over the current situation. "But it's going to be awhile before we can get anyone to Vista Del Mar. The best thing you can do is shelter in place in the meantime." And then he said something that surprised me. "I told you that everything is on the table until the medical examiner determines the cause of death. I'm not telling you to investigate anything, but if you could take some pictures and keep your eyes and ears open."

"Are you deputizing me?" I asked in surprise.

"No," he said. "But you did work for that PI and you have some skills."

"You're right," I said. "I already took pictures of the crime scene. Well, I suppose for now you would just refer to it as a death scene."

"I don't care what you call it, but good work with the photos. Now leave the room alone."

So, the voice in my head was right. I had won points with the lieutenant for taking the pictures. I agreed to set Audrey up in one of the phone booths and we hung up.

I looked out the window and saw that a steady rain was still falling as I went to find Audrey.

She was operating on automatic pilot as I took her to one of the phone booths and got the lieutenant on the phone. I closed the folding door on the small cubicle and left her to talk to the cop.

Chapter 11

As soon as Audrey Nicholson finished her phone call, she went back to her seat by the fireplace and resumed isolating herself from all that was going on. I had stayed by the registration counter doing a little gloating. I was feeling pretty good about myself after the phone call with Lieutenant Borgnine. He had said I had skills. Even if he said he wasn't deputizing me, he had asked for my help. I was thinking about calling Frank and telling him what the lieutenant had said, but then the bubble of my good feelings burst as my focus went to the guests milling around the main room of the Lodge.

"What are we going to do about them?" I said to Sammy, who had just joined me at the wooden counter. Cloris was still hiding out back from public view. "They're looking pretty edgy and it's going to be lunchtime soon."

"There's a more pressing matter, Case," he said, using the nickname he'd given me. "We can't just leave his body there."

"You mean because somebody will see it?"

"That, and I don't mean to be gross, but it's going to be awhile before anyone gets here to take him away, and there's going to be a smell and a situation with bugs. Even my magical skills won't help with that."

I knew he was right and chided myself for not thinking of it. "What can we do?" I said.

"We need to make him disappear from view and put him someplace cold. You know, like the morgue." We both looked at Cloris, who was almost hidden from view. The area behind the counter was generally off-limits to anyone but staff, but Sammy and I ignored the sign on the door that led to the business area.

"We need your help," Sammy said in a calm voice as we joined her in her spot in the corner. She heaved a deep breath.

"I want to help, I really do. What is it?" she said as she straightened. Sammy explained the situation and a look of horror crossed her face as she heard about the coming stench and hoard of bugs that would show up if we did not do something. I was worried that it was going to overwhelm her all over again, but the lights seemed to go on in her eyes and she nodded. "Of course, we have to do something."

Sammy laid out what was needed and she took a moment to think it over. She started to shake her head with a hopeless look, but then she stopped and brightened. "There is someplace that might work. There's a cold room in Hummingbird Hall." She explained that the auditorium was often used for special events and needed a refrigerated room to keep food and drinks. It was on the lower level of the place and most people didn't know it even existed.

"I think the keys are in Mr. St. John's office," she said. Sammy and I followed her back to the inner sanctum. She felt uncomfortable looking around his desk drawers, but I reminded her that it was an emergency situation. I had never been in there before and took the opportunity to nose around. He had turned it into his own personal space with a couch and several comfortable chairs. The walls were covered in photographs. There were pictures from the old days at Vista Del Mar and a lot from recent times. I was fascinated by the black-and-white photo from the time it was a girls' camp. A group of counselors were standing in front of the Sand and Sea building. Next to it was a more recent picture of a group of birdwatchers with binoculars hanging around their necks as they walked through the dunes on the boardwalk. Another featured a group doing yoga on the beach. I recognized one of the lobby rooms in the Tides building. A group was gathered around the fireplace and it looked very cozy. I sucked in my breath when I saw that the man who seemed to be the leader was Trent Nicholson. It was shocking to see him alive with an animated pose when I knew where he was now. I was reminded that I had heard he had put on weekend programs there before. I looked closer at the other people in the photo and picked out Audrey. There were several men and another woman off to the side. Something about her seemed familiar. But then it might just have been her clothes. The jeans and sweatshirt was such a common outfit among retreat attendees, it seemed almost like a uniform.

"Here they are," Cloris said, holding up a key ring. She seemed to have rallied a bit and I hoped she would stay that way as she led the way to check out the mysterious cold room.

Hummingbird Hall had been built in the same Arts and Crafts style, which meant the exterior was dark wood with local stones. The arrangement of the main area changed according to what it was being used for. It could be left open for dances, set up with tables for events or be filled with rows of chairs facing the raised stage when it was used for movies or other entertainment.

It was located just beyond the dining hall and built into a slope so that the lower floor was accessible from the outside. The three of us had to walk carefully to avoid sliding in the mud as we went down to the concrete pad around the door to the lower floor.

Cloris brought us inside and led the way past the bathrooms and the stairway that went up to the main space. We passed a storage area in a part of the building I'd never seen. She flipped on the lights, illuminating a windowless room. At one end there was what looked like a box with a serious-looking door on it. She said that they had used it to keep the champagne cold for the New Year's Eve wedding that had been held in the upper room. "There might still be some champagne," she said, telling us not to disturb anything.

She opened the thick door and let us go inside. The temperature immediately dropped and I shivered as I looked around. I assumed the bottles in the corner were the champagne she mentioned. Sammy was more interested in the metal table in the middle of the room.

"This should work out just fine," he said.

We returned to the Lodge and Cloris went back behind the registration counter, leaving Sammy and me to work out the logistics of moving Trent's body.

Audrey didn't seem to have moved a muscle while we'd been

gone. She seemed lost in her own thoughts and unseeing of anything going on around her.

"We better tell her we're going to move him," Sammy said. "We can't have her going in the room and seeing an empty bed with no explanation."

"Right," I said. "She'll either think that he's still alive and wandered off somewhere or that he somehow had risen from the dead."

"Either way is not good. You probably should be the one to talk to her. I don't have a lot of experience with stuff like this."

"And I do?" I said with a sigh. Really, none of us had experience dealing with all that was happening.

"You're right, you don't have experience either, Case," he said. "But you excel at handling bad situations." I took a mock bow and thanked him for the vote of confidence and went to talk to Audrey.

She barely looked up when I stopped in front of her. "I'm so sorry about your husband," I began. "Normally, someone would come to remove him." I didn't want to say *remove the body*. It sounded so impersonal. I looked at her to see if she was absorbing what I was saying. It was hard to tell as she remained expressionless. "With the problems because of the weather, we're cut off right now and no one will be able to come for a while." I paused and gathered myself to get to the next part. I didn't want to bring up the truth of smell and bugs. "We are going to move him to someplace cold in the auditorium building where he won't be disturbed." It seemed pretty lame but was the truth. In the cold room, he would not be disturbed by the natural process of decomposing.

She finally nodded. "Oh, thank you. I was afraid I was going to have to stay in the next room with him there in the bed," she said. "Then he really is dead?" she said, looking back at the fire. It was hard to read her tone. Was she resolved or relieved? I asked if she needed anything or wanted to join the others in the Lodge, but she shook her head. "I'd rather stay here and be alone while it sinks in."

Sammy and I went back to Trent's room. The door had been left unlocked and it looked like he was asleep.

"How are we going to do this?" I said. Trent was a big man, probably six feet tall.

Sammy dismissed the idea of us carrying him right away. "Case, he's way too heavy for us to manage. We need to find something to put him on."

"By the way, thank you for all this," I said. "It's not really your responsibility. I'm hosting a retreat and you were just visiting."

"Case, I'd do anything to help you and, uh, Cloris," he said. I reassured him again that I was fine with Cloris and him being a couple.

He let out a disappointed sigh. "Really? I guess I was hoping you'd be jealous."

"This is hardly the time to be thinking about stuff like that," I said, glancing back at the open door to Trent's room. "We better deal with this before people decide to go back to their rooms. It's one thing to tell everyone that he died, but another to see us moving his body."

"There has to be something we can use," Sammy said, looking down the dark wood-paneled hallway. With the rain and our task, it seemed even more forbidding. We kept opening closet doors until we found the double ones at the end of the hall that had the housekeepers' cart and supplies.

"That could work," Sammy said, pulling it out. He looked around the closet and found a box of black trash bags and some duct tape. I helped him clear all the towels and rolls of toilet paper off the top and we wheeled it down the hall.

Sammy positioned it next to the bed and looked at me. "Are you up for this?"

I had to admit that nothing in my past had prepared me for handling a dead body, even the time I spent working for Frank as an assistant PI. Sammy took his shoulders and he gestured for me to grab Trent's feet. When I recoiled at the touch of them, Sammy tried to help.

"Just think of it as an empty vessel," he said. "That's what I told myself in med school when we had to deal with cadavers." Maybe Sammy could do that, but it was still a man's body to me. I took some deep breaths, and when I was ready, at the count of three we both lifted him. Trent was literally dead weight. Sammy did most of it. He was hardly muscle-bound like Dane was and had a softer build. But he was stronger than I'd expected. He noted my surprise as he did most of the work draping Trent over the top of the cart. "All those card tricks and sawing women in half has built up my upper-body strength," he joked

Once Trent was positioned on the cart, Sammy pulled a trash bag over his head and another up from his feet and then taped the two bags together. He grabbed a couple more of the trash bags and used some scissors to cut head and arm holes in them before handing one to me. I glanced out a nearby window and saw that the rain had turned steady again.

"We can't use an umbrella or run through the rain with this," he said, looking at the cart. I pulled on the poncho and we each took an end of the cart and rolled it outside toward the back exit where there were no stairs. The path to the main part of Vista Del Mar was all downhill and we had to fight gravity the whole way. I could only imagine what would have happened to Trent if we had lost our grip on the cart.

The level ground was a little easier to navigate, but the terrain was bumpy and the plastic bags around Trent were slippery and it was a challenge to keep him from slipping off the cart. There was no way to avoid going past the Lodge and the windows of the café as we headed for Hummingbird Hall.

I shuddered thinking of how Lieutenant Borgnine would react if he could see what we were doing. He had told me to keep my eyes and ears open, but had not said anything about moving Trent. Or not moving Trent, for that matter. Would he consider it tampering with the crime scene? But what choice did we have. Was it a crime scene anyway? The lieutenant had said everything was on the table until the medical examiner had done their work. It was bad enough to have a natural death, but what if it was murder? I didn't want to consider how the group would react to that. Or how I would feel about being stranded with a killer in our midst. All my thinking had distracted me from keeping a hold on Trent. We hit a bump, and he started to slide off the cart just as we were passing the Lodge windows. I lunged for his legs as Sammy grabbed the upper part of him. I could only imagine what a sight we were, dressed in trash bag ponchos wrestling with the trash bags obviously filled with something. I glanced up at the windows hoping no one had taken that moment to look outside.

I could see heads and was glad they all seemed to be faced away from the window. But then one of them turned and looked out. It was Lucinda, and she did a double and then triple take. I put my fingers to my lips, hoping she would get the message not to say anything to the others. She nodded and gave me a thumbs-up.

We kept rolling and I let out a big sigh of relief when we passed the Sea Foam Dining Hall and I knew we were out of their line of sight. My arms were aching as we finally rolled to the lower floor of Hummingbird Hall. Sammy steered the cart in the door and back to the cold room. We lined the cart up with the metal table in the middle, and with a heave lifted Trent onto it.

We took the housekeepers' cart back to the Tides building, and while Sammy reloaded it with towels and toilet paper and put it back in the closet where it had been, I went to have another look at the room, wondering if we should put something across the doorway to keep everyone out.

With Trent gone, it looked like any other unmade room. The covers were pulled back and there were a pair of slip-on sandals by the bed, which he probably used as slippers. I took my time checking out the room. I stuck my head into the tiny bathroom and saw his incidentals were sitting on the little shelf above the sink. I didn't know Trent at all really, but it seemed sad to look at his toothbrush and imagine him using it the night before with no idea it would be the last time. I did another scan of his room. The pill bottle on the table next to the bed had gotten knocked over, probably when we were moving Trent. It was an automatic gesture to put it back upright. I glanced down at the amber bottle and saw the label. Something seemed odd about it and then I noticed that it was handwritten. I took a picture of it before leaving the room and closing the door. It was the only thing that I thought the lieutenant would approve of.

Chapter 12

"Mission accomplished," I said to Cloris when Sammy and I returned to the Lodge. We had stripped off the dripping trash bag ponchos before coming inside. I didn't know about Sammy, but the whole experience had left me feeling giddy. That and too much coffee and still being dressed in the same clothes from yesterday. My sneakers felt squishy from getting wet, again. The bottom of my pants leg seemed permanently wet, but neither seemed to bother me.

"Thank you, thank you both," she said. I was glad to see that she was trying to project her usual persona as assistant manager even with the crease in her forehead, as if her mind was whirling with all that was going on. She had a lot more to lose than either of us did. She'd been fired when some skeletons came out from her past. The Delacorte sisters, mostly Madeleine, and Crystal had prevailed on Kevin St. John and he had been forced to rehire Cloris, but it was under duress. He had taken it as a threat to his power as manager. Cloris and I both knew that he was gathering ammunition to let her go and have it stick. Letting everything fall apart in an emergency surely would count.

The mood in the Lodge was a little frantic. They'd had too much coffee and still didn't know exactly what the situation was, but obviously sensed that something was wrong. Cloris leaned against the counter for support when she admitted that she had not told the guests anything. "There was just so much noise and I couldn't get their attention," she said. "I know that's just an excuse." She put her head down, feeling bad that she was letting things slip.

The giddiness had subsided and I was back into focus and asked about Audrey. "She hasn't said anything to anybody as far as I can tell. She's staying in the shadows." We all looked at the area around the fireplace and it was true that she was barely visible. Cloris looked directly at me. "What do we tell the group about first—that the psychologist died or that we're stranded?" She turned to Sammy. "He died in his sleep, right? So it's natural causes."

Sammy shrugged. "That was just a guess." He looked to me. "Case, you worked for an investigator." He left it hanging.

"Lieutenant Borgnine said that nothing was certain until the medical examiner checked things out."

I heard Cloris swallow hard. "You mean that it could be murder?"

"We don't have to tell them that," I said, watching Mindy and Dorothy playing table tennis again. It was the same scene as before, with Mindy rushing around one side while Dorothy stood in one spot and hit the ball back.

"And you might want to cushion it a little," Sammy said. "I know about using patter from my work as a magician. I'm sure you have heard the 'cat is on the roof' story." He didn't wait for us to acknowledge that we had and went into what was actually sort of a joke. The point was that instead of announcing that there had been a death, you led up to it by saying that the cat was in a dangerous position on a roof, and then the story went on about the efforts to rescue the cat, but finally it came out that the cat had fallen and died. "That way, it's not such a shock," Sammy said.

"I don't know what we're going to do about lunch," Cloris said. Her brow was truly furrowed now. "And I'm supposed to tell them a convoluted story about Trent Nicholson." She shook her head. "I don't know how to do that."

"Maybe we should tell them about the situation with the weather first," I said. Cloris seemed overwhelmed with that suggestion, too.

"I'll do it," I said.

She gladly passed it off and we decided it would be easier to talk to them if they were all in the café. Cloris rounded everyone but Audrey up and got them into the window-lined room and turned the floor over to me.

All the coffee and unease about the bad weather had really jacked them all up and the din was impossible to speak over. I gave a nod to Lucinda and Crystal, who were sitting together at a corner table. Madeleine was sitting with Milton at their own table. I went to one of the stools in front of the wooden counter. Boosting myself on it put me a little above everyone, but it did not help to get their attention.

I thought of a trick I'd learned when I was the substitute teacher. Getting the rowdy class's attention was always a challenge. They were experts at tormenting a stand-in when their teacher was out. Instead of banging on something to get their attention, I had found something softer that worked. Singing softly. It wasn't that my voice was all that great, but somehow the musical tone cut through their chatter and got them to stop talking and look at me. I didn't know if it would work now, as the noise in the café was a lot louder and they were not even looking in my direction.

I chose the first song that came to mind, probably because of the circumstances, and let loose with my rendition of "Singing in the Rain." I wasn't sure of the lyrics and improvised, but it was the tune that cut through the chatter. The din died off and suddenly all eyes were on me.

"I know you are all probably wondering about how the weather is affecting things here. I spoke with the authorities, and for now they said we should shelter in place. Unfortunately, all the streets around here are impassable because of water, mud and debris. Vista Del Mar is an island at the moment. But the good news is that we have power and we are safe."

"What do you mean?" Lexie said, interrupting and looking at her friend. "Is this going to be like that island in that old TV show where we get stuck here forever?"

"You mean *Gilligan's Island*?" I said. The TV show was an ancient fantasy and I was surprised that someone so young and intent on being trendy would even know about it. But then what was old was now considered classic. I needed to calm her hysteria no matter how absurd it seemed. "No, we won't be stranded forever. The rain will end and the streets will get cleared." I left off saying *eventually*, afraid that would sound too distant.

"What does that mean about the program for the weekend? I suffer from anxiety," Bella chimed in. "That's how I got involved with making those crochet creatures. Concentrating on following the pattern is supposed to calm your mind. It helped being part of an online group, but I heard that it doesn't compare to being in a real in-person group. That's why we came." She looked at her almost twin, who nodded in acknowledgment.

"Don't worry. My yarn expert is here," I said, pointing out Crystal.

"We have the supplies we need. There won't be as many people as I expected, but we will definitely have a group," Crystal said.

"I was having special meal kits delivered for my retreat group," Dorothy said. Then she had another thought. "What about the rest of my retreat group?"

"They won't be able to get here," I said.

"What about food?" Mindy called out in a worried voice.

"I'm sure we'll be able to work that out," I said. I didn't give any more details, as I had no idea how we were going to feed them since there hadn't been the expected food deliveries and there was no staff to prepare the meals.

"Why didn't I eat those French fries," Mindy wailed. "This sounds like it was my mother's plan. Strand me with no food so I'll have to lose five pounds over the weekend."

Lucinda joined me at the front. "I think you overestimate your mother's power," she said to the distraught young woman.

Lucinda took over and reassured everyone that we would figure out the food. "I own a restaurant in downtown Cadbury." She left it at that, not mentioning that she was not involved with the cooking. She gestured toward me. "Casey is our dessert chef and she can do magic with even the most basic of ingredients."

"What about the Getting Unstuck retreat?" a man demanded. He was the one who had accosted Trent Nicholson in the dining hall the previous night. Someone had said his name was Leon Rissel. He had seemed agitated then and still did. He scanned the café. "Where is Dr. Nicholson, anyway?"

His question hung in the air and I realized I had to answer. I tried to think of what to say and Sammy's story was stuck in my brain, and the words tumbled out before I could stop them. "He's on the roof."

"Huh?" Leon said, giving me an odd look.

"I'm sorry, I don't know why I said that," I said. "With all that's going on, I'm a little distracted." I added a weak smile before continuing. "What I meant to say is that Dr. Nicholson is under the weather. He was taken ill during the night." There was a sound of concern from some of the people. "He's under the care of Dr. Glickner." I didn't want to make a lot of false promises about him being cured since obviously there was no chance of that happening. "He's been moved to a location where he can be kept stable," I added. That part was absolutely true. He was in a place where his condition was not going to change.

"What about us?" the woman in the floppy hat said. "I came here to change my life with Dr. Nicholson's help. He promised." She seemed apprehensive as her gaze moved over the group. "You don't know what it's like to be me. My name is Evie Delano." She paused and checked the group again. She seemed relieved when no one reacted, but only for a moment, and then she seemed annoyed. "Then none of you know who I am. Evie Delano, the lifestyle influencer with thousands of followers."

The trendy pair both reacted. "You're her?" Bella said. "That's right, the hat is like your trademark."

Evie took a step back. "Did you follow me here?" she said in a shaky tone. "Stay back. No one will let me alone. I have to keep making content and weird people think they know me. This weekend was supposed to be a chance to get away from all of it. No Internet, no cell phone. A chance for me to figure out what I'm going to do."

"You certainly got the part about no Internet or cell phone," Dorothy said. "If I were you, I'd be more worried about meals." She looked down at her watch. "It's getting close to lunchtime and breakfast sort of wasn't. A key part of the plan for my weekend program is not missing meals." Mindy nodded in agreement.

"We will get back to you on that," I said. I waved to Lucinda, Crystal and Madeleine to follow me and we went back to the main room to find Cloris.

Chapter 13

"The natives are getting restless," I said, glancing back at the crowd in the café. "The first order of business is food." Crystal, Lucinda, Madeleine and I were on our way to join Cloris in the area behind the counter to put our heads together.

I was about to follow them through the door that led to the business area when the outer door opened, letting the wind blow in some rain. I froze, afraid to look back. Since everyone was accounted for, I had an eerie feeling that it was Trent Nicholson, who had somehow become reanimated. It had happened where people had been considered dead and then came back.

When I finally looked, I saw that it wasn't a zombie Trent Nicholson. I felt a mixture of relief and disappointment. Relief that he wasn't angry about being wrapped in trash bags, slung on a housekeeping cart and left in a cold room, but disappointed that he was not still alive.

It was the hairy-looking guy I had seen when I was out checking the grounds.

He ignored me and went right up to the counter and started dealing with Cloris. "Any word when I can get out of here?" he said in a not too pleasant tone.

Cloris shook her head as she tried to find her voice. "I'm so sorry, James, but the road is still blocked and we don't know when it will be cleared."

"I'm not paying for any more nights in the cottage," he said in an annoyed tone. Cloris assured him that was a given and then she must have remembered that Madeleine had requested it for the weekend. She suggested that he might be more comfortable in a room in the Tides building and he shook his head vehemently. "No way am I trading that place for one of those tiny rooms. And what about meals?" he demanded. I felt bad for the way he was cornering Cloris and I tried to help.

"We're just working on that now." I introduced myself and explained that I hosted yarn retreats. "I sympathize with your situation." I pointed out that my house was just across the street and I couldn't even get there.

Sammy came out from the back and joined me. "Go back where you were," I said, dropping my voice. "We don't want anybody asking questions about you know who yet."

"Questions about what?" James said. I kept up with the charade and told him that one of the retreat leaders had been taken ill and explained that Sammy was a doctor.

"I thought he was a magician."

"I'm both," Sammy said and made a quarter appear to come from my ear.

James was not impressed. "You ought to use something bigger. A quarter doesn't buy anything anymore." He looked across the counter to Cloris. "Who got sick? Was it from something he ate? That dinner last night sat on my stomach like a stone."

"It was nothing like that," Cloris said defensively. "It was Trent Nicholson. Dr. Trent Nicholson." She looked to Sammy to take over.

"It was probably something with his heart. His wife said he was on some meds for it."

"The psychologist?" James said. "I heard him checking in. He seemed like an arrogant guy. Didn't he call you out for not addressing him as Doctor." He looked at Cloris.

"I didn't realize anyone overheard that," the assistant manager said.

"I thought it was my last night here and I was easing back into being around people. I had spent so many days keeping to myself, it's a bit of an adjustment. I'm working on getting used to talking again." He looked at the fireplace and picked Audrey out of the shadows. "That's his wife, isn't it? If the shrink is sick, she must feel bad for laying into him." James shrugged as he continued to explain why he had so much information. "There's not much entertainment here and I was trying to get used to being in the world again, so I eavesdropped. You have to take drama when you can get it. She was fussing at him about ogling another woman." He shrugged. "Makes me glad I'm single." As an afterthought he turned to Sammy. "You said the dude was sick, like how bad is he?"

Sammy looked from Cloris to me. James didn't seem to have anything invested in Trent or the rest of the group, so there didn't seem to be any reason not to tell him the truth. "Actually, he's deceased," I said.

"Whoa," James said. "Then she must really feel guilty for chewing him out." He leaned back against the counter. "Whew, that's the most I've talked to anybody in days. I didn't realize how much energy it took." He glanced over our little group and then to Cloris. "As long as I can't leave, I think I'll go back to my solitude. Let me know about lunch." And he went back the way he had come.

Talking to him about my house had suddenly made me concerned about Julius. His bowl of dry food would stay full thanks to the gadget I had gotten and he had water bowls all over the house, but still I wanted to know he was okay. I told the others I had to make a phone call before we dealt with lunch.

"I better make myself disappear," Sammy said with a wiggle of his eyebrows. "I wouldn't want anyone to think I was neglecting the patient." He went back through the door to the business area.

I had been operating on emergency mode and dealing only with what was right in front of me and I felt guilty about not thinking about the cat before. And my house. Though it was on a small slope above the street, which I hoped meant there was not a problem. Dane lived down the street from me. I was sure he had been called in because of all the storm problems, but I was also sure that he had kept tabs on his place. I didn't really want to call him due to the change in our relationship, but I felt like I had no choice. He answered on the third ring. As soon as I said hello, I could hear him tense up.

I had already decided to deal with the change in things head-on and get it out of the way. "I know about Stacy and who she is," I said. "Everyone in town has let me know about the situation and I get it. A second chance and all."

"This isn't really the time to talk about the *situation*, as you called it. Are you alright?"

I was used to him having a playful tone, but this time he was totally serious. "Yes," I said. "We're an island, but so far okay. Except . . ." I had the door to the phone booth open and I checked around me that no one was in earshot. "One of the guests died overnight."

"You should talk to Lieutenant Borgnine. He'll want to investigate—when he can get there."

"I already talked to him," I said.

"You know it might be a couple of days before anybody can get there." He left it hanging and I knew he was referring to the problems of having a body in a warm bed.

"It's already taken care of," I said.

"Really?" He sounded surprised. "Are you going to give me details?" It was hard to tell if he was speaking as a cop or as a friend. I gave him a full description, including all the trash bags we were all wearing. He let out a laugh, then stopped himself.

"I know it's serious, but you and Sammy pushing a body wrapped in trash bags had to be a sight."

"It was," I said. I described Lucinda's reaction when she looked out the window.

"She's there?" he asked. His voice had lost the official tone as he asked more about the situation with the guests at Vista Del Mar.

"We're just about to have a meeting to figure it all out," I said.

"I wish I could help, but the roads around Vista Del Mar are hopeless until we get some heavy equipment in."

"There is something you can do," I said, trying to keep my reserved tone. "I was calling about Julius and my house."

"Our side of the street is okay," he said. "It's just a problem getting there. I had to climb over the back fence to go through the Sea Spray Inn's yard to get to a street that wasn't a mess so I could go in to work. I can check your place when I go home. Will Julius be okay until then?" I told him about the dry food arrangement and he laughed. For a moment he seemed like his usual self.

"He's probably sitting in front of your refrigerator waiting for some stink fish. I'll figure out a way to get him some." He said he'd call me later with a report, but we realized it was easier for me to call him since I was relying on a pay phone. There was a moment of dead silence after that.

"We really need to talk. Not like this on the phone." His voice was dead serious and all at once it sank in that it really was all over between us and felt my heart sink. There would be no more teasing me about my flirting abilities, no more plates of his delicious spaghetti left at my door, and no more time spent just hanging out. I stopped myself before I got to the hot part and pulled myself back together.

"No need. I understand," I said, forcing my tone to stay neutral. "You just made it easier for me to do what I've been thinking about all along." There was silence on his end for a moment and then I heard him swallow.

"You mean leave Cadbury?"

"I don't have to worry about breaking your heart anymore," I said, trying to make a joke. I had used that as an excuse for not falling completely into a relationship with him—at least for a while. I thought back to how close I'd come to declaring my feelings for him, thanks to my ex-boss's advice.

"Don't rush and do anything," he said.

"Fat chance on that right now," I said. He seemed to hesitate then said he was on duty and had to go. We agreed that I'd call him later. I sat for a moment and thought over the phone call, pleased with myself for not wearing my heart on my sleeve, as the old saying went. Some people would have ranted and raved about being replaced. It wasn't my style. I tried to will my eyes not to fill with water, but even so a tear escaped and rolled down my cheek. I took a deep breath, wiped it away and got ready to meet with the others.

As soon as I joined Cloris, Lucinda, Crystal and Madeleine, they asked about the phone call and I tried to dismiss it and said it was about checking on Julius. I did not want to start talking about Dane and went right to why we were putting our heads together. "What are we going to do about feeding them?"

"We can get to that in a minute. Tell us what happened to the psychologist," Lucinda said. There was no reason to hold anything back. They had already overheard me tell James that Trent was dead. And Lucinda had seen Sammy and me pushing the loaded housekeeping cart. I spilled the whole story, including where Trent was at the moment.

"Are you so sure it was natural causes?" Lucinda asked.

"It seemed that way, but who knows. Lieutenant Borgnine said everything had to be considered until the medical examiner gave their report."

"You mean like murder?" Crystal said in a concerned tone. "Then it was one of them." She glanced at the guests spread around the area.

"You probably heard that guest say he heard Trent and his wife arguing. The spouse is always the first suspect," I said. "But there were others who had issues with him. There was that agitated guy who was dissatisfied with a past retreat."

"You mean Leon Rissel," Cloris said. "He seemed quite upset. There was a problem when he checked in. He wanted his room to be billed to Dr. Nicholson. I said that I'd have to have a credit card on file until I got an okay from the psychologist. He slammed it on the counter and said there better not be any charges on it."

"I overheard someone dissing his retreat program," Lucinda said. "She said she hadn't been helped at all. I wish now that I had caught the woman's name." She brightened. "But I think we can figure it out. It sounded like she came for the yarn retreat. She said at least she'll have something concrete to show for the weekend this time."

Madeleine didn't want to be left out and she brought up the woman in the floppy hat. "She seemed pretty crazed," Madeleine said.

"But it probably isn't murder," I said, trying to keep things calm. They all seemed relieved at my comment.

"We really need to figure out lunch," Cloris said, getting back to the immediate concern.

"You're right," I said. "We have to figure what there is to feed them, and who is going to make it."

"And there's cleanup to consider, too," Cloris said.

"I think I should go back to the café and act as host while you figure it out," Madeleine said. Giving her a title had really done something for her. She seemed to have a new sense of herself. I didn't know how much help she would be to us anyway, since she and her sister had been brought up with housekeepers and cooks, and I doubted she knew anything about actually making food.

"The first thing to do is see what we have to work with," Lucinda said.

I went back to Kevin St. John's office to get the keys to the dining hall. Sammy was stretched out with his feet hanging over the end of the couch, asleep. His eyes opened when I came in. "You have to grab it when you can." I took the opportunity to have another look around the manager's office and the photographs on the wall. I saw more familiar faces. Dorothy Spenser was surrounded by a group of women who I gathered were there for her diet retreat. She was in another photo, too, this time with Trent Nicholson and some others I didn't recognize. I recalled that I'd heard her talking to the psychologist about a seminar they had gone to regarding how to put on retreats. It hadn't occurred to me that it was at Vista Del Mar, though it made sense. I checked out all the pictures and most of them were of past retreats. Except there were none of mine. It only reinforced how much Kevin St. John wanted to get rid of them. If I left Cadbury, he would get his wish.

I joined Cloris, Crystal and Lucinda, and we went outside. There was a respite from the rain, but something about the way the air felt made it seem only temporary. We talked as we walked to the dining hall. "Once we've fed them, we're going to have to keep them busy or they'll start arguing among themselves," Crystal said.

"There are the board games and pool and table tennis setups," Cloris said. "We could set up some tournaments."

"Do you really think that is such a good idea? They are already agitated, and what happens if there are cocky winners, and sore losers," Crystal said. It didn't take much imagination to picture arguments erupting into fighting.

"We can deal with that after lunch," I said. "Hungry and agitated is a bad combo."

The dining hall was mostly lost in shadows when we walked inside. It was so gloomy that even all the tall windows did not bring in much light. It brightened when Cloris turned on the hanging lamps. Normally at this time of day, there would be lots of activity in the kitchen and smells of cooking food. The host would be settling into her space by the door so she would be ready to check meal cards as people entered.

At least all the round tables were cleared and the busing bins empty. The staff had finished all that before they left for the night, expecting to return the next day.

"The good news is that we don't have that many people," Cloris said. She was trying to sound encouraging, but as she glanced around the empty room, her anxiety returned. "We were supposed to get a load of fresh food delivered today," she said. "What are we going to feed them?"

Crystal tried to calm her by saying that since I was a professional chef—though desserts only—and Lucinda owned a restaurant, the food business should be left to us. "Cloris and I can go back to the Lodge and work on an activity."

I liked being called a professional chef and wished Crystal had said that in front of my mother. Maybe that would get through to her.

Really, with all that was going on, I was thinking about impressing my mother? I was sounding like Mindy. Even so, I realized I was going to have to call my mother when I had a moment. She called me all the time, and if I didn't answer my phone or her messages, she would freak out. But it would have to wait.

"It looks like it's just you and me," Lucinda said. "There's no shortage of space," she added, taking in the huge kitchen.

"Because there's usually a crew getting everything ready for the meal," I said. "Let's see what we've got to work with."

We made a tour, opening the massive refrigerators and freezer before checking the pantry.

The good news was that there seemed to be a lot of eggs, butter, milk and blocks of cheese. The freezer had frozen orange juice and bags of frozen vegetables. The panty was well-stocked with basic baking supplies. There were plenty of large cans of things like beans and peaches and a huge sack of rice. The bad news was there was no meat, chicken, fish, fresh vegetables or bread.

We checked the pots and pans and appliances, which were all industrial-size.

"Well," Lucinda said, looking to me. "There is food—any ideas what to do with it?"

It was true that I only made desserts, but during the time I had spent working in the bistro in Chicago, I had paid attention to what the other people in the kitchen were doing. And Dane kept prevailing on me to expand my repertoire, though mostly it had resulted in me brewing coffee and cooking oatmeal instead of using the instant envelopes of it. "It feels a little like we're on one of the food channel shows where they hand a chef a shopping bag of ingredients and challenge them to create a meal from it. I think I can figure out something for lunch, but we're going to need help," I said.

"I have an idea," Lucinda said. She laid it out to me and I realized it might work. Now, we just had to get them to agree.

Chapter 14

Lucinda and I went back to the Lodge. We cleared the idea with Cloris and she left it to us to present it to the others. She waved at the door to the café. "They're all still in there."

There was no din of conversations and it seemed almost eerily quiet as we walked into the café, and then I realized why as I heard Milton Carruthers's voice.

He was sitting on one of the stools in front of the wood counter, facing the group with a book in his hand. I couldn't see the cover, but I was betting it was one of his creations written under the pseudonym of Talulah Barnsdale.

He had a rapt audience and I imagined that it was a relief to them to have a distraction from all the problems. I didn't want to abruptly interrupt and I stopped to listen as he continued to read. Madeleine was sitting adjacent to him, as if trying to make it appear they were a couple. He looked up briefly at his audience and then continued to read.

> *She had carefully planned it. It was the perfect crime. No one would suspect it was murder and would certainly just see her as the grieving widow. She was already dreaming of what she would do with the life insurance. She wondered if the travels and luxury would blot out the years of his infidelity.*
>
> *She looked at the sleeping figure of her husband, blew out the pilot light on the heater and shut the door. What would his next stop be—heaven or hell?*

Milton finally noticed me standing in the doorway and closed the book. "I can read more later." They gave him a smattering of applause. "I have some copies of the book with me and I'd be happy to autograph them."

I took over the spot next to him and addressed the group. "The good news is that we looked around the dining hall and there is plenty of food to keep us going until more can be delivered. It may not be exactly what you want, but all we can do is the best with what we have."

I explained again that in addition to putting on the yarn retreats I was the dessert chef for Lucinda's restaurant and the muffin baker for the town's coffee spots. I stopped short of calling myself a professional chef because my mother's definition was stuck in my head.

"We thought that since you all have time on your hands that you could take turns helping with the meals and cleanup." I glanced over the small crowd, hoping hands would go up with people anxious to volunteer.

Madeleine raised her hand. "I don't really have any experience in a kitchen, but if you tell me what to do, I would be happy to help." She looked at Milton and volunteered his services as well. He seemed surprised at her offer and maybe not that happy with it either, but finally smiled and nodded.

"I could help, too," Evie Delano said. She still had the floppy hat on but had taken off the dark glasses, which had looked ridiculous on the rainy day. It took me a moment to remember her story. She was the influencer who had come for the psychologist's retreat and was worried about being followed. She gave off a frantic energy and didn't seem like someone into food, but I was glad for another pair of hands. I waved for my volunteers to join me and Lucinda, promising to ring the outdoor bell when lunch was served.

As soon as we got into the kitchen, Evie pulled out her phone and set it up on a stand. I expected her to take off the floppy hat, but she didn't, explaining it was her trademark look. She did roll up the sleeves on her taupe shirt, revealing the beginning of a tattoo that probably went up her arm. So many people had tattoos now that they hardly stood out or made them seem like a rebel anymore. I still didn't get it. Who knows, maybe that made me the rebel for staying ink-free.

"I need an apron," she said. "I have to look the part. Evie comes through in a disaster." She flipped the camera screen so that it was aimed back at her.

I was confused. Hadn't she made a fuss before about the pressure of having to create content, as she had called it. She was busy rearranging things and checking the light as I asked her about it.

"You're right. It's habit. I automatically think of everything as a way to create content," she said, suddenly stopping. "What am I doing?" She only stopped for a moment before it seemed as if she couldn't help herself and she began fussing with the angle of her phone. "I figure that it doesn't really count until I start Dr. Nicholson's program. Maybe I'll be cured of all this by the end of the weekend. I'll post it as my farewell to all my followers." She stopped for a moment as she thought it over. "I'm sure they'll harass me if I stop posting. They all love me so much."

Lucinda and I traded glances. At some point, Evie was going to find out that Trent would not be putting on his program. But for now, we would let her be. We understood very quickly her help was going to be marginal after watching the influencer crack one egg and drop pieces of shell into the bowl because she was so interested in talking to the camera. Lucinda took over for her and cracked all the eggs for her and then handed her the metal bowl with a whisk and explained what to do. Not that it mattered. Evie got in only a few turns with the whisk, as most of her attention was on the screen and her patter. It was all about the great adventure she was having almost on Gilligan's Island and how she was about to change her life. She reminded her would-be viewers that she had already told them about Dr. Nicholson and his weekend retreat.

Madeleine stuck close to Milton. Since he lived alone, he knew his way around a kitchen, while Madeleine admitted that the closest she had come to cooking was to press down some bread in a toaster.

It was a little different than the sweets I usually worked on, but I convinced myself that a recipe was a recipe, glad that I had found a book with directions for making a lot of their dishes. What was really the difference between chopping onions and cutting up apples—maybe the tears. I used my sleeve to wipe my eyes.

I loaded the ingredients into a pair of cast iron frying pans and gave Madeleine and Milton the task of sauteing them. I showed him the recipe and let him add the seasoning.

"Aren't they cute," Evie said, and I realized she was talking to her phone, though she had moved it so the couple was on the screen with her. They did look appealing. Despite all, Madeleine seemed perky in her denim outfit and he looked dapper with his silver hair and apron. "What's this we're making again?" she called over to Lucinda.

"A frittata," the restaurant owner said, bringing over the cheese she had grated. Some frozen mixed vegetables had been added to the frying pans. Lucinda poured in the egg and cheese mixture, explaining cooking would be finished in the oven.

I mixed up a batch of baking powder biscuits and worked on the dessert for lunch, hoping a sweet finish would add some cheer. I didn't need a recipe for the peach crumble that I made. I poured the canned peach slices in a pan and then made the topping of butter, sugar, and flour with a sprinkling of cinnamon.

With everything in the oven, we all shared in the setup. Evie had to leave her phone and worked alongside of me.

"How well do you know Trent Nicholson?" I asked.

"Well, enough to sign up for this retreat. We did an online session before I signed up. He promised me that I would come out of the weekend a different person. He didn't explain how and said I had to trust him." She shrugged and twisted her lips. "I had to do something. I was going crazy with having all the pressure. My followers hound me and I think one of them has been stalking me. But at the same time, I don't know how to stop. I have no life anymore. I can't sleep. All I think about is what I can make a video of."

I had an ominous feeling about how she was going to react when she found there was not going to be the program to change her life.

We arranged the food cafeteria-style, got drinks together and a stack of plates. Milton took it upon himself to go out in the drizzle and ring the bell to announce that lunch was ready.

The group seemed cheered when they came inside the dining hall and saw the fireplace going and smelled the hot food. I had a satisfied feeling as they helped themselves to the frittata and biscuits. They were like children at Christmas when they saw the peach crumble with the bowl of whipped cream to top it with. Lucinda and I toasted each other with cups of coffee. One meal down. We could deal with dinner later.

I went out into the dining area to check on everything. Leon Rissel waved me over. "You seem to be in the know. What's going to happen now?" I was trying to come up with an answer when he looked toward the door as Cloris and Sammy came in and headed for one of the tables. Leon zeroed in on the tall magician/doctor. "How's Dr. Nicholson? He must be better by now. Even if he isn't feeling one hundred percent, he could still put on his program. When will he be ready for the first workshop?"

Sammy's face went from his usual friendly expression to uncomfortable. He looked from Cloris to me for some guidance as to how to answer. I went over to confer with them.

"We can't keep implying that he's alive," I said. "Not when that man asked a direct question. Audrey Nicholson has kept to her corner in the Lodge, but eventually she's going to mix with the others. I think it's time to tell them the truth."

Cloris had a look of doom, but she agreed with me. "The majority wins," Sammy said. He stepped away from us and addressed the tables of guests.

"I'm sorry to report that Dr. Nicholson is deceased." He tried to end it there, but there was a barrage of questions about the cause.

Sammy put up his hands to stop them. "I don't know. All I can say for certain is that his heart stopped beating."

Leon jumped up from his chair. "That can't be so." His gaze went over the whole group. "I need to have a repeat of that retreat. He made a promise in the information about the retreat that everyone's life would get a kick-start from the program. Well, that's not how it worked out for me and I came here to find out how to fix it. There has to be some way we can do his program." He sounded desperate as he continued. "He told me that I should leave my wife and start over. I'm forty-one years old and now I'm living with my dad. I need Dr. Nicholson to tell me how to get out of this mess."

"I find it impossible to believe that Trent told you to do anything," JoJo Westerly said. Everyone turned to the petit woman, who had been staying in the background. "I've done his retreats and it's not his style to tell people what to do. Are you sure that he didn't just ask you if you thought that leaving your wife would fix your life?"

Her comment only seemed to agitate him more. I leaned into Crystal. "We have to do something to keep them busy. They're only going to get worse if we don't."

She nodded in agreement. "I have an idea for something that could work." She seemed ready to give more details, but was distracted when Leon overreacted to JoJo's comment.

"He did not ask me questions. He told me," Leon said, practically spitting the words out. "Why can't you people believe me. Ask that woman who is hanging by the fireplace. She was there."

"I don't think you should bother his wife. She's got a lot to deal with," Cloris said in a concerned tone.

Leon seemed surprised at the comment. "She's his wife now? What happened to the other one?"

I pushed Crystal to step in before things got worse.

Dorothy Spenser gave Leon a sympathetic smile. "My program is about dieting and food, but it's really about emotions. I'd be happy to try to help you."

Leon rolled his eyes and rocked his head. "My problem isn't about eating too much peanut butter. Thanks, but no thanks," he said in a disgusted tone.

"I was only trying to help," Dorothy said. "You could be a little more gracious. We're all stuck here together and we need to get along." Instead of soothing Leon, her comment seemed to incense him even more.

Lisa Montez seemed about to say something, and I worried that whatever the woman with the white-blond hair added would only escalate things. I nudged Crystal. "Go on and tell them your idea. We need to distract them."

She did not seem rattled by all the fussing. "When you live with two teenagers, you get used to a lot of arguing," she said. "Keep your fingers crossed that this doesn't make it worse." Leon's face was contorted in a mixture of anger and frustration and I saw her point. I held up my crossed fingers and urged her on.

She moved to a spot between all the tables and waved her hand to get their attention. She was still in her layers of colorful T-shirts from the day before and her appearance alone seemed to cheer things up.

She started by introducing herself as my workshop helper. Her natural charm immediately lifted the mood of the room except for Leon, who was sulking. "Since all the plans for the weekend are kind of destroyed, I thought of a way that we could do that turn lemons into lemonade thing, if you are all willing. We have kits made up for our yarn retreat. They have everything you need to make the project and it is aimed at novices. We can teach you whatever you need to know. And I can just about guarantee that no matter what else happens, you will leave this weekend with something to show for it."

"That's if we can ever get out of here," Mindy said, and they all laughed.

"I'm sure you will all find that working with yarn can be very therapeutic," Crystal said. She glanced over her audience for their reaction, but avoided looking at Leon.

"She's right," Bella said. "I can't tell you how much making these guys has helped me." She pulled out a handful of brightly colored animals and a doll. She picked a pink pig with wings out of the pile.

"She's the first thing I made and I carry her with me all the time to remind me that things that seem impossible do happen." She smiled. "Like me being able to crochet her." Just to make sure they understood what she meant, she explained that the phrase *when pigs fly* was supposed to mean that something wasn't supposed to happen ever. "She's like my support pig."

"Just finishing something makes you feel great," Lexie said. "We came here because we were part of an online group and wanted to see what it was like to make something in a real live group."

"I don't know how to do anything with yarn," Mindy said. "My mother said modern women don't do handicrafts." Crystal shook her head in disbelief at the comment, while some of the others chimed in with the same concern of having no experience with yarn. Only Milton said he had been to one of the yarn retreats before.

"I didn't know anything when I came," he said. "Except that the character in my mysteries did a lot with yarn. Crystal is an excellent teacher," he said. She smiled at him and took a mock bow.

"I came for the yarn weekend, so it's fine by me," Lisa Montez said.

"Me, too," JoJo Westerly added.

Leon seemed lost in his own thoughts and took a moment before he answered. "I don't know about doing something with yarn. I might just watch the rest of you."

Someone in a raincoat and hat came in the dining room. Cloris got up when she recognized the guy staying in the cottage and asked me to pack his meal to go. I took it to him and told him about the yarn workshop plan.

"You must have had enough of your own company by now," I said with a smile to let him know I was joking. "Since you're stuck here, you're welcome to join the rest of us."

"That's very nice of you," he said. It was hard to read his expression with the wild-looking beard, but I thought he was smiling. "I'll think about it." I couldn't tell if he meant it or it was just a way to brush me off.

With all that was going on, I hadn't noticed that Evie Delano had her phone out and was filming. Leon saw what she was doing and put his hand in front of his face to block it from her camera when she pointed it his way. "No pictures, no videos," he said in an angry tone.

Dorothy demanded to know why she was filming. Evie turned the phone toward herself as she gave them all an exasperated look. "It's what I do. I have to keep myself busy," she said, sounding frantic. "I was depending on Dr. Nicholson's workshop to help me deal with this and now it's not going to happen. I don't know how to stop being Evie Delano, Diva of Everything."

Cloris got in the middle of it, shaking her head. "Sorry, Ms. Delano, but you can only film yourself. You need permission from the others before you include them." She was definitely speaking as Kevin St. John's representative. That was exactly what the manager would have said, but in a less pleasant tone.

"You can film us," Bella said and Lexie nodded. They both struck a pose to show their willingness.

Crystal waved her hand to get everyone's attention back. "I didn't get a chance to tell you what the project is." She looked at Bella and Lexie, who had deflated after the filming ended. "Sorry, it isn't going to be amigurumi." She reached into her tote bag and started to take out the garland, but I stopped her. We had successfully distracted them from Trent's death and Leon's problems. But I worried that seeing a string of hearts was likely to start him up all over again about his broken one.

"It will be a surprise when we all meet to do the first workshop," I said in a bright tone. They all began to clear out of the dining hall until all that was left was Lucinda, Madeleine, Milton and me, with the table full of dirty dishes. Madeleine was going to have another new experience.

Chapter 15

With the dining hall back in order and ready for the next crew, I took a little time to regroup. I felt comfortable that Julius would get some stink fish eventually. Cloris had offered the group of us who were acting as staff rooms in the Pines building, which was closed for maintenance. The electricity and plumbing worked, but the lobby and rooms were in disorder. I had to rearrange the furniture in the room that Lucinda and I were going to share. Now that I knew where the housekeepers' carts were kept, I raided it and got towels and bedding. I glanced at the narrow bed, glad I would have someplace to sleep if I couldn't get home that night. Who was I kidding. There was no way the road would be cleared that day. The rain was still off and on, and until it stopped completely, I doubted anything would be done. In the meantime, I was grateful to be able to take a shower, even if I had to put on the same clothes. I wondered about a room for Madeleine since the cottage was not going to open up.

Even though she considered herself to be staff now, I picked a room and set it up for her.

The shower worked wonders and I felt renewed when I went back to the Lodge. It seemed that everyone had taken the opportunity to go back to their rooms and the cavernous space was empty. Almost empty. Audrey was still in her corner, though I saw that she had a plate of food and a cup of coffee. Now that everyone knew that Trent was dead, there was no worry that she'd contradict the cat is on the roof story. I considered inviting her to join the upcoming workshop, but let her be for the moment.

I looked at the row of vintage phone booths and accepted that I had to make that call to my mother. With the two-hour time difference in Chicago, I figured I would probably get her at work and she wouldn't answer. Leaving a voicemail explaining the situation and reassuring her that I was okay was preferable to an actual conversation. If it came up about Dane and Stacy, my mother would mean well, but instead of being sympathetic she would give me a lecture on how Sammy was so much better for me and that both of us should come back to Chicago. Plus, I did not want to tell her there had been a death. My mother was a cardiologist, and she would ask a lot of questions. I could just imagine her reaction if she heard we had wrapped Trent in garbage bags and hauled him on a housekeepers' cart.

The phone rang and rang and to my relief did finally go to voicemail. I was just able to get in all the important details before the voicemail cut off. I told her she could call Vista Del Mar if she needed to reach me, but I hoped she wouldn't.

I welcomed the privacy afforded by the cubicle with a folding door and took a moment to enjoy the time away from it all. There was even a little seat. It seemed a more civilized way to have a phone call instead of the current mode that had people walking around on their cell phones spewing their conversations on anyone in earshot. The row of cubicles had come from an independent drugstore that was going out of business—and from another time.

I wanted to talk to somebody who wasn't invested in what was going on. I wanted to lean on somebody's shoulder and have them tell me everything was going to be all right. The best I could do was call Frank.

"Okay, so when is the wedding?" he said before even a hello.

"Never," I blurted out before I could stop myself. "But the good news is that I may be coming back to Chicago to claim that job you've dangled in front of me."

I told him the whole story about the second chance with Dane's high school girlfriend.

"It's pretty hard to fight that. Isn't it everybody's fantasy to have someone who broke up with you come crawling back." The way Frank said it, I gathered he had some experience about being dumped, and not getting that second chance. I would have liked to ask him about it, but I knew he was too into playing the gruff PI to want to talk about it.

There was no sound of his office chair squeaking in rebellion as he pushed back in it, so I guessed he was out somewhere. When I asked, he said he was waiting for a guy to come out of a public restroom so he could serve him some papers. "It's a crummy job, but I need the dinero." He paused a moment. "About those plans of yours. If you want to get a license, you're going to need experience. We could work out an internship. Not sure about the pay."

Hearing him give details about actual plans made it suddenly feel too real and I wanted to change the subject. I told him about the storm and being stranded.

"Stranded at a brooding hotel by the sea. It sounds like a plot for a mystery. All you would need is a murder," he said.

When I didn't say something right away, he chortled. "Don't tell me there was a murder."

"There was a death," I said before giving him the details.

"I hope you notified the cops," he said.

"I did, but there's nothing they can do until the roads get cleared. But I took pictures. A lot of them." Instinctively, I took out my phone, thinking I could text them to Frank. It had gotten to be such a fact of life now that you could illustrate your conversation with pictures. Except for here. I suddenly understood the frustration some of the guests had at adjusting to being in an unplugged place.

Normally, I went home during the retreats, where I had Internet and cell reception. This was the first time I was in the same boat with all of them. "I'll describe them to you," I said. I began to scroll through them and tell him how Sammy and I moved the body. Frank chortled at the image of Sammy and me in our trash bag rain attire trying to keep the housekeepers' cart from getting away from us and rolling down the hill.

"The lieutenant said until the medical examiner does their investigation, there's no way to tell what it is, but it really seems like he died in his sleep. There was no sign of a struggle or any wounds." I mentioned his wife saying he took a pill for something with his heart and that the bottle was on the table next to his bed.

"Okay, Feldstein. Let's consider this as an audition for that job we just talked about. How could it be a murder?"

I flipped through the pictures again as I gathered my thoughts. As I looked at the pill bottle again, I had a thought. "What if the pills in the bottle weren't his regular medication? There were only a few pills left in the bottle. What if somebody emptied the real contents and replaced them with something else. Something that would send him off into the big sleep. Something like fentanyl."

"Excellent, Feldstein. Now put that pill bottle someplace safe."

As soon as I got off the phone, I rushed to the Tides building and went to Trent's room. The door was ajar, as if somebody had left in a hurry and not closed it all the way. I pushed it open and looked inside. The pill bottle was gone.

Chapter 16

My mind was swirling as I went back to the Lodge. The lieutenant had said that anything was possible, but I hadn't believed that murder was really a possibility until now. Why else would somebody take the pill bottle other than to hide evidence? What was I going to do with that information? Should I tell the group? A big *no* flashed in my mind. How would it help to let them know they were stuck at Vista Del Mar with a killer on the loose. I thought about how I felt being stuck with a killer on the loose and it wasn't good. But it was also a heavy burden to keep to myself.

Should I call Lieutenant Borgnine and tell him that it seemed like murder? He'd probably correct me and say homicide and then dismiss it, claiming my imagination had gone wild due to the circumstances of being stranded with a bunch of strangers. What if that was true? I was certainly stressed by the situation and Frank had gotten me thinking of it being a murder. I needed to air my thoughts with somebody.

I ruled out Cloris. She was on edge already trying to deal with all the guests' needs. Trent's death had only made it worse. Even though the possibility of it being murder had been brought up before, I didn't think any of us had taken it seriously. But now there was something that seemed like proof. I was afraid if I told her about the pill bottle, she would freeze up again and become nonfunctional.

There was the option of ignoring the missing pill bottle, but it wasn't my nature not to face a troubling state of affairs. Just like how I was handling Dane's choosing someone else by planning to leave and start another chapter in my life somewhere else. I couldn't just pretend I didn't know what I knew.

Lucinda came out of one of the phone booths. She was dressed in fresh clothes and appeared put together down to her lipstick. Lucky her to have brought her suitcase. Her expression was tense and I figured that she had just talked to Tag. He always got upset when she came to the retreats, but being stranded here had to make it even worse.

"The good news is that things aren't as bad in downtown Cadbury," she said when she saw me. "Just lots of puddles and business is slow at the restaurant. The bad news is that Tag is beside himself that I'm stuck here. He didn't even want to know how we had killed it at lunch. It was brilliant the way you made those biscuits."

She stopped talking as my troubled expression registered. "What's wrong? Did something else happen? What is it now?"

I looked for a spot where we would be assured of privacy. The cavernous interior was mostly empty. Dorothy and Mindy were sitting at one of the small tables near one of the windows, working on a jigsaw puzzle. James appeared to have come out of his solitude and was at the back playing pool by himself.

When I checked the spot by the fireplace, I saw that Audrey had finally left. The only mark that she had been there was her plate of half-eaten food. I felt a momentary annoyance at her expecting someone to pick up after her when she knew there was no cleaning crew. But then, she was the grieving wife, so maybe it was excusable.

I led Lucinda to Audrey's vacated chair and we both looked at the plate and silverware. "It's lucky Tag isn't here. He'd go nuts at an abandoned plate." I piled up the knife and fork on the plate and covered it all with a napkin and then pushed it back on the table so it was almost out of sight.

"I did that for Tag in absentia," I said and we both smiled as we sat down.

Even though we were virtually out of earshot of everybody, Lucinda leaned close. "It's about Dane, isn't it? You seem to be taking it too well. Nobody does that. You can tell me the truth," she said.

"It's for real," I said. "I already have a plan in place." I hated to tell her what it was since it meant leaving her and my job as dessert chef. Much as I tried to keep from getting too settled, Cadbury had started to feel like home. I liked doing the baking for the restaurant when the town had shut down for the night. I felt myself getting nostalgic about everything and momentarily my resolve weakened. But I knew that it was the right thing to do. "I'm going to leave. I can't stand having everyone looking at me and saying how sorry they are that Dane is with his old girlfriend. And that's now. What about going forward when they're living together down the street from me. When I have to see them cuddling at the Blue Door eating the apple pie I made."

I didn't mean to, but my voice had risen as I experienced the feelings I was talking about.

She shook her head with remorse. "Running away isn't the answer. Are you so sure it's a done deal with Stacy? Does he even know how you feel about him?"

I looked at her with surprise and she continued. "Just because you never said it out loud to me, there is no doubt what your feelings are. You know that you lo—" I interrupted her before she could finish the word.

"I'm certainly not going to tell him now. Maybe I did feel that way, but it's all over with. I am an expert at moving on. I've already talked to Frank. I could intern for him while I work on getting my PI license." I didn't want to talk about my feelings for Dane anymore. "That isn't what I wanted to talk to you about."

"You owe it to him to tell him how you feel," she said as a last shot. I didn't say it, but there was no way I was going to do that. Let him think that I still viewed our relationship as casual. What did it matter that he had declared his feelings for me. Obviously, it was only temporary until Stacy showed up anyway. Lucinda saw that I was not going to respond to her comment and moved on. "Okay, tell me what the real thing is."

"I know we talked about it being possible that Trent was murdered, but now I really think it's true," I said. I told her about my call with Frank and then my trip to Trent's room. I showed her the before and after pictures of the table next to his bed.

"Wow, I wouldn't have thought about something with the pills he took. I guess that's why you could become a PI and I just know how to run a restaurant. Except I do know from things you've said in the past, if it is murder, his wife is the most likely suspect," Lucinda said.

"She is the first person the police would consider," I said. "She does seem genuinely upset and I bought it as real. But she could be a great actress—or not." I brought up the fuss that Leon Rissel had made during lunch. "Remember how he seemed surprised when Cloris said Audrey was Trent's wife? I wonder what that means."

Lucinda nodded. "And then he said something about the other one."

"Right, he asked what happened to the other one. I didn't really think about it, but doesn't that sound like Trent had another wife?" I shrugged. "That still leaves Audrey as the person the cops would look at first. The good news about that is that she probably just intended to kill him and nobody else is in jeopardy."

"Unless she thinks someone isn't buying that he died in his sleep of natural causes and is investigating. Does she know you have those pictures?" Lucinda asked.

"I don't think so, but I don't really know." I stopped to think for a moment. "With the pill bottle gone, she probably feels safe. I guess I am just wondering what I should do with the information."

"You could just let it go, pretend you don't know what you know. Leave it up to the police to deal with when they finally get here." She looked intently at me. "You're not going to do that, are you?" my friend said.

"I can't unknow what I know," I said. "Not that there's really anything I can do anyway."

"That's true, but if you do figure out a way of doing anything and need help, let me know," she said.

Crystal came in at the end. "What do you need help with, Casey?" she said. We both looked at my yarn helper and our mouths fell open. Gone were the colorful shirts and black jeans, replaced by beige pants and a light beige sweater on top.

"What happened?" Lucinda said.

"You mean my change of looks?" Crystal said with a laugh.

"Pretty dull, huh. With the weather like this, if I go outside, I'll be invisible in the gloom." She gave her outfit a dismissive nod. "This is what Stephanie ordered online for me, so that according to her I would look more appropriate as her mother. I put all the stuff to return in the bin with the kits." Crystal shrugged. "It was my only choice for clean clothes." She reached around in her tote bag and pulled out a cowl made in pink, green and orange yarn and dropped it over her head. "There, that's better. I don't look like a cappuccino anymore." She smiled at us. "So what's going on? What does Casey need help with?"

"I'm not sure about telling something to Cloris since she already seems overwhelmed. You're a representative of the owners, so I'll let you decide who to tell."

"I'd be glad to advise you, but you know that I try to stay out of Vista Del Mar's business. It still feels strange that we are part of the Delacorte family."

I repeated everything I had told Lucinda. "I'd suggest keeping it to just the three of us. You're right about Cloris seeming overwhelmed, and Madeleine is being a good sport about being stranded and working in the kitchen, but your proof that makes it look like murder might be too much for her," Crystal said. "She's got enough going on with dealing with Milton. It's hard to tell how he feels about her from the way he's acting."

I mentioned that he had been concerned about being able to stay in the background. "Who knows what he meant by that."

She glanced in the direction of our plastic bins, which had been left in the Lodge. "Could we continue this while we finish up putting together everything for the workshop?"

I agreed with my helper. We had given the guests a time to meet and we needed to have everything ready. There was a discussion about where we should work on the kits, and we decided to move to the meeting room where my groups usually met. "I think we all need a change of scenery," I said.

The bins had lids so there was no worry about anything getting wet. It was a different story for us since a pelting rain was back. We opted for more of the trash bag ponchos topped with Vista Del Mar baseball caps that Cloris had made available to everyone. We managed to get to the Cypress building relatively dry.

The single-story building was a newer addition and built with the same brown shingles, which were beginning to get the same weathered look of the other Arts and Crafts structures.

The outer door was unlocked, but that was the only accommodation that had been made for our use of the meeting room. The interior was divided into two rooms. I always used the smaller one, as it had a fireplace and a window that let in more light. Normally, a fire would be going in the room, giving it some warmth in advance of the first workshop.

Nothing was normal right now and the room felt tomb-cold when we walked in. The chairs around the long table were haphazardly arranged. The counter that was used to hold refreshments had a stack of paper cups that had fallen on their side.

The three of us stood just inside the doorway and looked around. "Maybe we should rethink this and stay in the Lodge," Crystal said.

"We can fix up this room," Lucinda offered.

"I say we do what Lucinda said and hold the workshop here. They have already spent too much time in the Lodge."

"You're the boss," Crystal said. Her comment surprised me, but I realized she was right. I was the one in charge, but that also meant the one responsible, the one the buck stopped with and the one who would have to deal with any complaints.

I lit the fire and put the cups upright while Lucinda straightened the chairs with military precision. "I have been trained by the best for this," she said with a laugh. She did stop short of measuring the space between each chair to make sure it was the same for all as her husband would have done.

"What do you want to do about the kits and tote bags?" Crystal said. Originally, the red tote bags were for my retreat group only and we had put together a knit and a crochet version of the project kits and were going to give my yarn people their choice. "Both versions are designed for beginners," she added.

"But we are going to be dealing with some pre-beginners this time. They won't even know how to make a slipknot or what casting on means." I picked up two of the drawstring bags that held the kits and emptied the contents of one of them on the table. I looked over the pair of wooden needles and the two balls of cotton yarn, then unfolded the sheet of instructions that had a nice picture of the finished garland on the top. I dumped the other bag and the metal crochet hook made a ping on the table. The rest seemed a repeat of the other bag except there was also an envelope holding stitch markers and a tapestry needle. I looked over the contents of both kits. "The knit kit should probably have a tapestry needle, too, since the ends need to be woven in," I said.

Crystal appeared devastated at her mistake, while Lucinda offered a solution. "It's easy. Just offer the crochet kits."

I thought over who of my registered retreaters were already there. "Bella and Lexie are already into crochet so that should work for them." I shrugged when I mentioned Lisa Montez and reminded them that she was the one with the white-blond hair and bright lipstick. "It's kind of blinding and all you really notice about her," I said. "I don't know much about her beyond that, so I'm not sure where she's at yarn-craft-wise. And then there's JoJo Westerly. I know she has been here for retreats before. Cloris said she was what they call a retreat slut—someone who kept trying out different ones, hoping that they find the one that does the trick and fixes their life. I think she's a pre-beginner, so whatever would be fine."

I reached into one of the tote bags and pulled out a small bar of fragrant soap wrapped in cellophane. "Her company made this." I passed it around and they both admired the soap and packaging. The end was tied with a bit of hemp cord and a white label with what looked like handwriting, giving the details of the soap. I thought of how edgy the petite woman had seemed. "My impression of her was of somebody who is great at running her business but not so great with her personal life."

Just then Cloris poked her head in and then came inside. The tall slender woman still looked frazzled but a little refreshed. "It helped to have a shower and change into clean clothes. I keep a stock of them here for an emergency," she said. "It's the first time I've had to use them." She took in the situation in the room and appeared stricken. "Oh, no. I'm so sorry about the fire not being started and nothing set up for refreshments."

"No worries," I said. "You have more than enough more important stuff to deal with."

"Thank you all for being so understanding and all your help." She had let go of her professional persona for a moment and went around the table and gave each of us a hug. "Can I at least help you with what you're doing?" she said, looking at the array of red yarn on the table.

"We were just going over using only one version of the kits and how it would work with everyone." I picked up one of the tote bags. "We have plenty and can easily give one to everyone and not just the four people here for the yarn retreat," I offered. "That is, if they all show up." I glanced around the room at the empty chairs. "We told them what it was and when it was, but someone should encourage them to come."

"That someone should be me," Cloris said. "The guests are my responsibility."

"I told the guy staying in the cottage. Should we remind him?" I said.

"You mean James?" She thought it over a moment. "He's not so happy about being stuck here and doesn't seem to want to socialize even now. I say leave it be with him," Cloris said.

"Then there's Dorothy Spenser. She seems like someone used to being in charge. I wonder how she will feel about being a participant instead of the leader," I said.

"I bet she will be glad to have something to give Mindy to do besides worrying about what she's eating and if her mother would be upset," Lucinda said.

"Milton was here for a past yarn retreat because the main character in his mystery series knitted and he wanted some real experience with the craft. Maybe we can convince him to have one of his regular characters be a crocheter," I said.

"I keep forgetting that he isn't here for your retreat this time," Cloris said. "Why exactly is he here?"

"Madeleine appears to think that he's here to see her," I said.

"And you don't think that's true?" Cloris said.

"Honestly, I don't know what the situation between them really is. She said they have been communicating online. She is from a wealthy family and everybody knows that writers are always struggling unless they're James Patterson or Danielle Steele. What if he's forcing himself to court her with plans to marry her." I reminded them of his reading from his book. "It was all about a perfect crime and a woman killing her husband so she could get her hands on the life insurance, so you just have to reverse the roles."

"I'm sure they'd have a prenup," Crystal said.

"Don't be so sure. Madeleine might be too starry-eyed and inexperienced to do it," Lucinda said. "I know a little about being too lost in love to see what is right in front of you." We all knew the story that she and Tag had been high school sweethearts and then reconnected years later. She had been so caught up in the romance that she hadn't noticed the change in him. "I would have married Tag anyway, but I would have had a better idea of what I was getting into," she added quickly. She threw me a worried look, realizing that mentioning high school sweethearts reconnecting might remind me of Dane. I assured her it was okay.

"We really should try to get Audrey Nicholson to come," Cloris said. "It would be better if she was around people. It's a horrible situation with her husband, but it might help if she got her mind off of it."

I volunteered to talk to her.

"We can't forget Evie, the influencer," Lucinda said, shaking her head. "She's all over the place. She's paranoid about her followers and upset that she's pressured to make content and glad to be in a place that's unplugged where no one can bother her. But at the same time, she's addicted to filming stuff with her phone. And now that she's lost hope of a weekend program with Dr. Nicholson to fix it, she's even more frantic."

"One thing we can figure about her. She'll want to turn the workshop into another video," Crystal said.

"As long as she doesn't film anybody without their permission," Cloris added.

"And then there's Leon Rissel," I said.

Cloris let out a sigh. "We should make sure he comes even though he's most likely going to be a problem. He seems to be taking it personally that he won't have the weekend he'd hoped for." She stopped and her expression changed. "I try not to be critical of guests, but it's hard to be sympathetic when he seems so cold about Dr. Nicholson's death."

We finished up hiding the knit kits away and adding the crochet kits to the tote bags while we worked out the last details.

Lucinda offered to help put together the coffee and tea service. I said that I had made up a batch of the butter cookie dough and the chilled logs were waiting to be sliced and baked. Cloris said Sammy would get more wood for the fire. I momentarily had an image of him splitting logs, but then she mentioned there was a supply of wood ready to burn.

"Thank you again for all your help. Things seem to be moving forward." Cloris sounded back to herself. Lucinda and I shared a glance, glad that we had not told her the new development in Trent's death.

Chapter 17

Lucinda and I walked to the Lodge together. I was going to help her with the coffee and hot water for the workshop. As we cut through the building I saw that Audrey had returned, though she had changed to sitting on one of the sofas. "I'm going to pitch her on coming to the workshop," I said, looking at the sullen woman.

Lucinda assured me that she could deal with the drinks herself. "After that I'm going to call Tag again. With the emphasis on again." She made a face as if all the calls were tiring. "I have to keep reassuring him I won't be stuck here forever and in the meantime I will help him deal with everything by phone." Then she softened and let out a sigh. "It's hard to stay upset with someone when they keep telling you how much they miss you." She glanced at Audrey and wished me luck before she went on to the café.

I took a moment to evaluate Audrey's mood. If she seemed too depressive, I would reconsider trying to get her to join us. But she actually appeared a little better. There mere fact that she had moved out of the corner was a good sign. Her short brown hair appeared combed and she was wearing what seemed like fresh jeans and a white sweatshirt.

She looked up as I approached and almost smiled. "I wanted to see how you were doing," I said.

"Not so good. What am I supposed to do? I don't want to call his family. I don't really know his kids. They're grown and off on their own. And his ex." She swallowed hard and shook her head. "We've only been married a short time." She looked around the Lodge, as if remembering something pleasant. "This is where we met. I was here for one of his retreats. Our gazes met and there was like this spark that went between us, almost like in the movies. The way he was so passionate about helping everyone really got to me." She stopped to take a breath and I stepped in.

"I don't mean to interrupt your memories, but was the guy who confronted your husband at dinner at that retreat? His name is Leon Rissel."

Her face lit with an annoyed expression. "He was just a problem. In the group sessions, he kept taking up all the time complaining about his wife, and then he would ask Trent what he should do. I know Trent didn't give him advice in the group meetings. I don't know what he did during the one-on-ones, though," she said. "Trent was a stickler about patient privacy and he never talked about his clients, even without giving names."

"Then you and Trent were a couple at that retreat," I said tentatively.

"Not exactly," she said and seemed uncomfortable. "That would be unethical. It was more like we found each other." She looked up at me. "Is that what you're here for—to grill me? Are you working for the police since they can't get here? I heard that you are some sort of amateur detective."

What I did next wasn't very good, but I couldn't help it. I was tired of everybody calling me an aspiring this or amateur that. I was neither. "I'll have you know that I have worked for a PI and am planning on getting my license, which makes me a professional."

She backed away a little. "I'm sorry. You're awfully sensitive about it. If Trent were here, he'd probably say you were trying to make up for your lack of confidence."

"That's not true," I said. "I have absolute confidence in my baking skills. You weren't there or you would have heard how much everyone liked the peach cobbler and biscuits." I caught myself before I said anything about solving murder cases since I didn't want her to think I was investigating what happened to Trent. "I'm sorry if it seemed like I was grilling you. I'm more concerned about Leon Rissel being a problem. There's nothing to grill you about anyway. It's obvious that Trent's heart just gave out. I'm sure that's what the police will say when they do their investigation." She calmed down and nodded.

"I don't even know why they have to investigate. Like you said, he died in his sleep." She had a worn expression as she looked up at me again. "Is there anything else?" she asked.

"I wanted to tell you how we've expanded the yarn workshop to include all of you. It would be nice for you to be around everyone and help to get your mind off of things."

"I don't know how to do any handicrafts," she said in a dismissive tone. "I would just bring everyone else down. I'll pass." She seemed pretty adamant so I let it go.

Sammy was hanging behind the registration counter practicing fancy ways to shuffle cards. He stopped when I stopped on the public side of the counter. "I'm standing in for Cloris," he said. "Can I help you with anything?"

"Not unless you can wave your magic wand and fix it so we can get out of here."

"I wish I had the power, Case," he said. "This is the best I can do for now." He leaned over the counter and made a butterfly appear from my ear. It glowed and fluttered for a moment, enchanting me. But then it was back to reality. "I'm going to bake some cookies. I'll bring you your own supply."

I looked back over the room and saw that Audrey had left. I made a brief stop in the café to see how Lucinda was doing. She wanted my advice on drinks.

"Everyone is so edgy, maybe we should just give them all chamomile tea."

"That will just give them something else to complain about. But you can certainly put some chamomile tea bags in with the others."

"I don't know how we're going to get through this weekend," my friend said with a worried sigh.

I was actually feeling a little of the same, but still gave her a pep talk that we would manage to get through it and then we would have a good story to tell.

I asked her if she wanted to join me while I baked the cookies, but she said Tag was expecting her call.

A little time alone wasn't the worst thing, I thought as I went into the dining hall.

The days were short at this time of year and the light was already dimming, even though it was still afternoon. I turned on the lights to get rid of all the shadows and make the area appear a little less spooky. It must have been my imagination that we had left the dining hall in perfect shape. There were dishes in one of the busing pans that we somehow had missed.

It felt eerie going into the big dark kitchen. It was a space meant for a crew of people, not a single baker. Turning on the lights helped, though I saw that the kitchen too was in less than perfect order. But then my helpers had been Madeleine and Milton, along with Evie Delano. I had trusted them to do the job and had been too busy making the cookie dough to check on their work.

I put the oven on to preheat for the cookies and picked up the odds and ends of cookware that had not made it into the dishwasher and put them in the sink. The door to the walk-in pantry was ajar. I planned to just close it, but then I wondered if there was more disorder inside.

I went to check, and before I could turn on the light, the door shut behind me with a loud slam. Something fell off a shelf and I felt it whiz past my head and land on the floor with a thud.

I pushed the door open and the light from the kitchen illuminated a ten-pound bag of flour on the floor. Instinctively I checked my head, thinking that it had almost hit me. I was totally creeped out. I left the bag on the floor and went out into the dining room and saw that the front door was open. Had a gust of wind blown it open and the change in air pressure caused the door to slam, which in turn made the flour fall off the shelf—or was it something else?

I went back to check the pantry floor and noticed something strange. There was a piece of string laying on the floor.

Chapter 18

As soon as I had the cookies baked and packed in my tin, I went looking for Lucinda. She was in the café recovering from her phone call with Tag.

"You were there when we made lunch, did you notice some string on the floor in the pantry?"

She seemed mystified by the question and I realized I had just blurted it out with no explanation. I told her about the falling bag of floor and the slamming door. She didn't remember any string, but then admitted that she had not really checked the floor in the pantry. "It sounds like somebody could have set up a booby trap," she said with concern. "The way it works is you tie a string from something to a door and when it shuts, the string yanks it and it falls. My brother did it to me with a cup of water." She got me a cup of coffee. "The water was just annoying, but getting hit with a bag of flour could do real damage. Who knew you were going to be in the kitchen?" she asked.

"A lot of people," I said. "Milton, Madeleine and Evie Delano all knew I was coming back to bake the cookies." I shrugged. "I told Sammy, who was manning the registration counter for Cloris." I stopped as I remembered the dishes in the busing pan and asked her if she had collected Audrey's dishes from the Lodge and taken them to the dining room.

"Once you put the napkin over them, I forgot all about them," she said with a shrug.

"I think that if it was a booby trap, it could have been set up by whoever dropped off the dishes." I took a breath and told her about my conversation with Audrey. "The timing points to her and the fact that she brought up that she'd heard I was, as she called it, an amateur detective." I did not have to defend my status to Lucinda. She knew all too well that I had been successful in some past murder investigations.

"Sounds like she could certainly be the one," Lucinda said.

"She must have been expecting that the cops and medical examiner would have gone with the obvious. Trent was known to have a heart issue, which they could verify with his doctor. The investigation would have been superficial and his death attributed to natural causes. They probably wouldn't have even done an autopsy."

I mentioned the disappearing pill bottle. "Why would someone make it disappear unless it contained evidence that there had been a switch with his pills. She probably thought she didn't have to worry about the pill bottle since the cops couldn't get here to start an investigation, but then she got worried that I was poking around," I said. "If that bag of flour had hit . . ." I imagined what would have happened and it was not pretty. "Much as it does seem like Audrey is the most likely suspect, I'm not going to totally discount the others. One thing for sure, any investigating I do from now on will be super discreet." I turned to my friend. "I can still talk about it to you," I said. "I know it wasn't you that tried to off me with a sack of flour."

"Are you so sure?" my friend teased.

"Yes, you're not tall enough to have done it."

"Got me. Talk away," she said with a smile.

"Most of Frank's cases were about insurance fraud or cheating spouses, but he had aspirations about working for a criminal lawyer on a murder case. More than once we talked over sub sandwiches how he would investigate. He said he'd start with the basics of means, motive and opportunity." I waited while Lucinda got up and refilled our coffee cups.

"Means," I said, "is what the killer used. In this case, they could have used fentanyl to send Trent off into the eternal sleep. But that means they had to have planned it in advance."

"That could be any one of the people here. There was no secret he was going to be at Vista Del Mar. Though somebody would have to know about his nightly pill and figure out a way to get access," Lucinda said.

"That goes under opportunity. Audrey knew about the pill and had access, but then who knows if others knew about the pill he took? A number of people here have some history with him and he could have talked about having high blood pressure. There are people who think stress plays a part in it. And as for access—the locks aren't all that secure and a credit card could have been used to unlock his door." I took off the lid on the tin and offered her a cookie before I took one. I had gone basic this time. No chocolate add-ons or even colored sugar, and certainly no sandwich cookies this time. The sweet taste mixed nicely with the black coffee.

"And lastly, there's motive. Why somebody would want Trent out of the way." I thought of my conversation with Audrey. "She said they'd only been married a short time. It seems odd that she'd want to kill him even though someone did say that they heard them arguing. A psychologist might know a lot of secrets about people and a number of them appear to have had a past relationship with him. But I know what Frank would say. The most obvious culprit is the one closest to the victim."

"And that leaves us with Audrey," Lucinda said.

• • •

The rain had started again and we had to cover the cart with the supplies for the refreshments with more of the trash bags. It was a bumpy ride to get the cart to the meeting room and I expected we would get some weird looks when we rolled the cart in. We might have if anyone noticed us.

Most of the chairs were already full and there was a din of conversation. Crystal was standing at the head of the table being totally ignored. None of them even looked up at the rumble of the cart. Evie Delano had set up her phone on a tripod and was getting flack from Leon Rissel, who was next to her. He said something about not letting her post him fiddling with yarn and went into a diatribe about not being here for some handicraft. Mindy's gaze was locked on JoJo Westerly. The soap company owner started to protest until Mindy held up a sketch pad. I could not see her drawing completely, but it seemed like a caricature. Madeleine made a fruitless attempt to get their attention by waving her hand. Milton was ignoring it all and writing something down. Lexie and Bella were trying to show the others their creations. I was surprised to see Audrey after what she had said. She was sitting at the far end, staring out the window. Was she contemplating my demise from the bag of flour? I was going to pay extra attention to how she reacted when she saw me. Lisa Montez was the only one who noticed us and when she looked our way offered a helpless shrug.

I left Lucinda to do the arranging and joined Crystal. She usually took things in stride, but she seemed a little unnerved by everyone's behavior. "I think being stranded is getting to them. They all seem agitated. It's like I'm invisible." She looked down at the beige outfit her daughter had provided. "I do seem to blend in with the background. I guess that was Stephanie's plan." Crystal seemed defeated. "I'm not ready for that. Next, she'll make a fuss about the unmatched earrings. It's who I am. How people know me."

"You better do something," Lucinda said, interrupting as she came up next to us. "Or we'll have another murder." I gave her a look to shush her, not wanting the word *murder* to be overheard and cause more problems.

I turned to Crystal and apologized for not taking more time to listen to her clothes issues. "We need to get the group focused on hooks and yarn to calm them down."

"If we can get their attention," Crystal said with a helpless shrug. "I have clearly lost my mojo."

It had worked before, and besides, I couldn't think of anything else. I began to sing softly and maybe a little off-key, but then I wasn't auditioning for some TV talent show. In keeping with the current situation, I sang the beginning of "Raindrops Keep Falling on My Head." It worked, but not quite in the way I expected. "Stop that awful singing," Leon Rissel yelled out and the rest of them instantly went silent.

"I got their attention for you," I said with a smile and turned them over to Crystal, while keeping my eye on Audrey for her reaction to my presence. Her eyes had narrowed, making me think she was not pleased to see me.

Crystal's smile dimmed when they all gave her a squinty-eyed look and she realized they didn't recognize her in the bland clothes. She shrugged it off and tried to take charge, even though Leon had started to grumble again about his life being a mess.

She zeroed in on him with a fierce expression. "I understand that you came here for a therapeutic weekend and you're upset that it doesn't seem to be happening. A lot of other things have gone wrong for all of us." She let her gaze move over the whole group, stopping briefly on Mindy, who glanced up from her drawing with an unhappy expression. "I don't know exactly what the programs were going to be for your particular retreats, but I do know a little about getting unstuck. I was married to Rixx Smith." A hum of recognition went through the crowd at the mention of the rock singer's name. "When he dumped me and my two kids, I was in a funk. I was stuck."

I was surprised at what she was saying. It wasn't as if she kept it a secret, but I'd never heard her talk so openly before about being left. She had definitely gotten their attention. "I couldn't seem to do anything and I felt adrift. Until . . ." She let it hang in the air, building suspense. "My mother handed me a kit to make a pair of handwarmers and told me to just concentrate on making them until they were finished. It worked. I focused totally on working on what was right in front of me and forgot about trying to do all the things I needed to do, like taking care of my kids and starting up my life again. And when I finished, I felt this huge sense of accomplishment that I had completed something. My anxiety and depression level had gone down, too. It turns out that my mother isn't the only one to have figured out that doing handicrafts is helpful to your mental health. After my experience, I did some research and it turns out that experts have said it is true. The added bonus is that you can all share your feelings as we're working." She took a moment to check their reactions. Opening herself up to them had gotten some sympathetic reactions and their attention. "I guess the proof will have to be in the doing," she said. She gestured toward the bins in the corner and I got a handful of the tote bags and began to distribute them, while she held up a finished sample of the garland of hearts and did a pitch on it. "We designed this for absolute beginners and it has the most basic of stitches. We picked it since Valentine's Day is the next holiday."

"That looks like a girly thing," Leon said, using his fingers to snap at one of the hearts so it started to twirl.

"You can give it to your girlfriend," Crystal said. Too late she realized her mistake.

His lips curled in annoyance. "I don't have a girlfriend or a wife anymore. What do I want with some valentine thing. If I had Cupid's arrow, I'd shoot it to kill somebody with it."

Crystal tried to smooth it over. "I understand how you feel. I've been there myself. But you never know what is around the corner. Completing the garland and hanging out with the group may change everything for you."

"Hey, it's worth a try," JoJo said, speaking to him. "I've been to a lot of self-help and wellness retreats and they all make a bunch of promises to change your life forever. No matter how great the weekend is, it all fades as soon as you go back to your regular life. This time we could learn a skill that keeps with us and we get a prize of something we made at the end."

Dorothy nodded. "It certainly isn't what I planned to do with my group of diet people, but that whole plan went splat with us being cut off. Mindy is the only one who even got here." She looked toward her charge. "And the food situation has destroyed my menu plans. Sorry." She patted Mindy's hand. "I don't know anything about yarn beyond wearing sweaters made of it, but as long as we're stuck here, it seems like something to do. I do like the idea of completing something. It will make this weekend not feel like a total washout." She realized how apropos to the situation her word choice was and let out a weak chuckle.

"It works for me, too," Lisa Montez said. She had put a baseball cap over her short white-blond hair, and even with the shadow it threw over her face, the bright red lipstick was visible. "I agree that completing something helps your self-esteem. I just started working with yarn recently and it helped me get through a pretty dark time."

"You don't have to convince us," Lexie said. "One of the selling points to learning how to crochet and make those little amigurumi creatures was just what she said. I have had anxiety issues since I was a kid. Working with yarn did more for me than all the pills." She pulled out a little penguin. "He was the first thing I made and I carry him with me everywhere. He's like my support animal," she said with a smile. "Just looking at him makes me feel calm." Bella had the little pink pig with wings she considered her support animal sitting on the table.

Lucinda put a hand on Audrey's shoulder and the woman finally looked up. "It should help you, too."

"I made a mess of everything. If I had known it was going to turn out like this . . ." She let out a heavy sigh. I held my breath, wondering if she was going to confess, but instead she got up and went to the cookie tin, saying something sweet might help. The rest of them got up, and as they made their way to the counter someone said, "You can't escape karma." I looked around to see who said it, but all I could say was that it was a woman's voice.

I felt someone brush past me as Audrey rushed out the door.

Was it because of the karma comment? But who said it and what did it mean?

Chapter 19

"We better deal with what's for dinner," I whispered to Lucinda. We had started the crochet project with the rest of them, though mostly we had helped the non-crocheters learn how to do a single crochet stitch. It helped that the kits had the first heart already started so that once they learned how to do a single crochet, all they had to do was to keep going. I kept looking for Audrey to come back, but she never did, and whoever had made the comment did not say any more.

"You are right. We better get on it," Lucinda said. They were all so wrapped up in what they were doing, no one even noticed when we pulled away from the table.

We slogged through the puddles, and when we reached the driveway I detoured toward the street. I so wanted to go home and see Julius and find some clean clothes. I was hoping for a miracle, but the fallen trees still blocked the way and beyond the street was a river cluttered with cars and muck. My house was so close and yet so far.

"Sorry," my friend said.

"I'm sure that Dane will check on Julius, but these clothes feel pretty rank."

"I can help with that," she said. She offered me one of her Eileen Fisher outfits that was very forgiving, and it would not matter that I was taller with a fuller build. We agreed to wait until after dinner since it was already late.

After my last trip to the dining hall, I was a little worried and glad to have company. But this time everything looked just as I had left it, including the bag of flour still being on the floor.

"Be glad it didn't break," Lucinda said as we replaced it.

I had thought over the incident with the flour bag. One way or another, their motive seemed to be to stop me from poking around. I would simply have to make sure I kept quiet about any more investigating. Then I put it out of my mind.

"I think we should go for comfort food and something everybody likes," I said. Lucinda agreed and we began to go through the pantry. When I saw the package of pasta I thought of Dane and the pots of spaghetti he made for the kids who came to his place to practice karate.

I brought it up to Lucinda and she agreed. "Who doesn't like spaghetti?" I said. "I wish I knew how to make his sauce." I fought the urge, but memories of him floated through my mind. He was such a good guy. That is, except for now. I used that thought to keep me from getting sentimental and went back to focusing on the meal.

"I know I said I don't do the cooking at the restaurant, but I do know how to make a basic spaghetti sauce," Lucinda said. She checked over the canned goods and gathered some cans of tomatoes. There was a huge unopened container of Parmesan cheese, too.

"I can make this cheesy garlic quick bread," I said, holding up a recipe I'd found in the kitchen's book. "There's frozen broccoli we can roast with garlic, olive oil and grated cheese. And chocolate pudding for dessert." I'd found cocoa and cornstarch. "There's plenty of milk."

"Who are we going to get to help?" Lucinda said, reminding me that we had said they were going to have to take turns helping with the meals. "Milton has already helped. We could ask Madeleine again since she's supposed to be staff," Lucinda said, but I shook my head.

"The cooking was fine as a novelty and something to do with Milton, but it might be better to leave her to act as a host."

The workshop had ended and they had all drifted back to the Lodge when we went looking for helpers. A loud thwacking noise was coming from the back of the large room. Leon and Sammy were involved in what seemed like an aggressive game of table tennis. The aggressive part seemed to belong to Leon, who was slamming the ball with Sammy lobbing it back to him. Finally, my guess was that Sammy got tired of the game and ended it by catching the ball in his hand and making it disappear.

"It's a magician's curse," he said with a smile. "No ball means game over." Sammy was trying to be friendly, but Leon seemed to take it wrong.

"Ha-ha, Mr. Magician. Make the ball reappear so we can finish the game and I can win."

Sammy shrugged as Lucinda and I approached. "It was supposed to be a friendly game." He put the paddle down on the table. "I'm done. We can say you won if it makes it better for you."

"No way. I don't want any favors. I want to win fair and square," Leon said. It was a bad situation. Sammy was trying to end it peacefully and Leon was using it to vent his frustrations.

"You can finish the game later. For now, it's your turn to help in the kitchen," I said, looking at Leon directly.

"What?" he said in a complaining tone. "I don't know how to cook, and besides, I'm a guest. Meals are supposed to be made for me."

"Normally that would be true," I said. "Normally, I wouldn't be making the meals either. But you may have noticed nothing is normal right now. Everyone has to step up and take a turn helping." I must have gotten through to him because he finally agreed and followed the two of us as if we were leading him off to a dungeon.

I had him fill a huge stockpot with water to boil for the pasta and carry it to the stove. When he had finished, he came to me. "Is that it? Can I go now?" he said. He appeared agitated and I tried to start a friendly conversation.

"This must be a very different experience for you than when you were at Vista Del Mar before," I said.

"Yeah. This really sucks. I know what that woman said. But I'm not sure doing something with yarn is going to help me. It might even make it worse. I kept dropping the hook. My brain doesn't work that way. I'm sorry Trent is dead, but sheesh, he should have had some kind of backup plan."

His total self-centeredness floored me and I didn't know what to say. But I didn't have to worry about it because Leon kept talking. "His wife seems out of commission so she can't do anything." He rocked his head and rolled his eyes. "As if she would know what to do anyway. The last time I was here, she was one of the participants and he was married to somebody else."

I was anxious to hear more and he obliged by going on about how Audrey had played up to Trent. "She was so obvious. But you know that saying about what goes around comes around—I saw the one who had the flying pig making googly eyes at Dr. Nicholson. Who knows what would have happened if he'd lived. Maybe she would have been his assistant next time."

"What about his ex-wife?" I asked, remembering he had mentioned her before with no details.

"I wasn't really into paying attention to her, but he had her handing out stuff and bringing us tea. Now that I think about it, maybe it was her own fault that he fell for somebody else. She was kind of drab-looking." He hesitated. "All you saw when you looked at her was that nose." He gestured with his hands and I got the message that it must have dominated her face. "She wore baggy cargo pants and a sweatshirt, while Audrey was kind of dolled up looking. By the way, the guy was a babe magnet. The women treated him like he was a rock star. Like he knew what was going on in their heads and how to fix their lives.

"He had us all call him Trent and he talked about his own issues with some kind of heart problem and how it made some people get fearful and put off doing things. He said how important it was not to put off living. I think his line was something like live every day as if it is your last because one day it will be." Leon realized what he had said. "Wow, it came true for him." He looked around the room. "Am I done? Can I leave now?" he asked.

Lucinda came by and looped her arm in his and directed him to set up the table with cutlery and pitchers of water. "Thank heaven Tag isn't here to check his work," Lucinda said with a chuckle.

Leon took an inordinately long time with the setup, and when he came back into the kitchen, the sauce was simmering on the stove. I had watched with interest how she put it together with what we had available. She simply put in the tomatoes, a quartered onion, a lot of butter and some seasoning and put it on to cook. It smelled delicious.

Before Leon could ask if he could leave again, I gave him the job of testing the pasta to see when it was done, while I poured the pudding into individual cups and the rest of the meal finished in the ovens.

"Yeah, you just throw it against the wall and when it sticks, it's done," he said. "This is the kind of cooking I can get behind." He made some gestures as if flinging something overhanded, then underhanded.

"That's a myth," Lucinda said. "Any pasta will stick to the wall. Your job is to wait until the timer goes off and take out a few noodles and cut into them to check for doneness." He seemed disappointed but went to hang by the stove with the timer in his hand.

He ended up staying until everything was ready to be served and we let him ring the bell to announce dinner. He stood by the door playing maître d' and made sure everyone who entered knew that he had helped with the meal.

"All those carbs. My mother would have a fit if she was here," Mindy said, inspecting the pan of spaghetti and tray of garlic bread. "What am I supposed to do?" she said as she went through the cafeteria line we had set up.

"I'd suggest that you take a plate of food," Lucinda said as Dorothy pushed her way through the line until she was next to her charge.

"Calm down," the diet leader ordered. "I keep telling you that there are no good or evil foods. You keep mentioning your mother. What do *you* want to do?"

"Have a plate of that spaghetti and the bread. Even the broccoli looks delicious."

Dorothy seemed frustrated with the whole situation and let out her breath. "Then go ahead and do it."

"But I feel so guilty," Mindy said.

"Feeling guilty isn't going to change anything besides taking away any chance of enjoying the meal," Dorothy said. "It's about moderation. Eat everything, but simply not too much."

I couldn't help but think how different this dinner was from the one the night before, when everything seemed normal. Luckily, the food was a big success. When I finally sat down with a plate of my own, I understood why. It was absolutely delicious. "I may have a future in what comes before dessert," I said, twirling some of the long noodles on my fork.

Leon tried to leave with the others, but I snagged him. "Not so fast. Part of working on the meal is the cleanup." The group had cleared their dishes and left them in the gray busing trays sitting on folding stands against the wall.

"That will be it, then? I won't have to help with another meal, right?" he said in a grumbly voice. The best I could tell him was that it was probably true.

I had something on my mind about Audrey and Trent. "Did they, uh, you know, get together during the retreat?"

He chuckled at the question. "You could just say what you want to know. Did they sleep together?" He stopped and thought about what he'd said. "That's not really being straight either. You want to know if they had sex." He looked at me for a response and seemed amused at my discomfort at him saying it so bluntly. "I really don't know. I didn't come to watch what other people were doing, but I don't think so." Trent talked about needing his own space during the weekend so he could recharge and deal with the group. "I would guess they had some walks on the beach." He looked at me again. "Why do you care?" He untied the apron I'd given him and handed it to me. "That's right." His face brightened with a thought. "I heard you fancy yourself as an investigator." He looked at me directly. "I get it. You don't think his death was natural." He glanced around the empty dining hall. "You should keep that to yourself. If there's a killer among us, they might not be happy with you mucking around."

Chapter 20

Everyone had gravitated back to the Lodge after the meal. Where else was there to go? The rooms were small and plain and meant for sleeping only. Once inside the cavernous interior, they scattered around looking for something to do. Leon was already holding one of the table tennis paddles looking for another player.

JoJo Westerly was sitting at a table under one of the windows. She had taken her tote bag with her when the group left the meeting room and was taking out the ball of red yarn and the beginnings of a heart. She seemed a little lost and I went over to see if I could be of help.

She held up some red yarn hanging off a crochet hook. "I thought I knew what to do, but I'm not sure where to put the hook." Her voice was choppy and I noticed that her stitches seemed a little tight. She tried to get the hook into the next loop and couldn't. I was not the expert that Crystal was, but by now I knew my way around a hook and offered to sit with her.

She seemed more agitated than when I had first met her and I worried that learning how to crochet might be having the opposite effect than she hoped for. She appeared to be a perfectionist and it was all or nothing with her. I knew the type. They were either a super success at doing something or a complete zero, in their minds. I'd met people like that in school. They were hysterical at only getting ninety-five on a test instead of one hundred. Anything above passing was okay with me. I had never understood what a burden it was to have to be number one.

Due to the tightness of her stitches, I took out several rows while explaining that it was called frogging. She wanted to know why it was called that. "Because it's rip it, rip it," I said with a smile, "like the sounds a frog makes."

Her face relaxed and she let out a smile until she looked back at her work. I thought she might have an easier time with the heart if I explained how it ended up with the shape, since for now it looked like a rectangle. I held up a finished one that I had kept in my pocket and showed her that the slipknot would turn out to be at the bottom point of the heart. I assured her that when it was finished and blocked, it would be fine. "It also helps to remember to relax your shoulders and breathe as you are crocheting." She took her work back and worked on a row as I watched. She was doing much better and gave me a thumbs-up. She wanted me to stay to make sure she had it right.

"You never explained what happened to Dr. Nicholson's body," she said as she moved to the next row. "It's shocking that he died. You said it was natural causes, right?" She sounded upset. "But I guess things like that happen." She had an expectant expression when she looked at me.

After the story about him being sick and all, I did not want to say anything that would contradict it. "He was treated with the greatest respect," I said. I cringed as I said it, thinking back to his bumpy ride to his current resting place. "As soon as the road is open, someone will come to take it, I mean him." After the episode in the pantry, and then Leon's comment, I was even more determined to say as little as possible about what happened to Trent.

"I really think this yarn weekend is going to be much more beneficial for me."

I asked her about the others she had been to and she got an uncomfortable smile. "I'm not so sure sharing tawdry details of your life is any help. Then you're viewed differently. And I know that professionals are not supposed to give out information about you, but who knows really." She brightened after that. "If this was one of the weekend programs I went to before, they would have probably turned the disaster into the theme. You know, like turn your life around by having to make due in an emergency."

I asked her about Trent Nicholson's retreat. She shuddered and I wondered if he was the one whose confidentiality she was concerned about. My next thought was what would she do to keep him from talking—ever?

She seemed to have no idea what I was thinking and continued. "It was smaller than most of the ones I've attended. That was good and bad. There was more personal attention, but more dealing with the personalities of the other people." She looked around the room and focused on Leon, who was still looking for a table tennis opponent. She held up her hand to shield that she was pointing at him.

"He was at the one I attended and he acted like he was the only one there. He dominated every group session and we all knew what a mess his life was. He was the kind who blamed everybody for his mistakes. It was the doctor's fault for giving him the pills for his shoulder that gave him the addiction. It was the rehab place's fault that he'd had to go through the program twice."

I remembered that Leon had had a confrontation with the psychologist at dinner the previous night and asked about it.

"Trent did say something about promising that we would all get something positive out of the weekend and if anyone felt they got nothing out of it, they could do it again. I didn't hear anything about the repeat being free. Once was enough for me," she said. She put her attention back on the crochet as she got to the end of the row and seemed at a loss what to do, and I showed her how it would become a heart shape.

"I get it. Thanks," she said, feeling triumphant. I watched her crochet for a few more minutes before I excused myself.

Crystal came out of one of the phone booths and assessed the situation. She waved me over. "If they're going to finish the garland over the weekend, we better keep them working on it." I agreed and was going to offer to help gather them up, but saw that Cloris was leaning on the wooden counter, looking distressed.

"Mr. St. John called for an update. When he asked about meals, he was upset that I let you deal with the food prep and that you got the guests to help with the cooking. He berated me for not handling things better and said Vista Del Mar was not a do-it-yourself kind of place."

I tried to calm her. "What else could you do?" I said. "Does he understand that there's no staff here, but you and the ones like me and Lucinda who have stepped up?"

"He said there would be consequences."

"That's ridiculous," I said. "Madeleine and Crystal are owners and technically his boss. I'm sure they will stand up for you."

"He was angry about that too. According to him, I am making him look bad to them."

Crystal was attempting to gather up everyone and bring them to sit around the fireplace. Other than her unhappiness about the beige clothes, she didn't seem particularly upset, and I doubted she had even thought about the missing manager. Madeleine seemed to view it as a big adventure and her chance to be with Milton, even if it didn't seem to be working out as she had expected.

I thought, but didn't say, that Kevin St. John would probably be more upset to realize that nobody had remarked on his absence.

Somehow my assurance that everything would be okay worked and Cloris calmed down.

Lucinda let me know that she was going to check in with Tag.

When I rejoined Crystal there was a new problem. Most of them had left their kits in the meeting room. "It's my fault," Crystal said. "I should have said something. We're making it up as we go along due to the rain and all." She had a light tone and friendly smile. She looked across the cluster of seated guests to me. "I hate to ask you, but could you get the rest of the bags?"

Sammy heard her and offered to help. He was all smiles as he handed me one of the trash bag ponchos. "I never thought I'd appreciate these so much," Sammy said. He did one of his corny tricks and made a fake butterfly seem to appear out of my pocket. "I'm adding this to the show when I do table magic. It seems appropriate, huh?"

This plastic butterfly had the markings of a monarch and I nodded. "Nice touch since Cadbury is known as the place where the orange and black butterflies winter." I knew they were presently in the area that had been set aside as a sanctuary. "I wonder if the rain bothers them," I said.

"They certainly don't have to deal with flooded streets," he said. "How nice to be able to fly above it all."

"You don't seem to be upset by the circumstances," I said as we walked through the rain to the meeting room.

He laughed. "I like the chance to be the hero," he said. "Even if it's just going through the rain to get some crochet stuff." He held up a couple of spare black trash bags. "And they will be delivered dry."

Crystal had remembered to have them write their names on the bright red bags, so that Sammy and I were able to get the bags to their owners. Crystal was giving more advice about working on the hearts. Lexie and Bella nodded with recognition when she talked about keeping track of the rows with checkmarks done in pencil. The rest of them seemed a little overwhelmed with everything. Except Madeleine and Milton, who were having their own conversation.

Crystal was an excellent teacher and after a few minutes had them all on track with the red yarn and their hooks. The best part was that it kept them distracted from the rain, which had turned to another steady downpour.

It didn't take long before the talking began. The crochet work might have distracted them from the rain, but not their troubles. Mindy was the first, bemoaning the situation with her weight. "My mother would kill me if she saw what I had for dinner. All those carbs."

Dorothy let out a weary sigh and made an effort to be patient with the food fuss. She spoke in a measured tone. "Your mother isn't here, Mindy. You have to stop thinking about her and pay attention to yourself. I hate to tell you this, but you are never going to have your mother's bony build. You have curves."

"But she told me that you guaranteed that people attending your weekend program would lose five pounds," Mindy said.

Dorothy's eyes went skyward. "No, dear, I was very clear that attendees *could* lose some weight. The plan is more about changing your relationship with food." It seemed to be an effort for her to keep with the measured tone. "I never guaranteed anything. It was the first thing I learned when I went to the seminar about putting on seminars. You never guarantee anything and you always have a disclaimer with any testimonials saying basically that whatever success someone claimed was only true for them and results would vary." Dorothy looked down at the red heart she was working on. "I'm going to have to add a disclaimer that I'm not responsible if the program gets upended by an act of God."

"Or a death," JoJo said. Leon's head shot up and he turned to look at the speaker.

"That's the truth," Leon said. "I came here hoping he could fix the mess he made of my life and now he's not even here." He had stopped working on the heart and his hook slipped out and fell on the floor. "If he hadn't told me to leave my wife and that it was all her fault that I was so unhappy, everything would be different." He added a shrug. "I probably wouldn't even be here." He noticed the hook on the carpet but did not bother to pick it up. "I trusted him and did what he said and everything is worse."

"Are you sure Dr. Nicholson told you anything? More likely he asked you a question about what you wanted to do based on what you told him," Audrey said. Nobody had noticed until she spoke that she was standing just outside the group "That's all he had to go on. You must have made it seem like she was the obstacle."

"She's right," JoJo said. "I doubt that any therapist would tell you to do something so extreme." She turned to address the group. "I have been to enough of them to know."

She looked at Dorothy. "You are right about the disclaimers in small print, but nobody pays attention. You go believing that you're going to hear some magic that will change everything forever. But it never worked, at least for me. I finally got it on my own." She looked at Leon. "You can't blame him for your life still being a mess. Nobody else can fix you but you, and the first step is taking responsibility for your own happiness, or in my case, getting some balance in my life."

"I don't think so," Leon said. "He just gave me bad advice."

Lucinda had joined us, having finished her phone call. "I wonder what Dr. Nicholson would have said to me." She looked in my direction and smiled. "I do go on complaining about my husband's peccadilloes." She gave them a quick story of how she and Tag had reconnected years later and that he had changed a bit since high school. "Or maybe I just didn't notice it then. He is a perfectionist, fanatical, and some may say he has OCD. It drives me buggy the way he follows the servers around and adjusts plates and cups they have just set down. I am beginning to understand why he does it, but it's still hard to take. I just have to get away occasionally."

"Dr. Nicholson would have told you to lose the guy," Leon said. Lucinda seemed shocked at the comment.

"If he had said that, I simply wouldn't have listened," she said. "Tag has his shortcomings, but I'd rather have him with all his quirks than be without him."

"Sometimes you have to find your own way to deal with problems," Lexie said. "I got a lot of advice about how to deal with my anxiety, but nothing really helped until I started crocheting these little creatures. I concentrate on making them and the world melts away."

Leon made a face at her. "Well, then good for you. But nobody told you to dump your spouse and start over again."

"He didn't tell you that," Audrey said. "He wouldn't tell you that."

"Are you calling me a liar?" His voice was rising and he had a scary look on his face.

The whole group stiffened, wondering what he was going to do next. Dorothy stood up and walked to the front. "Let's all take a deep breath and let it out slowly. I'm the closest thing you have to a therapist and we need to take a step back and calm down." She paused as most everyone followed her suggestion. "Leon knows his own truth and it is best that we don't question it." She turned her gaze to the upset man. "And you need to accept that no matter what Dr. Nicholson said, he's not here to fix it." She looked from Crystal to me. "I don't know who I should be saying this to, but maybe you can serve something to ease the tension."

Someone suggested wine, but then Lisa interrupted. "What about that blue tea?"

"That's what Trent did as a nightcap," Audrey said, taking over. She said that the psychologist had brought a supply of it and given it to the assistant manager when they checked in. I thought she was going to follow through and see about the tea, but Audrey seemed to think that whatever she had said was enough. I went to check with Cloris.

Cloris sparked as soon as I mentioned it and said she had left the canister of tea bags in the café. "I hope it settles them. It sounded like things were escalating."

"I think all their nerves are on edge. I wonder what's in the tea. We don't want to give them something that is going to cause other problems," I said. "Let's have Sammy look at the ingredients just to be sure."

I found him sitting at a table practicing something with cards. "I'm glad to help, as long as you don't try to get me into the yarn thing," he said with a good-natured grin. "I heard what you said about it being therapeutic, but it wouldn't be for me. I've had a problem with knots since I tied one in my favorite basketball shoes and couldn't get it out."

"I didn't know you played basketball," I said. With Sammy's teddy bear build, I had never thought of him as an athlete.

"I was pretty good." He did a mock toss of a ball toward an imaginary basket. "The knot was only a problem when I was a kid," he joked. He came with us and read the label. "It's fine. Just herb tea with some blueberries in it to give it an unusual color." He offered his assistance in making the brew. Cloris went back to her station and we set up the cups while the water boiled.

Cloris rushed back in with her brow furrowed. "Mr. St. John called again. He wanted to know what we were doing about housekeeping. What we had done about all the damp towels in the rooms. In this weather, they won't dry." She looked like she was going to cry. "And they'll get moldy." I hated to see her looking so defeated.

"Sammy and I did a good job with the housekeepers' cart before," I said. "If he's willing, we could take care of it while you take over the tea. Don't forget the chocolate pudding left from dinner. Chocolate is supposed to be a mood lifter, too."

"How can I ever thank you," she said. She wasn't usually a hugger, but she reached out and spontaneously wrapped her arms around me and handed me the master key. Lucinda came into the café and took over helping with the tea and pudding as we left.

It took a few moments for my eyes to adjust to the darkness so that I could separate the silhouettes of the cypress trees from the sky. There were only small lamps to light the walkways. The lights from the Sand and Sea and Tides buildings stood out like beacons. The rain had changed to more of a heavy mist, but everything was supersaturated and whatever towels had been used would never dry out on their own.

We went to the Sand and Sea building first, where the retreat people in my group were being housed. According to the list Cloris had given us, the first room belonged to Lexie and Bella. I followed Cloris's instruction to knock first even though I knew there would not be an answer and then we went in. It felt strange to go in their room. When the housekeepers did it, it was impersonal as they did not know who was staying in what room or care.

"If my parents saw me now," Sammy said as he went on into the bathroom to collect a pile of wet towels. "I can hear my mother going on about all the years of medical school and I was wasting my time on magic shows and now helping as a housekeeper at a hotel."

"It's not like you turned your back on being a doctor," I said, trying to make him feel better. "They should be proud of how much character you have and how willing you are to help." He dumped the load of wet towels in a bag attached to the cart and turned to me.

"Case, it's like I always say. You're the only one who gets me."

It always made me uncomfortable when he said that, even though I knew it was true. I got a load of fresh towels and gave the room more than a cursory glance as I went through to leave them on the beds. They had all their incidentals on the sink and had decorated the room with a bunch of the little amigurumi creatures they had made.

We moved on to JoJo's room. The first thing I noticed was the smell of roses, and I realized it was coming from the pink bar of soap on the sink in the room. It was clear with blocks of pink and red mixed in. The smell was heavenly and I made a mental note to use the bar that she had given me with her business card. It would definitely soften the edges of being stuck at Vista Del Mar. She apparently traveled with a whole selection of amulets and charms. A God's eye was hanging by the window. The woven yarn on the piece was a beautiful combination of turquoise and rust color. There was a bowl of crystals and a dream catcher. There was also a pill bottle next to her bed. I checked the label and saw that it was Xanax, which made me believe that even with all the retreats and trinkets, she still relied on chemicals to help.

The last room that had my people in it was Lisa Montez's. She had stayed in the background and I really didn't know much about her. Her room offered only a few clues. She had a book about beginning crochet and what appeared to be some practice swatches. She had set up some photos to personalize the room. I only glanced at them. One had a plain-looking woman with a caption that said *Never Forget*. Sammy got the wet towels and I left a stack of clean ones on the bed.

The trash can in the lobby was full of paper cups and other refuse that had overflowed onto the floor, and I emptied it into one of the large plastic ones. Done with that building, we rolled the cart the short distance to the Tides building. Dorothy's room was our first stop. She had folded the wet towels and left them neatly stacked on the floor. She had a collage that she had set up on the table next to her bed. It had catchphrases that were all like mini rah-rah speeches, like *Remember You Are Your Own Best Friend, You Are Unique Like a Snowflake, There Is Only One of You.* There was also a box of chocolates that had *For Emergencies Only.*

Mindy's room had a book of cutouts from magazines of bony-looking women in stylish clothes. A note was attached to it. *Here's some inspiration to get you through the weekend. All those clothes could be yours.* It was signed Love, Mother. It made me wonder about Mindy's mother. Did she really think that losing weight was going to turn her daughter into a model look-alike? Dorothy was right. Mindy needed to make friends with her curves. As I was putting the towels on the bed, I noticed the sketchbook next to it and opened it. She had done sketches of the Lodge and even drawings of the rain. Beyond those were some caricatures she had done of the group. I knew Cloris would love the one of her as it portrayed her as a superhero saving the day. I stopped when I got to the drawing of Leon. She had made it look like a volcano was erupting out of the top of his head. We did the towel exchange and moved on.

Evie Delano's room was as I would have expected. She had rearranged the furniture so she had a corner where she could video herself addressing the camera. I glanced in the closet and was surprised at the amount of clothes she had brought and the selection of floppy hats. I guessed it was all for costume changes during her stay.

Milton's room was orderly. He had brought a small stack of his latest book and some colorful bookmarks. His laptop was charging on the nightstand. He always seemed to be handwriting, but my guess was he put whatever into his computer later. I was curious what he had entered into it, but it was closed up and I was sure had a password. He had actually hung up his used towel and it was almost dry, but we took it anyway.

I took one look into Leon's room and let Sammy deal with it. There were clothes left all over, as if he'd flung them around the room when he took them off. There was a sock hanging on the lampshade. Sammy showed me a psychology magazine that was on the table. A photo of Trent Nicholson was on the cover with a big X drawn over his face.

Last but not least was the adjoining rooms that belonged to Audrey and Trent. I wondered if Lieutenant Borgnine would consider it tampering if we took the used towels out of Trent's bathroom. We did Audrey's room while I thought about it. It looked as though she had rushed out of the room. There were some clothes on the floor and the stuff on a small table was in disarray. I noted that mixed in with her assorted creams and cosmetics there was a small plastic bag that contained capsules and pills.

Finally, I weighed the wrath of Lieutenant Borgnine with Cloris's worry if we left a pile of wet towels, and chose to help her and take Trent's towels. It turned out to be pointless as the towels were unused. He had died before he showered. I glanced around the room a last time. It appeared the same as when I had last seen it and noted the missing pill vial. I had to wonder where it had gone.

We were done with all the rooms and about to roll the cart outside when I noticed the trash can in the main lobby. "We should empty this one too," I said as I had a thought.

I picked the small plastic container up and poked through the paper and stuff, glad that I had on rubber gloves. And then I saw it, or really them. I extracted two amber pill vials and a plastic bag with some white pills in it.

One of the plastic vials was full and one had a few pills at the bottom. Both of them had Trent's name on them. Sammy confirmed that they listed blood pressure medicine. Then he noticed something odd. "There's no doctor's name on this one," Sammy said, holding up the almost empty vial. And the pills are different." He compared both vials with the plastic bag of white pills. They matched the ones in the almost empty vial. There was a label stuck to the plastic bag with a large *F* written on it.

Chapter 21

"What do we do with these?" Sammy said, looking at the pill vials and plastic bag of white pills. "You probably know more than me since you worked for a detective and know about investigating."

"Shush," I said, looking around, worried that someone might hear. "We have to do something now. They will be coming back here soon." I thought of Lieutenant Borgnine's order not to touch anything. I had followed what he had said and left the vial in Trent's room. And look what had happened. "We need whoever to think that they are getting away with it," I said. It was seeming more and more like the *whoever* was Audrey, but I wanted to keep an open mind. I thought it over and came up with a plan.

First, I took more photos. We backtracked to Trent's room and I took more pictures of the empty spot where the pill vial had been. I got shots of Audrey's room and the plastic bag of her vitamins and took shots of the full trash can before I dropped the whole thing into a plastic bag and put it on the cart. I rushed to another of the other lobby rooms to get a receptacle to replace it.

"You better hurry," Sammy said, looking out the window. "I hear voices."

"Done," I said, coming back breathless. We pushed the heavy housekeepers' cart toward the back entrance. We didn't even have time to grab the rain ponchos, but rushed out as the first people came in the other door.

"All they'll see is an empty trash can," I said, letting out my breath. "And think it was emptied and the evidence will be lost in the garbage." I patted the heavy cart, knowing the small trash can with its contents was packed up safely behind all the wet towels. We rolled off into the darkness and waited until the pathway was clear before moving on.

Sammy and I were giddy by the time we rolled the cart past the Lodge. Being wet had become a fact of life, so we didn't even care that we didn't have the trash bag ponchos. There was no one to see us now as we maneuvered the cart to the maintenance building and dropped the towels into the washer. Then we pushed it back to Hummingbird Hall. Sammy stood guard as I rolled it inside and quickly put the evidence in the cold room with Trent's body.

"We did it," I said, giving Sammy a high five.

The Lodge was a lot quieter now that most of the guests had gone off to their rooms. Crystal was helping Lisa Montez finish crocheting her heart.

We handed back the master key to Cloris and said that the towels were in the washer. I thought about telling her the rest of it but did not want to take a chance that Lisa would hear.

I had a fleeting memory of her talking to Trent. Since I had no idea what was going to happen I had not paid much attention, and now I wished I had. All I could recall was that there had been some discord between them.

"I'm ready to call it a night," I said after helping Cloris clear up the teacups. She started thanking me again for all my help.

"Let me do something for you." She led the way back to the closed gift shop. "These are emergency circumstances." She opened the door and turned on the light. "Help yourself."

There was no way I was going to turn down clean clothes, even if everything did say Vista Del Mar all over it. I grabbed an oversized T-shirt to sleep in and a mishmash of clothes for the next day. They were not as nice as the Eileen Fisher outfit that Lucinda had offered to lend me, but the leggings and sweatshirt would be fresh and comfortable. And who knew there was Vista Del Mar underwear as well.

I went through the lobby of the Pines building, barely looking at the torn-up lobby. The furniture was piled in a corner and covered with a sheet, making it look like a ghost who needed Dorothy's weight-loss program. All I wanted was to get a hot shower and bed. I was glad that I had gotten the room in order earlier. Thanks to the piece of scented soap that JoJo had given me with her business card attached, the room had a floral fragrance and I looked forward to using it in the shower.

When I came out of the tiny bathroom wearing my advertisement for Vista Del Mar, Lucinda had just come in. I was glad we were sharing the room.

"This feels like camp," Lucinda said as she sat down on the made-up bed. She had just finished another call with Tag, who needed to be reassured that she was okay. "Where did you and Sammy disappear to?"

I told her the whole story and took out my phone to illustrate it with photos, starting with the ones I'd taken before we moved Trent.

She had a hard time looking at the picture of him in the bed. Even though he appeared to be just asleep, she knew he was actually dead. I told her what Sammy had said about viewing Trent's body as an empty vessel. She still didn't want to keep looking at the picture long enough for me to point out the drug vial and swiped to the next picture.

"It looks to me like someone switched his pill bottle with one that looked enough the same that he wouldn't notice that it was different. The pills in both bottles were white," I said with a shrug. "I'm guessing these are fentanyl." I had swiped to the photo of the trash can contents and pointed out the plastic bag of white pills with the *F* on it.

"Somebody sure came prepared," Lucinda said. She looked at me. "I guess we both know who the somebody is."

I nodded. "It's looking pretty bad for her." I flopped onto my bed, letting out a contented sound as I put my feet up. "The main thing is that I have the evidence packed away so I can hand it over to Lieutenant Borgnine when they finally get access. And hopefully, Audrey thinks she's safe now that the evidence has disappeared, so I don't have to worry about any more booby traps. She can't go anywhere. We just need to concentrate on keeping everything going until they can open up the street."

There were no phones in the room and the only amenity was an ancient clock radio with terrible reception, unless you were into listening to static. I wondered how well the alarm function worked on it and chose to use my phone's alarm instead. There would be no sleeping in for me. I had to see to breakfast.

• • •

When I awoke in the morning, I didn't know where I was. There was no Julius cuddled next to me ready to race me to the kitchen for his morning snack of stink fish. The light coming in the window was bleak, and with no sun it was impossible to assess the time other than it was after dawn. I looked at my phone and saw that I had awakened two minutes before the alarm was to go off.

After another shower, I emerged dressed in the things from the gift shop. Lucinda looked at me and laughed. "Maybe not Eileen Fisher, but it does have a label." I agreed to go on ahead while she got ready.

Cloris was stretching behind the counter when I came into the Lodge. She was using a couch in the business office to sleep on and had placed a bell on the counter if anyone came in during the night. There was a bathroom and shower in the business area and she had a stash of clean clothes for a situation like this. As soon as she saw me, she came out from behind the counter and the two of us went to the café as if a caffeine magnet was pulling us.

She set the drip pot on and we waited impatiently for the brown liquid to fill the glass pot. We were on our second cups when Lucinda came in. I don't know how she did it, but she looked perfectly put together. "You're even wearing lipstick," I said to my friend. I patted my head, thinking about how I must look with my damp hair pulled back and not even lip gloss.

JoJo had agreed to help with breakfast the night before, but we weren't sure if she would actually show up and we decided to go ahead without her. The dining hall lost the desolate feeling as soon as I turned on the lights and got some heat going to burn off the chill.

Breakfast had always been my favorite meal at Vista Del Mar and I regularly ate it with my retreat group. It was a lot closer to the kind of food prep that I did and I was actually looking forward to making it.

We had already come up with a menu based on what was available. Thanks to the staples we had found, there would be oatmeal with brown sugar and dried fruit, along with waffles with butter and syrup. The scrambled eggs would balance out all the carbs. We had located cans of frozen orange juice to go with the coffee and tea.

I was used to making everything from scratch, but under the circumstances was glad there was a big sack of waffle and pancake mix and we just had to make a few additions to it and heat up the waffle irons.

Lucinda handled setting up the oatmeal and when Cloris arrived, she started on the scrambled eggs.

"You should probably tell her what you found," Lucinda said.

Cloris recognized that she was the *her* Lucinda was talking about and stopped what she was doing. "What did you find?" she asked. "I hope it's something good." She had a hopeful smile and I hated to have to crush it by telling her about the evidence in Trent's death, but as the person in charge she should know where it was stashed and that it made it even clearer that his death was not by natural causes.

I laid out what I had found and where it was. I repeated what I had said to Lucinda, that all we had to do was keep things together until the cops could take over.

Lucinda put some butter in the frying pan while Cloris began to crack the eggs. The assistant manager was preoccupied and pieces of shell fell in the bowl with the egg. Lucinda stopped her from doing more and took over.

"I suppose it is reassuring that if it was Audrey then there isn't a killer on the loose, but still, a murder is different than someone dying in their sleep," Cloris said with a heavy sigh. "What do I tell Mr. St. John?" She had an apologetic expression as she looked at me. "If I say it appears to have been murder, I'd have to tell him all the presumptions are yours. It's not as if she confessed."

I nodded with understanding. "Maybe you leave it as is and don't mention murder."

"But he will hold it against me if he finds out I kept something from him."

While we were talking, Lucinda had made a big pan of scrambled eggs and I had stacked up more waffles.

JoJo arrived just in time to set up the coffeepots on the table and set out the silverware. She apologized numerous times, explaining her alarm didn't go off. "I don't like to make excuses when I fall short."

She seemed so distressed even though the three of us kept assuring her that everything had worked out. She insisted she would not have peace of mind unless we let her do the cleanup. We were glad to oblige.

Chapter 22

Unlike dinner, when they had all arrived at once, breakfast had been a scattered affair, with people wandering in at their own leisure and I was glad we had used the heated serving pieces. Everyone went back to the Lodge when they were done and there was a feeling of *now what?* Lisa stood up and addressed the group. "I don't know why I didn't think of this before. I'm a yoga instructor. I could give a session now. Under the circumstances it might help get rid of some of the tension." Once she promised that they could modify the moves to their own ability, most of them agreed. Only Leon balked.

"I didn't do yoga at Trent's retreat and I'm not going to do it now."

"Suit yourself," she said without even looking at him. Cloris volunteered to get yoga mats that were on sale in the gift shop.

I didn't resist when Lisa encouraged the so-called staff to join in. We probably needed it more than the guests. She kept it simple and had us do what she called Sun Salutations, which worked the whole body in a series of moves that were repeated a number of times. I only wished there was some sun to salute. The rain had stopped but there was no telling if it was permanent or just a short respite. It was sweet to watch how Milton helped Madeleine when she almost lost her balance.

With the yoga mats rolled up and the furniture moved back in place, Crystal suggested going right into working on the crochet project. I joined them since I felt responsible for the yarn activities, and spending some time with a hook and yarn would do me good.

I grabbed one of the extra kits and began working on the beginnings of a heart. I felt myself let out a big gush of breath and realized that even with the yoga, I was holding my body in tense mode.

As before, it did not take long for the conversations to start. Mindy went right for fussing about the breakfast, particularly the waffles.

"They were so delicious. My mother never let me even taste one before." Her shoulders sagged. "I felt so guilty, but every bite was wonderful." I heard someone groan. I was sure it was Leon.

Dorothy seemed distressed by her comments. "It's getting pretty obvious that your mother is a big part of your problem."

Mindy nodded. "Ever since I was little, she was obsessed with what I ate. Her mantra was 'you don't want to get fat.'" She glanced around at everyone. "She always looked so glamorous dressed in stylish clothes. My father is a venture capitalist and they are always going to fancy events."

Someone asked if she had a boyfriend and she appeared stricken. "I had one but my mother chased him away. She said it was for my own good. He managed an electronics store, which didn't measure up to her standards. That's why she wanted me to come here. She said I needed to get myself down to a lower size if I wanted to attract the right kind of men."

Someone else asked what kind of work she did. "I'm a commercial artist," Mindy said. She pulled out a sketchbook and showed off some of her work. She had done sketches of the beach, obviously done before the rain started. She flipped the page to one of the caricatures I had seen. All I saw was that it was of a man and I worried that it was the drawing I had seen of Leon with the erupting head. I went to block the view of it, thinking it might make the picture come true if he saw it. Then I saw it was the hairy guy staying in the cottage and let her show it off. She had drawn him holding his hand out, as if keeping everyone at bay. Since he was not part of the group, no one paid much notice and she flipped the page to a drawing of Sammy. She had him doing a magic trick while dressed in a doctor's coat and captured his warm smile.

"I hear you," Bella said, picking up the topic Mindy had started. "My mother hates my boyfriend. I couldn't take it anymore and finally I told her I broke up with Seth just to keep the peace. He wants to get married, but I don't know if I do."

It was turning into a therapy session again. All the talk of boyfriends that mothers didn't like brought me back to thinking about Dane. My mother had been against him from the moment I mentioned he lived down the street. She was pushing for Sammy. I had finally told her about the no chemistry thing, but she dismissed it as being unimportant in the long run.

I ventured making a comment. "I had a boyfriend like that—that my mother didn't like."

"What did you do?" Mindy asked.

"It doesn't matter now. His high school girlfriend showed up and that was the end of us." I made a gesture with my hands as if wiping it away from life.

"You don't sound very heartbroken," JoJo said. "I'd be sobbing for days if that happened and it would take a lot of chocolate."

"I guess I'm pretty good at accepting my fate and moving on. I have a lot of experience at it." I gave them a rundown of my many professions.

I was surprised when Crystal made a comment. "If it was me, I wouldn't just accept it without a fight. It makes it seem like you don't really care." She went from there to talking about her life as a groupie and then briefly wife of a rock star. "I did my share of trying to hang on when he told me he'd found someone else." She smiled at the group. "I didn't say it would work, but at least I gave it my best shot."

"It's not my way," I said. I felt so blah next to Crystal. She still had a presence even with the beige clothes. It wasn't just the unmatched earrings or her black curly hair or all the makeup. She had a kind of confidence and wasn't afraid to seem vulnerable. It was my MO to keep my cool and move on when something did not work out.

There was silence after that until Milton spoke. "I understand what Casey is saying. Some things just aren't meant to be and it's better to accept that." It seemed obvious he was talking about Madeleine. I forgot all about my problem when I saw the dip in her expression. I wanted to hug her and tell her it would be all right, but it seemed like the best thing to do was to change the subject.

I asked if anyone had seen Audrey.

"Her husband dying like that has to be a big shock," Milton said. "She must need time to deal with it. She was in here earlier talking to someone."

"That was me," Lisa said. "I was telling her about the yoga class and then she did the Greta Garbo thing and said she wanted to be alone."

"You can't help people when they shut you out," JoJo said. She directed her next comment at Crystal. "Maybe you can get her to come to the workshop. She probably needs it more than any of us."

The hooks had all stopped moving with the conversation. Crystal said she would try to seek out Audrey, but in the meantime urged the rest of them to get busy.

I understood the Greta Garbo thing. Being stuck inside at Vista Del Mar with endless company was getting to me. I needed some time alone, outside, even if there was rain. When the group broke up, I found the trash bag poncho and headed outside.

I went to the boardwalk and took the path that led through the dunes. The fresh air and solitude gave me time to think. I barely noticed that the white silky sand was compacted by the rain and appeared a dark tan.

Cloris's concern about calling Kevin St. John had made me wonder if I should call Lieutenant Borgnine and tell him about what I had done with the evidence and what I thought it meant. It seemed like damned if you do or damned if you didn't and they find out later. By the end of the walk, I had realized one thing—that Cloris and I either had to call both men or neither of them.

I found Cloris and told her what I thought and she agreed. "If we only tell one of them, he's sure to call the other," she said.

"And then make a fuss that we didn't call him directly," I said. "I say we call them."

She used the Vista Del Mar phone and I went into one of the phone booths. As I was afraid of, the lieutenant said I should have called him before I moved the evidence. "What would you have told me to do?" I asked.

"Part of the evidence is where it is found," he said. "You may have contaminated it when you handled it."

"Sammy and I were wearing gloves," I said. "And we were careful how we handled the pill containers." I reminded him that I had taken pictures of where we found the trash can. "I left the pill vial in Dr. Nicholson's room even though it was definitely evidence and look what happened. You do understand what this means," I said.

Lieutenant Borgnine let out a grunt. "Of course I do. I'm a cop. But why don't you tell me what you think it means."

Everything was getting to me and I probably sounded a little snippy. "I think it means that someone switched pills on him and the pill he took killed him. The most obvious suspect is his wife. She has an adjoining room so had easy access. And the spouse is always the most likely suspect. If I hadn't been so observant, it would have ended up in the dumpster, which might have been emptied before your people did their investigation." I was finding it hard to contain my irritation. "You should really thank me for what I did."

"I wouldn't go that far," he said, sounding weary. "But I see why you viewed what you did as protecting the evidence. Don't get carried away and try to confront the woman. And don't start bragging to the others about what you did. Don't talk about it at all. Try to keep them all calm until we can get the road open."

I wanted to tell him that I had no intention of confronting Audrey and I wasn't about to start bragging, as he called it. And that I had already planned to do exactly what he had told me to do. But I decided that it was best to keep that to myself. "Thank you, that sounds like a good plan," I said.

"Okay, then," he said. There was a little surprised sound in his gruff voice. He must have expected me to argue. "And be sure to call me first, if you find anything else." Before I could comment, he ended the call.

With the calls completed, Cloris and I met up to discuss. We wanted to be sure no one heard us and went back to Kevin St. John's office.

"He reacted as I expected," Cloris said. "He dismissed the whole idea of it being a murder."

"He probably said it was all a figment of my imagination because I thought that I was a detective," I said.

She seemed uncomfortable, but finally nodded. "That's what he said, more or less."

I told her what the lieutenant had said and what he had told me to do.

"That's just about the same as what Mr. St. John said." She was worried about staying away from her post for too long and we went back to her usual spot behind the counter. Once she looked over the rest of the large room and saw that everyone seemed to have found something to do, she suggested we check on the café.

I glanced at the windows as we went into the smaller space. Rain was splattering against the windows again. We had the place to ourselves and we both needed a pick-me-up, and I offered to show off my new skills and make us cappuccinos using the espresso machine.

It really wasn't that hard. It was all push buttons now. The strong coffee dripped into the two demitasse cups while I held the container of milk under the steaming nozzle and watched the foam build up.

"You're hired," Cloris joked as I handed her the cup. I had tried to make a heart shape in the foam as a lot of baristas did. The important word here was *tried.*

We sat down at a table and deliberately looked away from the windows. It was too dismal looking out at the dunes through a rain-soaked window.

"I still can't believe that she did it," Cloris said, keeping her voice low even though we were clearly alone.

"Trent Nicholson held other retreats at Vista Del Mar," I said. "You must have gotten to know something about him and his wife as well.

Maybe if we can come up with a motive."

Cloris took another sip of her drink and it seemed to energize her. "I always try to keep a professional distance with the guests—take care of their needs but not be intrusive. Dr. Nicholson did put on a number of his retreats here over the years. A lot of them were before I was assistant manager."

I reminded her there was no one listening but me and she did not have to worry if she seemed nosy.

"I stayed in the background and most of the guests ignored me when I worked in the dining hall and filled in where needed in other positions. Except Dr. Nicholson. He always asked how I was doing, and told me to call him Trent. The way he looked at me made it seem like he really cared." She seemed a little embarrassed. "Women seem to fall for him. Even me, though just a little." She looked stricken. "Don't tell Sammy." Then she appeared even more stricken. "I'm sorry—"

"It's okay," I said. "I know about you and Sammy and I'm fine with it. You're both good people who deserve each other."

She seemed relieved.

"I know what you're talking about," I said. "There's a name for it—transference—and it's very common with therapists and their clients. I gather that's what happened with Audrey, only she took it a step further. More than a step. She was one of the participants at his last retreat. It must have been hard on the woman he was married to then," I said. "All I know about her is what Leon said. She was forgettable except for a big nose. Do you remember anything else about her?"

Cloris shrugged. "He was the star and his wife kept to the background. I don't have much memory of her other than someone dressed in functional clothes with brown hair. I'm sure Leon is right about her nose, but I really didn't notice."

"But why would Audrey want to kill him? She was the victor." I took a sip of the cappuccino.

"For the moment, anyway. He could have found somebody to

replace her. Isn't there some saying about what goes around comes around," Cloris said.

"You mean like karma?" I said and she nodded.

Why did that sound so familiar?

Chapter 23

I looked at the clock and was shocked to realize how late it was. When the weather was this gloomy time got away from you. The mealtimes seemed to be coming faster and faster. I pushed the thoughts about Audrey, the trash can of evidence and the call with Lieutenant Borgnine to the back of my mind as I wondered what we could come up with for lunch. The first order of business was to find Lucinda.

She was in one of the phone booths with the folding door open. I waved to get her attention and she put her hand over the phone and rolled her eyes. "Business has picked up and Tag is having a hard time explaining why there aren't any of your fabulous desserts."

"Tell him to give out rain checks. I'll do a courtesy baking session when I get out of here."

She went back to the call and passed on what I said before ending it. "Thank you, it worked. Tag is beside himself. You know how he is. He wants everything to be so perfect. But life just isn't."

I reminded her of lunch. "We need to figure out the menu and who we can get to help us," I said.

"Is everything else okay?" she asked.

I shrugged. "Cloris and I were trying to come up with a motive for Audrey killing her husband."

"Any luck?" she asked and I shook my head. She brightened. "I think I know who we're going to get to help us with lunch."

• • •

It would have been a good plan if we had found her. When Lisa heard why we were looking for Audrey, she volunteered her services. I wondered how much help she would be. With her slender build, flashy white-blond hair and blood-red lipstick, she didn't give off a vibe of being into cooking.

It felt like I had just left the dining hall as I turned on the lights and led the way back to the kitchen. "Now what?" Lisa said, looking around at all the massive cooking equipment.

She followed Lucinda and me as we did a quick appraisal of the pantry and refrigerator. I was totally surprised when she was the one to come up with a menu.

She chuckled, figuring out my reaction, and patted her short, slicked-back hair. "It's kind of extreme. I think I overcompensated." She pulled out a big can of black beans and one of tomatoes and dumped them into one of the large stockpots. Lucinda found some frozen onions and I added a bag of frozen mixed vegetables. Lisa added the spices and we set the pot on to simmer.

"I used to make chili and corn bread for my daughter's school carnival," she said. "I think we need an extra kick to lift the mood of this group." She poured in some extra seasoning as she described the benefits from spicy food. Lucinda was already working on the corn bread and I was mixing a chocolate chip pan cookie.

The mention of a daughter made me think of Crystal and her daughter's reaction to her clothes. "I gather your hair and all is a new look. How did your daughter take it?"

"Not well," she said with a smile. "She said it looked like I was trying too hard. But I had to reinvent myself after the divorce." I waited to see if she wanted to say more, but she seemed to shrug it off and went to talking about the weekend. "It certainly isn't what I expected."

"I'm so sorry about that and thank you for your help with lunch and the yoga class." As an afterthought, I apologized that everyone hadn't taken part in it. "Leon and Audrey were the ones who needed it the most," I said.

"Isn't it always that way," Lucinda said, and we both agreed.

Lisa was the one who brought up Trent's death and told a weird story about a woman whose husband died from an overdose of fentanyl, and she insisted he had taken it himself. She had appeared grief-stricken and had even written a children's book about grief.

"Though she insisted she had nothing to do with him taking the drug, she ended up getting charged with murder," Lisa said. "I'm sure that nothing like that happened here."

"It's not for me to say. But the police will investigate," I said.

"When they finally get here. And who knows what will be left for them to investigate," Lisa said. "It seems like a perfect situation for someone to get away with murder."

I swallowed a little hard at her comment, but keeping my resolve not to talk about it, said nothing.

We forgot to ring the bell, but people showed up anyway, drawn by the smell of the cooking food.

I took over handing out the bowls of chili in the cafeteria line. I had my eye out for Audrey since nobody had seen her all morning. Could she have found a way to escape?

Then there she was at the end of the line. I watched as she approached the food station I was manning. Her eyes darted around at the others and finally at me. Her expression had changed from grief-stricken to threatened. I had to make her believe that no one suspected her.

I turned on my smile and offered her a bowl of the chili. "It's spicy, but nice," I said. "The heat will get your endorphins going and lift your mood." I hoped my expression didn't give a clue to what I was really thinking as I dropped a dollop of sour cream on top of the chili.

Chapter 24

The lunch was a big success. It wasn't just that their worries of being starved were fading away, but they were pleased with the food. I liked that there was more than dessert in my repertoire. I had fleeting thoughts about wanting to share it with Dane after all his teasing me about living on frozen entrées despite my cooking skills. But it was too late for that.

With lunch done, we needed to get them occupied with something. Crystal and I rounded them up to work on the garlands. We decided they needed a change of scenery and took them back to the meeting room. Audrey tagged along and I offered her some assistance on the crocheting. She seemed more relaxed and I wondered if the chili had done it or if it was that she finally felt safe now that she thought she had made the evidence disappear.

No surprise that Leon caused a problem. He threw down his half-done heart and went to grab one of the samples that Crystal had on the table. "I'm done. All finished," he said triumphantly as he held up the completed garland.

"No cheating," I said and grabbed it out of his hand and stuffed the whole thing into my jacket pocket. It was only after much cajoling that he went back to working on the heart he had cast aside. He wasn't the only one having a problem. Evie Delano seemed restless and complained she had taken enough videos of her being excited about learning how to crochet. Dorothy seemed fidgety and complained about all the sitting. Mindy was drawing the group sitting around the table. She was shielding it from sight and I could only imagine how she was depicting everyone. Even the four that had come for my retreat seemed edgy. I glanced at the window and saw that not only was it not raining, but the sky seemed a little brighter. I remembered how getting some outdoor time had refreshed me.

"Let's go outside while we can," I said. "And take a walk."

The suggestion took them all by surprise, but as soon as they saw the weather situation, all left their tote bags and got up to go. Milton helped Madeleine on with her coat and even took her arm. She seemed pleased but uncertain about the gesture. Evie was excited to have something new to video herself doing. Dorothy exclaimed how good it was to move. Mindy didn't have to say it, but I was sure she was thinking about burning off some of the carbs from lunch. Lisa suggested everyone take deep yoga breaths of the damp fresh air. JoJo seemed happy to be outside and said that all the retreats she'd been on incorporated walks to shake out the tension. Audrey stuck by herself. Bella and Lexie seemed to enjoy the change. Even Leon was okay, for a while, but after we had done the loop through the dunes and were on the way back, he saw how the driveway was blocked with fallen trees and the street beyond was clogged with cars, and he started to go on about being stranded and the worry that it could get worse and Vista Del Mar could get flooded. His fussing got the rest of them on edge and I knew there was no way we could go back to crocheting just then.

I got Crystal to take them back on the loop through the dunes, hoping that some more exercise would calm them down. I went to talk to Cloris.

The first thing she did was to tell me that Dane had called for me. "He wanted to let you know that your house is fine and that Julius has been given several snacks of stink fish. He wanted me to make sure to tell you that you could call him."

"That's not going to happen," I said. I had the uncomfortable feeling that he had taken Stacy with him when he went to my place. What if Julius did figure eights around her legs and decided he wanted her to be his human instead of me? I ordered myself to snap out it and turned to what I had come to suggest.

"I know there's usually a movie shown on Friday evening," I said.

Cloris got a stricken look. "I forgot all about that." She started apologizing for the forgotten movie and all the things that hadn't gone as usual, like the outdoor roasting of marshmallows and nature walks. "If you and Crystal hadn't gotten them all crocheting, there would have been no activities."

"It's okay," I said, trying to calm her. "I was thinking we could move it up to this afternoon. We need something to distract them and keep Leon from stirring everybody up."

She agreed and we discussed logistics. There was no choice but to use Hummingbird Hall since that was where the equipment was. She said that she and Sammy could set everything up. I was hoping for a comedy, but the selection of movies the manager had left were *Titanic*, *Poseidon*, and *Jaws*.

By the time I brought the group to the auditorium building, it was all set up with chairs and a refreshment area with a selection of candy and a popcorn cart filled with a freshly made batch.

Sammy started it off with a few magic tricks and then waved his arm, and *Jaws* began on the screen behind him. We shut off the lights on the way out and left them to enjoy the movie.

Lucinda, Crystal and I went our separate ways. I went back to the Lodge and took a spot near the fireplace. I had my tote bag and went to work on making some hearts. I ran out of steam after a while and thought of what else I could do with the time. The meal prep was a strain, but baking never was. I went to the dining hall with a plan to make bread for dinner. Working with dough was therapeutic and I wondered if any of the wellness weekends that JoJo had gone to had incorporated it in their program. If not, they should. I felt much less stressed by the time I had kneaded the dough and it was doing its first rising. I waited around until it was time to punch it down and shape it into loaves for a second rising before I left the kitchen. I had even come up with the menu.

All the relaxed feeling went away when I got back to the Lodge. The movie would be done soon, and then what? The rain had started again, making hopes of the road opening feel bleak. I had figured out dinner, but what about the meals on Saturday?

Cloris was doing her best to hang on, but I knew it was all getting to her, too. Lucinda had her own worries with Tag, and it was hard on

Crystal. She was only supposed to be here for the workshops, and I was sure she was anxious to go home and get back to her life and her clothes.

They all had enough to deal with and I did not want to share my feelings with any of them. I went to the café and made myself a cappuccino, hoping it would give me a boost and banish my mood. Madeleine came up to me just as I was looking for a place to sit.

"I couldn't stand another minute of that movie," she said. "I thought Milton would leave with me, but he just told me to go on." She took the seat next to me. "I thought it was going to be like a date. We'd share the popcorn and maybe he'd put his arm around me." She seemed distraught. "All I know about contemporary romance comes from Hallmark movies." She looked longingly at my cappuccino and I offered to make her one. She followed me to the espresso machine as I got out the coffee and milk. "This is all a bit much. Being stuck here. Cora said it's my own fault. My sister thinks I'm silly for wanting to be part of your yarn retreats. How it must look that the café here is named after Cora and me, and I'm acting like a common worker." Madeleine realized that it sounded a little condescending. "Those were Cora's words, not mine. Being part of things here has made me feel useful." Her brow furrowed. "What do you think about the way Milton is acting?" she asked.

I wanted to make a joke and say he was not exactly acting like a duke in disguise, but she seemed too serious about the situation. I did not want to say anything to upset her, but I didn't know what his intentions were or what she thought they were. I did not even know how his visit had come about. "Did you invite Milton to come for the weekend?" I asked finally.

"No. I would never do anything as forward as that. I saw him a little when he came for a writers' conference and we kept in touch. He let me know he was going to be here for this weekend and said maybe we could get lunch or dinner together." She seemed uncomfortable. "I did tell him the weekend would be comped."

"That's it?" I said and she nodded. I didn't say it, but it sounded like seeing her was not his primary reason for being there. I didn't want her to feel bad and tried to smooth it over. "The weather and being stranded is getting to everybody," I said, and she instantly brightened.

"I bet you are right. He's probably just upset about being stuck here. Thank you. I feel so much better." She leaned back against the cushion at the back of the chair. "He kept talking about that psychologist dying."

"Really? What did he say about it?"

He said that he thought somebody might have helped him to go to . . ." She stopped and said she wanted to get the words just right. "He called it the big therapy session in the sky."

"Did he say anything else, like who he thought had done the *helping*?" I asked, trying to sound casual.

"He said something about a heated interchange and that the tea proved something." She glanced around the room nervously. "Then you think it was murder, too," she said. "I was hoping that it was just his imagination." It would not do to have her getting all panicky, and worse, telling anybody. I momentarily forgot my own issues and focused on getting her to relax.

I didn't want to lie to her about whether I thought it was murder, but I didn't want to discuss it either. I took the politician's way out and simply ignored the comment and went on about something else.

"I know that you and Milton already helped with a meal, but do you think that you two could help with dinner?" I asked. She beamed a big smile.

"That's a wonderful idea. It's something we can do together." She started to back away. "I'll tell him after the movie."

Too bad all problems couldn't be handled that easily, I thought, watching her go. I wished she'd had more details about what he had said. Could there be clues that I missed?

With her gone, my gloomy feelings resurfaced. Was there anyone I could talk to about the situation at Vista Del Mar without being worried that I was upsetting them? I considered my parents. My mother was a definite no. She already did not approve of what I was doing and would be happy that Dane was off with someone else. My father was also a doctor, a pediatrician. He was softer than my mother, but also a worrier. Telling him what was going on would only upset him.

I went to the phone booth and called the only other person I could think of. Frank answered on the third ring.

"What's up, Feldstein?" he said instead of a hello.

"How did you know it was me?" I asked, since the caller ID on his phone would just show the number of the pay phone.

"I'm a PI," he said with a chortle. "You're the only one I know who would be calling from that area code." He paused a beat. "Still stranded? Any more bodies to put on ice?" I played detective and listened for background noises, trying to figure out where I had reached him. There was no squeaking of his office chair as he pushed it back to its limit, which meant he was not in his office. The was no rustle of paper, which usually meant he was in the midst of eating one of his favorite sub sandwiches. I heard water being turned on and maybe the sound of a pan. None of it seemed familiar.

"Where are you?" I asked finally.

"If you have to know, I'm in my kitchen." He stopped and lowered his voice. "And I'm not alone. Someone is helping make dinner."

"You have a date," I said in surprise.

"Correct," he said curtly. "Now, why is it that you called?"

I almost just hung up. Even Frank had someone. He knew all about my life but kept his mostly a mystery. He wanted to maintain his tough image. I had only found out that he had a cat named Mittens by accident.

He was right about being a detective because he figured out what my silence meant. "Something's wrong, isn't it?" There was another pause and it sounded as if he had moved to another room. "Go ahead.

I'll let Vicky work on dinner without me."

It was a relief to be able to just dump everything on him. "It's all gotten to be too much," I said. I went on about being stuck in Vista Del Mar and having to deal with the meals and playing housekeeper. I mentioned distributing the towels and the trash can with the evidence.

"I hope you did something with it," he said, and I told him about putting it with Trent's body in cold storage. I described my call with the lieutenant.

"It sounds like you have things under control," he said.

After he said that, I did not want to seem like a crybaby and tell him I was afraid I could not keep up the cooking and dealing with everything. I figured the call would be ending soon and I mentioned that they were all watching a movie in the auditorium building.

"Isn't that where you said the cold room is?" he said with sudden attention. "That sounds like a bad idea. You think the wife is the killer and she knows where you've got his body. What if she takes a look and finds the trash can with the evidence? It would sure be egg on your face if it disappears after you told that cop about it."

I heard some more background noise and knew he was getting close to ending the call. "Feldstein, you're slipping. You shouldn't have let that woman in that building where she could have access to the cold room." I thought he was going to end the call there, but instead of a hang-up, he changed the subject. "Situation the same with the cop?"

I mumbled a yes.

Frank softened. "I'm sorry."

After we hung up, I tried to dismiss it. Audrey could not possibly know about where I had put the evidence, or could she? She knew where we had moved Trent's body. What if now that she was in Hummingbird Hall and had access, she decided to check. Frank was right, I had slipped up.

Chapter 25

I wanted to rush to Hummingbird Hall to check on the evidence, but I got waylaid before I could leave the Lodge. The movie had finally ended and everyone had come back to the Lodge.

"They're getting restless again," Cloris said, stopping me as I came out of the phone booth. She sounded uneasy. "The only thing that has pleased them is the food. I heard them talking about dinner and what might be for dessert."

I saw them all looking at me. "Fine. I'll get right on dinner," I said.

"Tell them there will be dessert," she said. I followed her to the café, where she picked up a carafe of red wine and a bowl filled with bags of chips and cheese crackers.

"Maybe you should toss the snacks to them," I said. "Like they throw meat into wild animal cages." Cloris laughed, but I could tell she was thinking about it.

I called out a promise that there would be a delicious dessert and grabbed Lucinda to help. I left Madeleine and Milton to show up on their own.

When I'd been killing time in the kitchen while the bread rose, I'd found some frozen lasagna hidden at the bottom of the freezer. While the lasagna and bread baked, filling the kitchen with delicious smells, Lucinda showed me how to turn the bags of frozen vegetables into a treat with garlic butter and Parmesan cheese. I threw together a fast dessert, taking canned peaches and covering them with a cobbler crust. I would whip up the cream later.

Madeleine and Milton showed up in time to help set everything up. There was no need to ring the bell. Everyone was already waiting inside the dining room as we set up the food.

I waited until they were all eating and then I slipped out and went to Hummingbird Hall with my fingers crossed that Frank was wrong. I regretted how cocky I had been to Lieutenant Borgnine. What would I do if after all that I had nothing to show him?

I went into the upper floor and saw that everything was still set up for the movie. I had not considered the stairway that led to the lower floor where the bathrooms were located when I hustled them there for the movie. I almost tripped down the staircase and went into the storage area where the cold room was. As soon as I opened the door, I knew the worst was true. The fresh towels I had used to hide the bag with the can were on the floor. When I checked the cart, there was just an empty spot where the plastic bag with the trash can of evidence had been. The evidence I had promised the lieutenant was gone.

I had to rush back to the dining hall to whip the cream for the peach cobbler and act like nothing was wrong. As I went around topping the plates with the cobbler, I tried not to stare at Audrey, and she certainly didn't look at me.

Crystal got them to work on the hearts after the meal. But it didn't work for long. Leon threw down his hook and the yarn attached to it in frustration. "Whoever said this was therapeutic is nuts." He glared at Bella and Lexie. "Maybe it is for you two since it was your choice to do this, but it's just making me feel more edgy. When are we going to get out of this place?"

Audrey was keeping herself separate from the group and was back to playing the grieving widow. All she needed was a black veil to complete the image. The rest of them were used to it by now and simply let her be. She glanced up and for a second our eyes met. She appeared panicked.

"They need another movie," I said to Cloris, "and it's got to be something funny this time." Cloris started to say that Kevin St. John had only left the three disaster movies and then she remembered something and we went back to his office.

She opened a desk drawer and showed me a stack of DVDs. "He can't know that I know about these or he'll know that I have been in his desk." She went on with how it had happened when she had needed something when the manager had been off the grounds. She was giving too many details and I wondered if she was trying to cover up her nosiness.

"I won't tell," I said and grabbed a handful of the plastic cases. "This is perfect," I said, picking one out. We made a run for Hummingbird Hall. I knew that everything was still in place from the afternoon, but acted surprised. I didn't want Cloris to know about my mistake. I was too embarrassed. We did a little spruce up and set the popcorn cart up to make a fresh batch before we went to gather everyone up.

Crystal mouthed a heartfelt thank-you to me as the group vacated the area by the fireplace and followed Cloris to the auditorium. She had snagged Sammy and told him to repeat what he had done earlier.

When she returned to the Lodge, she joined Crystal, Lucinda and me on the couch. "We made it through another day," I said. They all nodded and we gave each other high fives.

• • •

I had gone along with the smiles and high fives, but I certainly didn't feel it. I was so upset with myself for not realizing that Audrey would have access to the cold room. Did she go into the box-like room to check if Trent's body was really there? Whatever her reason, she must have figured it out when she saw the housekeepers' cart. All I could think of was how I would drop in Lieutenant Borgnine's estimation when I had to admit that the evidence had been taken.

I had to find it. Since Audrey couldn't leave Vista Del Mar any more than the rest of us, it had to still be there. I didn't think she would take it back to her room since she must have realized someone had been there to deal with the towels. Would she take out the two vials and the plastic bag and put them in her tote bag to carry with her? I didn't think so because it was too easy for someone to grab hers by mistake and look inside. The more I thought about it, the more it seemed like she would repeat what she had already done—try to throw it all away. Throw it where she thought it would end up when she put it in the trash can in the Tides lobby. A place that nobody would go hunting for it.

I looked up at the window and let out an ugh sound when I saw there was more rain. Going through the dumpster was bad enough without being pelted with raindrops. But if I intended to become a PI, there would be icky jobs.

Cloris had gone back to her post behind the counter figuring Kevin St. John would call for an update. Crystal pulled out her crochet things and went back to working on a heart. "I don't care what Leon says," she said, letting out a relaxed sigh. "Working with yarn would be good for him, if he gave it a chance."

Lucinda went back to one of the phone booths to see how dinner had gone at the Blue Door. I slipped away and went back to my room to prepare for my expedition. I had done it before, but in better weather.

I was glad that Lucinda was occupied and couldn't see what I was doing. I didn't want to explain, even to her. I couldn't afford to mess up the leggings and sweatshirt I was wearing since I had nothing to change into. It was time to be creative. I went to the housekeepers' closet and found a box with different-sized trash bags and a roll of duct tape. The poncho part was easy to make, but the bottoms were more of a challenge. I made pants out of two trash bags with holes for my feet. I held them up with duct tape suspenders. I added rubber gloves and a long stick with a claw at the end. I was going to use towels held in place with rubber bands to cover my shoes just before I climbed in the dumpster. The final touch was pulling the strap with a headlamp over my forehead. I went out into the night looking like a cyclops.

For obvious reasons, I didn't want to be seen by anyone and took a circuitous route through the grounds. The dumpster was next to the back gate and I noticed with distaste that the wind was making the top go up and down, which meant the inside would be wet. The street beyond was swirling with water, mud and debris. I leaned against the dumpster and fashioned my shoe protector booties. I was already planning that they were making a one-way trip. So much for any illusions that being a PI was going to be glamorous or fun like *Charlie's Angels*, *Hart to Hart* or *Moonlighting*. I found a plastic pail and used it to climb on to raise me up to the lid of the dumpster. It was slick with the rain and my hand slipped as I tried to lift it and it fell back with a crash. I did not even want to think about any critters that might be hiding out in there.

The second try was successful and I pushed the lid all the way back and hoped the wind would leave it there. All my experience with the stink fish came in handy and I was already holding my nose as I shone the light around the dark interior. There were mounds of food scraps and other trash because the storm had kept it from being emptied. I tried using the grabber to poke through the piles of ick, but my reach was limited. There was no alternative other than climbing in. I checked that the rubber bands holding the towels around my shoes were snug and I climbed in. I slid over the slippery plastic bags and squished on some over-ripe bananas. As my headlamp illuminated the piles of refuse, it felt a little hopeless. I used the grabber to poke around and I heard it hit something hard. The headlamp confirmed that it was one of the amber pill vials. Then I saw the small trash can and checked the area around it and found the other vial and the plastic bag of pills. Of course, Audrey had just thrown it all in quickly and not thought about trying to bury everything. The grabber was only good for so much and I had to use my hands to pile stuff back into the small trash can. Thank heavens for rubber gloves!

This time I wasn't taking any chances. Once I had lost the trash bag outfit, I used one to protect the trash can with the pill vials. I didn't explain, but told Cloris I needed to leave a package someplace secure. She offered me the vault where guests could leave their valuables.

I mentally gave myself a high five. It was a little worse for wear, but I had the evidence back.

Chapter 26

I knew exactly where I was when I awoke Saturday morning and I wished it wasn't so. The first thing I did was look out the window to check the sky, hoping for a change. It seemed to be a little brighter and at least there were no slashes of rain on the glass. I would have liked to pull the covers up and gone back to sleep, but food was the only thing that the group seemed to be pleased with and they would be expecting breakfast. It was funny that I—the person who had relied on instant oatmeal and frozen dinners—had become the center of creating the meals.

At least I had clean clothes. Even with my concocted rain suit when I went dumpster diving, my leggings had gotten some ick on them. I hadn't explained how it happened to Cloris, but she let me go wild in the gift shop again. There were no more leggings and I'd had to settle for navy blue sweatpants that were a little small and a maroon sweatshirt that was way too big. Both were emblazoned with the Vista Del Mar name and logo.

Lucinda laughed when I came out of the bathroom in my outfit. We made an odd sight as we went to the dining hall. She was wearing the Eileen Fisher outfit she had offered me and had on makeup. My hair was pulled up into a topknot and there was a flash of my ankles below the too-short sweatpants.

Crystal joined us in the kitchen. She gratefully tied an apron over her gray outfit. "And I thought the beige was bad. Now I look like the sky."

Part of me wanted to tell them about my escapade the night before, but a larger part told me to keep it to myself. Audrey might think I knew something, but she probably felt safe now that she had thrown the stuff into the dumpster, never considering the lengths I would go to to find it. All I wanted to do was keep things even until Lieutenant Borgnine could get there and take over.

We had managed to find food to create the impromptu meals so far, but we were running low on the basics. Lucinda found some sausages in the bottom of the chest freezer. After the coffee cake I made and the pan of scrambled eggs sprinkled with cheese that Crystal and I concocted, there were barely any eggs left.

Cleanup had gotten easier. They all scraped their dishes and put them directly in the dishwasher. I had made an extra coffee cake to leave in the café. I was setting up air pots with coffee and hot water when someone walked in.

"Oh," I said in surprise when I looked at the door and saw the guy who was staying in the cottage.

"There's no one at the counter. I was looking for some breakfast. And some clean towels." He asked in a nice way and I felt bad realizing that when we'd done the towel exchange we had not thought about him. I explained that breakfast was over but offered him coffee cake and a cappuccino.

"I'm getting pretty good with the espresso machine. I guess there is a silver lining to every cloud. If I wasn't stuck here with no one to stop me, I never would have gotten a chance to use the machine. So, are you game?"

"Sure. It sounds great." I was surprised when he accepted my offer for him to sit. "It would be nice to drink it here. I'm pretty sick of my own company."

I smiled at him as I loaded the coffee grounds in the machine. "You are welcome to come to the dining hall. You could even volunteer your services to help with a meal."

The long hair and beard made it hard to read his expression, but there was light in his eyes. "I'm not going that far." He punctuated it with a chuckle. "Any word on when we'll be able to get out of here?"

I shrugged as I steamed the milk. "Hopefully soon. At least it's not raining."

While I finished the drink and cut him some coffee cake, I asked him about himself. After so much time alone, he seemed glad to talk. He was from San Jose and had a job in tech that was too boring to talk about. Then he asked about me. That rarely happened when I was putting on a retreat. It was always spotlight on the group I was responsible for. It was even more so this time with all that had happened. I handed him his drink and pulled out the stool next to him to join him and drink the cappuccino I had made for myself.

I gave him the short bio of my assorted jobs and move to Cadbury, which ended up with me inheriting the yarn retreat business.

"Working for a detective must have been interesting," he said.

Somehow, I ended up telling him how much I liked it and that I was planning to go back to it.

"Why leave Cadbury?" he asked. "It seems pretty dreamy if you ask me."

"It was until my boyfriend took up with someone else," I said.

"Understood. Been there myself," he said with a heavy sigh.

"To getting out of here," I said, holding up my cup to make a toast.

"You can say that again," he said before taking a sip of foam-covered drink. I was tempted to repeat what I just said, but accepted that it was way too corny. I invited him to join the yoga class that Lisa was going to give in the main room, but he declined, saying he was not ready for that much company.

Lisa was organizing the group when I went into the larger room. "Is that everybody?" she asked as she got ready to start.

"Audrey's not here," Mindy said, checking over the group. "I didn't see her at breakfast. Maybe she decided to sleep in."

I felt myself go on high alert. What if she had found a way out? I offered to find her and left them to begin the sun salutes while I rushed off to the Tides building. I knocked, and when there was no answer, tried the door. I had a bad feeling as it pushed open.

At first, I thought the room was empty, and then I saw there was someone in the bed. Mindy must have been right about her sleeping in. After the episode with the disappearing evidence, I had wanted to keep a low profile with her. I thought about backing out of the room before she noticed me. But as an afterthought, it seemed okay to remind her about the yoga class. I called out her name and brought up the class, but there was no response from her. I repeated it with the same result. Finally, I touched her arm. It was cold to the touch. I ran to get Sammy.

The yoga class was in the midst of doing a pose called downward dog, which amounted to turning the body into an upside-down V shape. The only part of Sammy that was accessible to tap for his attention was his butt. Instead, I called out to him and said it was urgent. My tone of voice got everyone's attention and they followed us back to Tides, hanging in the hall outside Audrey's door while Sammy and I went inside to check on her.

Sammy swallowed hard before he turned to me and offered a solemn shake of his head. "Are you sure?" I whispered. "What about CPR?"

He shook his head again. "It's too late for that. She's dead."

Even with the whispering, the group in the hall heard us and someone called out that she must have died of a broken heart. Sammy shook his head again.

"I did a stint in pathology," he said, trying to keep his voice low. "It looks to me like she suffocated." He pointed to red dots on her face around her eyes and on her ears. "It's called petechiae and is a sign of asphyxiation." He did a quick survey of the room and pointed to a pillow on the floor. "Don't quote me, but that's probably what did it."

"You mean, somebody killed her with that?" I asked, thinking how it looked just like an ordinary pillow that had lost a bit of its feather fill and hardly a murder weapon. He nodded. With a bad feeling of déjà vu, I took out my phone and, trying to be as discreet as possible, began to take pictures of the crime scene.

Sammy and I came out of the room and shut the door. Despite their clamoring, we did not offer any details of what Sammy had noticed. All they understood was that she was dead. The chance for the yoga class to pick up after an interruption like this was hopeless, and I herded them back to the Lodge pitching another crochet workshop, as if not mentioning Audrey would make them forget what they saw.

The only enthusiasm came from the four who were actually there for a yarn craft weekend.

Leon was the worst grumbler, but then he relented. "What else am I going to do."

Crystal came out of the café with Madeleine and Milton, who had chosen another cup of coffee instead of the yoga class. I pulled them aside and gave them the news. "Not someone dead, again," Madeleine said. Milton gave her arm a supportive pat and thankfully did not ask for details. Crystal offered me a sympathetic nod as I explained the need to get the group busy crocheting while I took care of things.

Cloris had figured something was up when she saw me interrupt the yoga class, but stayed at her position behind the registration counter. She was trying to be stoic, but her expression dimmed as I approached the counter. She must have sensed that I had some bad news.

"Do you want to call Lieutenant Borgnine?" I said after telling her Sammy's assessment of Audrey.

She shook her head rather vehemently.

"Please. You do it," she said. "You're so much calmer than I am. And you were the one to find her."

I went into one of the phone booths and shut the door before I placed the call. There were endless rings at the police station before someone answered. I was surprised at the female voice, but then realized she was one of the two women on the force.

I asked to speak to Lieutenant Borgnine, but she insisted on knowing why before she would put me through. "There's been a death at Vista Del Mar," I said. I couldn't believe it when she almost mirrored what Madeleine had said. "A deceased person, again?"

There were no more questions and she put me through to him. "What happened this time? Is it weather-related?" he asked in a tired, gruff voice.

I gave him the facts with no editorial comments other than to pass on that Sammy—though I referred to him as Dr. Glickner—had said she appeared to have died from asphyxiation.

"We could move her to the spot with her husband," I said, dreading the whole process of the housekeepers' cart and using trash bags as body bags.

"Hold off on that," he said. "Leave everything be. We have heavy equipment on its way and the plan is to get things partially cleared by late today." There was a pause. "And don't even think about finding the perpetrator. And don't mention you think her death was homicide to the rest of the guests. They might panic if they thought there was a killer among them."

"There might be a connection between the two deaths," I said, but he cut me off.

"We'll take care of everything. Just try to keep everyone calm until we clear the road."

"Sure," I said, wishing he could tell me how to do it.

Chapter 27

I left Cloris to deal with passing the news on to Kevin St. John and went to join the group. My worries that they would think there was a killer among them went away when I heard JoJo talking about broken heart syndrome. "The other spouse dies shortly after the first one because their heart just breaks at the loss of their partner," she said.

"It's true," Milton said. "I used it in one of my books."

"But isn't that when they were together for like sixty years?" Dorothy said. She stood out from the other women with her stylish gray hair and height, along with her teacher-like demeanor. "My specialty may be diets and such, but I'm interested in how relationships work." She let out a sigh and mentioned her ex-husband and how she certainly wouldn't be dying because he did. "We were married for forty years before he decided he preferred to be single."

"How long was Audrey married to Trent?" Mindy asked. "I thought she said something about them being almost newlyweds."

Milton looked at Leon. "You were at the last retreat the psychologist did. Were they together then?"

"I don't want to talk about him anymore. I came here to fix my life," Leon said, sounding annoyed. He might have been nice-looking if his expression wasn't always stuck in a scowl. "And now there's no chance I'm going to get any help this time."

"What was your reason for going to Trent's retreat?" Dorothy said. "I'm used to dealing with food issues, but maybe I can help."

Leon hung his head and let out a snort. "Where should I start?" Apparently, he decided to start at the beginning, which had to do with his mother wanting a daughter. He went on from there and it seemed that all of his problems were somebody else's fault now, including Trent, who had told him to break up with his wife because it was her fault that Leon's life was stuck in neutral. "I should have never listened to Trent. I miss her and her family. I worked in their business," he said. His scowl changed to a pout.

"Just a suggestion, but you need to stop blaming everyone for your unhappiness," Dorothy said when he finished. "But how to do that is really beyond my expertise. Sorry." She turned her attention to Mindy. "I'm not used to doing it one-on-one," she said with a shrug. "I have my set pitch I give to the group. When there is a group." She stopped and sighed. "Sorry if this isn't what you expected."

I was relieved that the subject had been changed back to the problems of the people that were there.

Mindy gave Dorothy's arm a reassuring pat. "Don't feel bad. I have really enjoyed the carbs and you telling me not to feel guilty," she said with a genuine smile. She was wearing pink slacks and a matching sweatshirt that had a bunch of flowers in the middle. Her outfit brightened up the gloom.

"This is certainly different than any retreat, self-help, or spa weekend that I've gone on," JoJo said. She seemed so put together in her fancy name jeans and black turtleneck, it seemed at odds with the turmoil going on inside. "It's been more about survival than learning meditation techniques."

"As for Bella and me, this is a little more than we expected. We wanted to learn more about crochet and what it was like to do it with a group. We never expected to be stranded and having people die." Everyone flinched at the last part. I looked over the faces and wondered for which one of them it was just an act.

I stepped in and apologized for everything and they all rushed to say it wasn't my fault. I thanked them for their understanding and then passed on the possible good news.

"I heard they hope to get the road open later today," I said, and there was a hum of excitement from all of them. I gave them the details I had, and when I saw Sammy stop at the edge of the setup of chairs and nod to get my attention, I excused myself to talk to him.

"I'm here to volunteer my morgue services," he said. "Say the word and we can meet up at the housekeepers' cart."

"Not needed," I said and told him what the lieutenant had told me about dealing with the body.

Cloris waved us over. Instead of being cheered by the apparent end of the rain and the imminent arrival of the equipment to clear the road, she seemed more agitated. "Mr. St. John is on his way back. He said that everything better be okay here or someone was going to have to pay."

"He's the one who is going to have to answer," I said. "He's the one who left for his seminar without checking the weather."

My comment did not do much to calm her. "I hate to ask you to do it again, but if Mr. St. John decides to inspect the rooms and sees that the used towels have not been removed, he will throw a fit." She didn't have to say the rest. He would blame her to get the heat off of himself for being gone.

We both gave her a salute and went to load up a cart with the freshly laundered towels and attached a bag for the used ones before rolling off to make our rounds.

I thought about asking Sammy if he had any ideas who the killer was, but I was too concerned about us being heard. Besides, I had made a deal with myself to stay out of it and leave it for the lieutenant to handle. We had rolled through the two adjacent guest room buildings. No one had responded to our knocks on the doors and we had to use the master key to make the towel switch.

He adjusted the bag of used towels hanging off the cart. "What do you think my parents would say if they saw me on towel duty again?"

I shrank at the thought. I knew his parents only too well from when we had been dating. "They would blame me, of course. They'd say that I somehow had spirited you away to come to Cadbury and waste your time with magic. And this is what it had led to. You, a renowned urologist, was reduced to playing housekeeper." I looked at the bag on the side. "We better throw these in the laundry."

"You think I'm a renowned urologist?" he said with a humble smile.

"You're outstanding at whatever you do," I said, and then gave him a thankful smile. "Including everything you've done here."

He smiled back at me and repeated what he had said so often about me being the only one who "got" him.

I wanted to change the subject before he said any more sweet stuff. He might be with Cloris now, but I knew he still had feelings for me. I brought up Evie Delano. "For someone who complains about the demands of her followers and her desire to break free, she has been spending a lot of time making video," I said.

"People can get addicted to more than drugs," Sammy said as we rolled through the more rustic area of the grounds. The maintenance building was up ahead and then I noticed the cottage. "We better get the ones from his place. He complained to me that he'd been neglected."

"Sure," Sammy said as he steered the cart toward the small building. Somehow we started talking about JoJo Westerly. "Do you think she has some past history with Dr. Nicholson? She did say she had been to his retreats before," he said.

"I didn't realize you knew about her," I said.

"Even though I didn't join the crochet group, I heard a lot of what was going on," he said.

"It could be more than once, too," I said, and realized that without even meaning to, we were going through the group trying to figure out who could be the killer.

I glanced at the small structure with the same weathered shingles the others had. Back in the day when it was a camp, it had been set aside for the head counselor and had always intrigued me. It did seem perfect for someone who wanted to be left alone. "Should we just leave some towels on the porch?" Sammy asked.

"No, Cloris seemed worried about a mountain of mildewed ones inside." I knocked at the door. After a second knock with no answer, I used the key to unlock it. "He must have decided to get some outside time." Sammy went to get the towels out of the bathroom and I took the opportunity to check out the interior. No wonder Madeleine had wanted to stay there. It was the perfect spot for a romantic rendezvous with Milton. The living room was charming in a rustic way. A cozy couch faced the stone fireplace. A small round table and chairs sat near a window that looked out on trees and the wild part of the grounds. There was a mini kitchen area with a small sink, refrigerator and microwave. I was caught up with looking around now and went on into the bedroom. Instead of the spartan look of the regular guest rooms, it had nice touches. There was an eye of God hanging on the door, the bed had a colorful quilt and the walls were adorned with paintings and photographs.

"What's this?" Sammy asked, coming in behind me. I looked and saw he was touching a circular thing with a netted middle and feathers hanging off the bottom near the bed.

"It's a dream catcher," I said. "It's supposed to protect the sleepers from bad dreams." I pointed to the eye of God on the door. "That's a symbol of divine watchfulness and care from the universe. Too bad that Madeleine didn't get to stay here. I am sure she would have liked showing off those touches to Milton."

"And maybe she wanted to show him more," Sammy said with a wink.

"I thought about that, too," I said. "Not much chance of anything like that happening. She is totally disappointed in how he has acted." I went into the bathroom to see that Sammy had gotten all the damp towels before they began to mildew. On the way out, I noticed some dirty dishes left from his meals packed to go.

"We might as well take these, too," I said. Sammy obliged and picked them up, not realizing he had knocked something off the chair next to the table. He was already on his way out the door when I went to pick it up. It was an unfamiliar gadget. There wasn't time to ask him if he knew what it was, so I snapped a picture. As I came outside, Sammy brushed his hand against my hair and I thought he was going to do his usual thing of making something magically appear, but instead of a butterfly there was just a bit of something from the dream catcher.

"The dynamic duo does it again," Sammy said as we walked back to the heart of Vista Del Mar after loading the towels in the washer and leaving the cart.

When we reached the driveway, we saw something that made us stop and look.

Chapter 28

The trees were still blocking the road, but there was activity on the street beyond as big pieces of equipment moved back and forth. For the first time, I believed the road was going to get opened up. But it wasn't going to be instantaneous and, in the meantime, we had to keep everything going.

"How do you feel about helping with lunch?" I said.

"Sure," he said in a happy tone. "I don't know how to cook, but if you tell me what to do . . ."

I thanked him and was hoping to snag some more help from Lucinda, but she was locked up in one of the phone booths, gesturing wildly. Poor Tag was probably suffering more than we the stranded were.

This was not the Saturday lunch I had expected when I organized my retreat. I certainly would not have expected to be the one coming up with a menu from a dwindling food supply and also the one to prepare it. This was usually a happy meal. By now the group all knew each other and whatever project they were making was well on its way. Okay, that part was sort of true.

"This is where we have to get creative," I said as we walked into the kitchen. I explained the situation and he seemed surprised.

"I never thought about how you had to figure out what to make. I think it qualifies you as a magician creating meals out of thin air."

I took a bow and said I'd had help and it wasn't exactly thin air. "More like odds and ends," I said.

I started to look around the kitchen, checking the pantry and refrigerator, along with the chest freezer. I had hoped there would be another surprise entrée stuck in the bottom like the lasagna had been, but all that was left in there was some ice cream that was so hard it would have to be left out of the freezer before a scoop could even make a dent.

We looked around the pantry and at the assorted cans, hoping to find something for the meal. I saw a big can of black beans and considered making them with rice. It would take care of their hunger, but probably not be very pleasing. I let out a sigh of relief when I found boxes of macaroni and cheese mix along with some cans of fruit cocktail and boxes of Jell-O and instantly had an idea.

"We'll make a retro meal," I said.

"Huh?" Sammy gave me a quizzical look.

"Old-fashioned. Like what people ate in the 1950s," I said.

"I get it." He picked up the gelatin dessert box and read the label. "My grandmother used to make this for me. Red was my favorite. I think it's kind of timeless. Who doesn't like to eat something that is sweet and jiggles."

I gave him the job of dealing with making the Jell-O and checked the back of the box for the macaroni and cheese, already thinking of how I could make it even better. I checked the refrigerator and saw there was still plenty of butter and a wedge of cheddar cheese.

I took the cans of fruit cocktail and racked my brain for a cake I used to make when I worked at the bistro. They used to have themed nights with food that matched it. I'd come up with the cake for *Happy Days* Night. It was named for the TV show that was supposed to take place in the 1950s with a middle-class family. No matter how much of the cake I made, we always seemed to run out. And best of all, it was easy to put together.

I heard the sound of a buzz saw starting outside and hoped that it meant this would be the final meal I would have to worry about.

The baking cake filled the air with its sweet scent as I worked on the macaroni and cheese. Once I'd boiled the pasta and sprinkled on the cheese mix and milk, I dumped in a hunk of butter and grated the cheddar cheese over it. I thought there ought to be something on the side and made a salad out of a can of mixed vegetables with mayonnaise and seasoning. Hardly a light meal. My thoughts went to Mindy and how she would react to it. But it was the best I could do.

Sammy had used the speedy version and the red liquid was already jelling when he showed it to me.

"You haven't said any more about the two people who died." He was whispering, but then saw there was no one to hear and went back to a normal voice. "More than just died—two people who were murdered. Are you really just going to drop it in Lieutenant Borgnine's lap and let him figure it out?" Sammy said. He put the Jell-O in the refrigerator to finish. "You know that by the time he gets here and accepts that they were homicides, whoever did it might be long gone. I bet they make a run for it as soon as the road is open."

My head shot up from arranging the macaroni and cheese in a casserole dish and I saw that Sammy was looking at me with a smile.

"I get it. You're trying to push me into playing detective," I said as I put the ceramic dish in the oven to keep it warm.

"You're really good at it and I can't imagine you not caring if someone gets away with murder or murders."

I smiled at the praise. It was just what I needed to hear at that moment. Ever since the whole mess with the disappearing evidence, I had been doubting my skills. "You're right, I am good at it a lot of the time, and I do care if someone gets away with murder." I cocked my ear to listen to the sound of the equipment working outside. "But it seems that time is running out," I said.

"Then you better make the most of what you've got," he said. "I'd be glad to help." We started to go over what we knew as we finished getting the food ready for serving. Instead of having a cafeteria line, I decided to put bowls of everything on the round tables and serve it family-style.

"Trent's death took advance planning," Sammy said.

"And it was somebody who knew about his medication," I said. "Everything pointed at Audrey. She had access and the spouse is always the first suspect."

"Right," Sammy said. "It did seem like she was the one who dumped the pill bottles and bag of pills."

"But now that she's dead and you think that she was suffocated, I would guess that someone had planned to set up Audrey. Someone wanted to frame her." I thought back to what I'd heard about Trent. "Someone said that Trent had a different wife when he came here the last time." I put up my hands. "But I guess that is a dead-end street."

"Didn't Dorothy say she knew Trent from a seminar on how to put on seminars?" Sammy said. "Maybe they had a past relationship and she was upset he had married Audrey."

"Or what if Trent was meant to be the only victim and something happened to make the killer take out Audrey?" I stopped a moment to think. "I heard that how someone is killed says something about the killer. Just a guess, but suffocating someone might be the ultimate way to keep them from talking."

"What about who had opportunity?" Sammy said. "Isn't that how it goes—means, motive and opportunity?"

I looked at Sammy with a hopeless shrug. "That leaves everyone."

"It doesn't take any special skill to smother someone," Sammy said. "She was probably asleep."

The outside door opened and someone called out and asked if lunch was ready. We had been too busy talking to think about the bell. Mindy walked in the kitchen and sniffed the air and repeated her question about lunch. It was the end of Sammy's and my conjecturing. We got Mindy to help with the setup and then let her ring the bell.

They all filed in and smiled when they saw the food on the tables. I had tasted everything while I was cooking and even taken a slice of the cake to make sure it was okay, and wasn't hungry. I nursed a cup of coffee and watched them eat, waiting for the thumbs-up or -down. The room had windows all around and I groaned when I saw that the rain had started to fall hard again. The sounds of the buzz saws had stopped.

I couldn't really make out any of the conversations until I heard a loud yelp. My first thought was that it was something with the food, like a fork had gotten baked in the cake or something. Sammy and I had been talking about murder and might have been distracted.

There was another yelp and I saw it was coming from Mindy. She stood up and looked around at the group. "Did you hear that?" she said in an excited voice. "Someone asked me if I wanted another piece of cake and I said no. Actually, I said no thank you, I've had enough. *Enough.*" She emphasized the word in almost a squeal. "I have never in my life said that. It was always my mother telling me I couldn't have any more. I never ever thought about whether I really wanted more."

Dorothy came over and hugged her. "That's more important than all that carb nonsense. I didn't really get a chance to give you my program, but it seems like you got it on your own."

"Good luck on it lasting," JoJo said. "Take it from me, who has been to every self-help seminar, retreat, and spa weekend, there's always that big aha moment and you leave thinking you're fixed. But then you go home and all your good intentions fade. That's why this time I came for the yarn retreat instead of wasting my time on another of the ones like Dr. Nicholson's. At least I will leave with a new skill."

Dorothy rushed to reassure Mindy. "Just because that's been JoJo's experience doesn't mean it has to be yours." I noticed that Evie was holding up her phone and had been capturing the moment.

They all began to attack her at once and she put up her hands in a helpless manner. "I need content." She sounded a little desperate.

I waited to see if anyone would add anything, but they just let it be.

• • •

The downpour had stopped by the time they were dropping off their plates for the dishwasher. When I shut off the lights and walked outside, the air felt different. The clouds had thinned and there was an actual bright hint that there was indeed a sun up there. Did I dare think that that last burst of rain was the final hurrah.

This time no one rushed to get inside and instead basked in the almost sun. Some of them headed to the boardwalk. Even if they could still not get through to the beach, they could take the looping path through the dunes. The best news of all was that when Sammy and I went to the driveway to check, men were back to working with buzz saws on the fallen trees.

When I finally went back inside the Lodge, Madeleine and Milton were standing outside the café. I had become the emergency barista and thought I would offer my services. Madeleine was already looking through to the tables, but Milton's eye seemed stuck on the hanging wooden sign that read *Madeleine and Cora Delacorte Café*. What could he be thinking? Was it a reminder that she was part of the wealthy family that was like Cadbury royalty. It regenerated my concern that he might be more interested in her money than in her. I went to join them. It turned out that my barista services were unnecessary. Lucinda was filling the air pots with freshly brewed coffee. "I'm sorry I missed helping with lunch. I thought I'd make it up by setting up the coffee and tea."

The three of us found a table near the window, where we had a good view of the grounds. Already there were some dry spots on the pavement, even though there were plenty of puddles. I was hoping to feel out how Milton really felt about Madeleine, but he took over the conversation, starting with complimenting me on the lunch. "They ought to put it on the menu. The retro meal goes perfectly with the retro atmosphere here." I thanked him for the comment but doubted that Kevin St. John would agree to it if I was the one to suggest it.

"It certainly brightens everything to have the rain stop," Milton continued. "You and the others managed to keep everyone busy and fed so they didn't have a chance to dwell on the two deaths." He looked at me intently. "I know it seemed like they were from natural causes. Maybe Dr. Nicholson's was, but while a spouse dying of a broken heart is legit, it seems more likely for a couple who have been together for decades." He looked at me. "I saw you whispering with Dr. Glickner when you were checking on her. I'm betting that you saw something that made you think it was murder."

I looked around and urged him to keep his voice low. "You certainly are observant," I said.

He smiled. "A writer's curse. I eavesdrop on conversations all the time and consider what they are saying really means."

I remembered a comment that Madeleine had made about some of his observations, but all I could recall was that it had something to do with the special blue tea we had served and I asked him about it.

His face took on a self-satisfied demeanor as he began to talk. "It wasn't the tea itself, but who suggested it." He paused to ratchet up the tension. Meanwhile, I was berating myself for not having picked up on whatever he had, and was making excuses to myself. Maybe he had been able to focus on exactly who was saying what, but I was too scattered trying to keep everything together to get every detail. If I intended to have a future as a real PI, I needed to get my act together. Instead of giving up, I closed my eyes and went back to the other evening. I saw them all gathered around the fireplace. The rain was pelting the windows, putting everyone on edge. We were going to serve hot chocolate, but someone mentioned a special tea that Trent Nicholson served his group. And then a face popped into view.

"It was Lisa Montez," I said, relieved that I'd been able to figure it out. He seemed disappointed that I had messed up his moment. He started to say what it meant, but I had an aha moment and cut in before he could speak.

"If she knew about the tea, she must have been to one of his retreats before."

"I don't think it went well either," Milton said. "The first night they had a moment in the dining hall. I heard him tell her she should leave."

"I'm going to talk to Cloris and see what she knows." I asked Milton if he wanted to come, but he put up his hand.

"I'm just a detective on paper, I'll leave the real stuff to you."

Sammy had gone off somewhere and Cloris was back to pacing. I was glad to give her something else to think about, and as I expected, her mood lifted as soon as I started explaining. It was her nature to set aside her own troubles when someone else needed something.

I told her that I thought Lisa might have been to one of Trent's weekend things before. "Does she look familiar to you?" I asked. She wondered why I was asking.

"She knew about the tea that was served at Trent's retreat and apparently had an angry exchange with him that first night," I said.

"I have a pretty good memory for faces," she said before taking a moment to think and then shrugged. "She doesn't look familiar. Too bad we don't take photos of the guests, then I could check that. All I do remember is that Audrey was at his last retreat."

Her comment stirred something and I was trying to get what it was when Mindy came up to the counter. She was still excited about what had happened at lunch. She was holding her sketchbook and said how good it was to finally spend some time outside. She showed me some drawings she had done and I recognized the location she had sketched. She had captured the backs of several people taking the fork in the walkway that led through the dunes. Even though their faces were not visible, I recognized Leon and JoJo. When I commented on it, she said it had to do with capturing their shape as a whole.

She glanced toward the phone booths. "I was thinking of calling my mother and telling her what I'd done about refusing the cake." The way Mindy was hesitating, it seemed she wasn't sold on the idea. She looked at me. "What do you think? You met her."

She had broken my train of thought just as something had popped into my mind. I tried to stall her, knowing what I wanted to check, but she simply followed me as I went through the door into the back area and Kevin St. John's office.

I checked over the pictures on the wall until I found the one that featured Trent Nicholson and some other people. The last time I'd looked at the photo I had been struck by seeing Trent very much alive when we'd just found him dead. And now it was the same with Audrey. She was so animated in the photo and then there was the memory of how we had found her. *Just an empty vessel,* I said to myself, remembering Sammy's words. I moved on quickly to the rest of the people in the shot. I dismissed the man and focused on the woman next to him. She was just as dowdy-looking as I had remembered. But there was something about her face. Mindy was behind me rattling on about how she wondered if her mother would appreciate how important turning down the cake was. I interrupted her and asked if she could do me a favor.

Chapter 29

"Do you know who this is?" I held out the photograph I had taken off the wall and showed it to Cloris.

Cloris had a blank look and started to shake her head, but then she hesitated, and after a moment her face lit with recognition. "Of course, that's Dr. Nicholson's wife. Or more accurately the woman who was his wife." She dropped her voice to be discreet. "Who could forget that nose." The assistant manager let out a nervous laugh. "I guess the answer to your question then is that I do. In the jeans and sweatshirt, she blended in with the crowd."

"How about this. Do you recognize her?" I asked, holding Mindy's sketch in front of her.

Cloris glanced at Mindy. "Very nice, but I thought all you did were caricatures." Cloris turned to me. "This is Lisa Montez."

"Tell Cloris what you did," I said to Mindy.

"Casey showed me the photograph and asked me to draw her with a smaller nose and different hair. When I realized who it was, I added the red lipstick." She looked over the picture and brushed off a speck of something. "Lisa mentioned that she'd gone through a change recently. She wasn't kidding."

"She must have gone back to her maiden name. I wonder why she didn't say anything."

I certainly knew why. How about it made her a suspect. Talk about motive—the husband who dumped her and the woman he left her for. I was not about to explain. As far as everyone but Sammy, Lucinda and I knew, both deaths seemed to be from natural causes. It seemed best to leave it that way.

I needed to think and excused myself, saying that I was going to take advantage of the better weather and get some outside time. I knew that the other walkers had taken the path that led through the dunes. I didn't want to get caught up with joining them and took another route that I knew would be solitary. Yellow tape had been used to block the roadway that led around the buildings closed for maintenance. It was easy to get around it and I followed the path up the slope until I got a view of the ocean. Even with the clear sky, the water hit the shore with an angry fierceness. There was a drone of the engines on the heavy equipment working on the street that separated Vista Del Mar from my house. A whine from the buzz saws meant they were still working on the fallen trees. Only the street that ran between the Vista Del Mar grounds and the beach was being left as is for the moment.

There were bits of blue showing between the clouds and the sun was actually visible. It felt like the scene in the *Wizard of Oz* when it went from black and white to color. I felt my brain clear as I thought over everything I knew about Lisa Montez. She had registered for my retreat, but was that really why she had come or was it just a cover to give her access? Even with the change in her appearance, Trent must have recognized her and that was why they had the fuss the first night in the dining hall. I wondered if Audrey had recognized Lisa or if Trent had mentioned that she was there. Lisa had to be angry with both of them. I had thought before that whoever killed Trent might have tried to frame Audrey for Trent's death as a way to punish her. But why kill Audrey, unless she figured it out and was going to talk? Smothering Audrey with a pillow didn't take advance planning the way all the pill switching had been in Trent's case. It only reinforced my feeling that one death had been planned out and the other was a spontaneous reaction.

I considered just telling Lieutenant Borgnine my thoughts and letting him deal with it. Somehow it seemed incomplete, like the quitter's way out. I had quit things before without a problem, but as I stood there, it felt like something had changed—that I had changed. I straightened my posture and took a deep breath of the fresh air. I was determined to see it through myself and then I would hand Lieutenant Borgnine the killer.

The photograph and Mindy's drawings did not really mean anything. There was no law against getting a nose job and sprucing up your appearance. What if I got Lisa to talk and she spilled it all and I got it taped on my phone. My mind was clicking as I walked on top of the hill. A cloud had blotted out the sun and the light instantly dimmed. The trees cast dark shadows over the roadway and with all the closed buildings, it felt a little desolate. I started walking back to the main part of Vista Del Mar trying to come up with a plan.

I could try using what I had learned when I worked for Frank. Much as I liked to make it sound like I was out doing surveillances and tailing cheating husbands, most of what I did was phone work related to finding people. My job was to get information from people who did not want to give it. I had to get it out of them without them even realizing what they were doing. There were tricks that Frank had taught me. I was always friendly, which helped, and then seemed to be looking for confirmation on information I already had.

All I had for Lisa was the drawing folded in my pocket. Somehow, I would have to convince her that it was proof of what she had done. I turned away from the view of the ocean and looked over the grounds. Time was of the essence. The trees laying across the driveway were being cut up and moved to the side of the road. The street crew was making progress and they would have it cleared soon.

I surveyed the area near the Lodge and the small parking lot. Madeleine's golf cart had a puddle on the awning and I imagined the inside had gotten wet. I was thinking that we would have to get it dried off before she drove it home, when there was some movement nearby. Someone in a baseball cap was pulling a suitcase toward the cars. The trunk on a gray car opened, and as the suitcase was lifted into the trunk, I saw a bit of the white-blond hair.

I rushed down the hill to the Lodge to call Lieutenant Borgnine, but all I could do was leave a message. That meant I would have to do what I could on my own. There was no chance to plan my strategy, I would have to wing it.

She looked startled as I ran into the parking lot. I stopped and jogged in place as if I was cooling down from a run. "Are you going somewhere?" I said in a friendly voice.

"I want to be ready when the street is cleared," she said, looking toward the noise of the equipment.

"But there's still tomorrow. Don't you want to finish your garland?" I said.

"I learned enough to be able to do it on my own," she said. "I just want to get out of this place." She made a move to the car's door. I threw out all my plans of being friendly and catching her off guard and went for the direct approach.

"I know who you are," I said. I pulled the folded drawing out of my pocket. "Mindy drew this from a photograph taken at Dr. Nicholson's last retreat—with a few changes." I opened it to show her while I continued talking. "You dropped his last name and changed everything about yourself, but Dr. Nicholson still recognized you, didn't he?"

Her shoulders sagged. "The nerve of him telling me that I should leave because he and that wife of his might feel uncomfortable. Like I was going to care." She looked at me. "I didn't even know they were going to be here. If I had known, I never would have come. I wanted the chance to get away from it all, but without all his self-help nonsense." She chewed on the inside of her lip. "It's too bad what happened to them both. I had no idea that Trent's condition had gotten that bad. And as for Audrey—" She left it hanging. "With all that, I'm even more anxious to leave this place."

"I know that Audrey didn't die from broken-heart syndrome," I said. "In fact, someone smothered her with a pillow."

Lisa's eyebrows shot up in surprise. "That's ridiculous. Who would want to kill her?"

I didn't say anything, but kept looking at Lisa. After a moment she got my drift. "You think I killed her?" She shook her head vehemently. "She did me a favor. You have no idea how tired I was of being his assistant. Always in his shadow, his helper as he dispensed his wisdom. By the way, he definitely did not tell Leon what to do. There have been lots of Leons over the years who don't want to take responsibility for their own lives." She blew her breath out. "I turned my life around," she said, striking a pose. "And it's a lot more fun being the new me."

I was beginning to think she had gotten more out of being married to a shrink than I realized. She must have thought that she could use complete denial to get me off her case. There had to be something I could say that would get her off-balance.

"I have proof that someone switched Dr. Nicholson's pills. The cops know all about it. Who you are and your rush to leave makes you look suspicious."

"So, you think I killed both of them. Ha! I heard that you like to play detective. Well, you're wrong and it would be better for everyone if you kept your crazy ideas to yourself."

We were at a standoff and she made a grab for the drawing. She got hold of it and seemed about to tear it up. But she looked at it and said something that changed everything.

I had to think fast. The driveway had an open path between the fallen trees now and the last of the cars were being hauled away from the street as trucks lumbered through their chores. Something that looked like a snow plough was pushing away the mud and water. Any moment there would be a way out.

Once the killer made it out of the grounds, they would be out of sight, out of mind. Lieutenant Borgnine would dismiss whatever I said and his investigation would never focus on the right person. It would end up being a perfect crime. Maybe it was not exactly their original plan, but the two people had gotten the ultimate punishment.

I hid behind a stack of the cut-up logs near the stone pillars that marked the end of the Vista Del Mar grounds. And then I waited. The street cleaning continued with its repetitive rumble and then the sound got softer as the truck began to pull away.

I felt my adrenaline start to pump as I prepared for my single shot at stopping the killer. Someone else had been listening to the truck and now that it was gone, was ready to make their exit. I heard the sound of rushing footsteps and I peeked out of my hiding place just in time to see a figure pulling a suitcase toward the exit.

Now it all came down to timing. I had dismissed the idea of trying to tackle the person. All I could use was my ingenuity and what little else I had available.

I waited until the someone was almost next to my hiding spot and then I jumped out and yelled stop. It was enough to startle the wannabe escapee and distract them as they continued to move toward the exit. I held my breath as they took a few steps and there was a loud cry of surprise as their progress came to an abrupt halt and they fell forward, hitting their head on the pavement.

For once, the timing was perfect. A police cruiser turned into the driveway and stopped short and Lieutenant Borgnine jumped out.

The lieutenant rushed up to me and looked at the person on the ground.

"She tripped me," the person said in a childish whine as they rubbed their head and tried to untangle the garland of hearts from around their feet. It had been my turn to make a booby trap by tying the garland in a loop to a fallen tree branch so it would catch their foot as they tried to flee.

"Casey, do you want to explain?" the lieutenant said in his gruff voice.

Chapter 30

"Who are you?" Lieutenant Borgnine said, looking at the man seated in the mission-style chair. We had moved into the Lodge. The group was sitting right behind him and had put down their crochet hooks to hear what was going on.

"My name is James Wilson," he said. "And this crazy woman set up a booby trap. You should arrest her for assault."

"That's not your name and you know it," I said. I addressed the lieutenant and the assortment of officers who were with him. I did my best to ignore that Dane was one of them. "His name is Wilson James." I looked at the shaggy-haired man. "You should have come up with something better than just transposing your first and last names." I shrugged and continued. "He's your kil—I mean alleged killer."

I had to do a hasty show-and-tell with photographs to illustrate what I had managed to figure out. "He was staying in the cottage," I said, showing one of the photos I'd taken of the interior. "See the dream catcher with all the feathers? Remember that." I flipped ahead to the photos I'd taken of Trent's room and pointed out the bit of gray fluff on the pillow. I kept flipping until I got to the photos I had taken of Audrey's room when I had found her. I had taken a close-up of the pillow on the floor, which had some of the same gray feather fluff as was in Trent's room. I didn't mention that I had put the pieces together when I had remembered what Sammy brushed from my hair.

"I get it," Lieutenant Borgnine said. "We're supposed to believe that the gray stuff in the victims' rooms came from the dream catcher. Continue."

"The plan was to switch the pills that Trent took every night so that instead of his blood pressure drug, he would take something laced with an opioid that would overdose him." I showed the picture I'd taken of the pill bottles and plastic bag when Sammy and I had first found them in the trash before they made their trip to the dumpster. "But what's important is who James, I mean Wilson, is." I paused as they all

211

listened with rapt attention.

"All the hair and beard were a disguise," I said.

"Get to the point," Lisa Montez said impatiently. "He's Audrey's ex-husband." She looked to Mindy. "When Casey showed me the drawing you had done from that photograph, you drew Audrey's ex, too. Either you somehow recognized him as being Wilson or just decided to give him longer hair. But it was enough that I realized who he was." She glanced over the crowd. "I'm Trent's ex-wife." There was a sound of surprise from the group, most loudly from Leon, who mentioned her former nose.

I explained that Audrey and Trent had met at his last seminar weekend and then married. "I kept thinking about Trent's ex and never stopped to consider that Audrey had an ex who had been with her that weekend and who might want revenge." I looked directly at Wilson. "That's what it was all about. You wanted to kill Trent and have Audrey get the blame. You switched the pills and then probably planted the pill bottles and bag of opioid pills in her room. Your plan was to check out the next morning and be gone before anyone realized Trent was even dead."

Cloris chimed in. "That's true. He had been here all week on what he said was a personal retreat. He didn't want his meals in the dining hall or to hang out here." She gestured around the main room of the Lodge. "He was supposed to check out Thursday morning."

"But it had started to rain Wednesday night, and by Thursday morning Vista Del Mar had become an island and he couldn't leave," I said. "So what happened? Did Audrey figure out that someone was trying to frame her and tried to get rid of the evidence? Then what—she recognized you and you were afraid she would talk? The first alleged murder took planning, but Audrey's was spur-of-the-moment, probably in her sleep. I imagine that you hoped that by the time the police got here, both deaths would be chalked up to natural causes since by then the evidence was gone and the story was circulating that Audrey died from broken-heart syndrome." He turned to the lieutenant. "The alleged killer didn't realize that there is something called petechiae, which is a sign of suffocation. I'm sure the medical examiner will recognize the red dots on Audrey's face."

Sammy put up his hand to get their attention. "That was me that pointed it out," he said and did a quick bow of his head at his moment in the spotlight.

"Even with all that had happened, you believed you could get away with it. You had stayed under the radar even when we were all stranded. No one knew who you were and you thought you could slip out unnoticed. And if you were gone no one would even consider you a suspect." Wilson stayed silent.

Finally, he collected himself and spoke to the lieutenant. "It sounds like conjecture to me. Some fluff on a pillow hardly seems like evidence." His head swiveled toward me and back to the cop. "It's more like a flight of fancy from someone who thinks she's a detective."

"That's it," I said, getting annoyed. "It's no flight of fancy." I glared at Wilson. I admit I was a little thin-skinned about being dismissed as a Nancy Drew wanna-be, and I also worried that the lieutenant might believe him. I held my phone up so Borgnine could see it. "Do you know what this is?" I asked, and showed the picture of the gadget I had seen in the cottage when we went to get the towels. It was actually a trick question and the kind that cops asked. I knew exactly what it was thanks to Sammy. The lieutenant gave me an unimpressed look. "It's a handheld tablet press. What does that prove?"

"How about I took that picture in the cottage," I said. "I bet that's what was used to make the blood pressure pills laced with the opioid.

"That's ridiculous. It doesn't mean anything," Wilson said defiantly. "Who knows when she took that photo. I don't have anything like that." He was trying to sound confident, but it was beginning to wear thin. Two of the cops moved on either side of him, ready to stop him if he tried to flee.

Just then Kevin St. John stormed into the Lodge. He took a long look at all of us and then he focused on Cloris. "What's going on now? Did something else happen?"

Tag rushed in behind him and in a big romantic moment swept Lucinda into his arms and kissed her.

. . .

It took a warrant but Lieutenant Borgnine got a look in Wilson's suitcase, and no surprise, to me at least, the handheld pill maker was found wrapped in a pair of Hawaiian-print boxer shorts. The lieutenant took it in as evidence as he had a uniformed officer read Wilson his rights.

Dane came up to me. He looked around at all the commotion. "We'll have to talk later, but good work," he said under his breath before he followed the officers out. Everyone else stayed in the Lodge while I showed the lieutenant where the bodies were, and he made arrangements to have them picked up, and blocked off the two guest rooms and the cold room. I didn't bother telling him about the booby trap with the flour as I had already figured out that Audrey had done it. She must have realized she was being framed and wanted to scare me off the case.

The cops had to get statements from everyone there, which Leon found more interesting than working on the garland. The lieutenant took mine.

"What about that evidence you told me about?" he asked after he'd gotten my information. Kevin St. John watched with horror as I went back to the business area and pointed out the vault.

The stuff in the small trash can did look a little worse from being fished out of the dumpster and there was a strong scent of banana from the brownish peel that had gotten scooped up with the pill vials and papers. The lieutenant shook his head.

"I understand that you did what you thought you had to," he said.

He glanced at the can and finally continued. "It would have been better if we had found it in its original location, but it also could have disappeared." I bit my lip to keep myself from telling him how true that had almost become.

When it was time for him to leave, he leaned in close. "Thank you. You did good." His voice was gruff as usual, but I knew he meant it. He glanced up at me. "I don't suppose there are any baked goods."

I laughed and sent him off to the café for some coffee cake.

It was too late for the staff to come in and prepare dinner and the manager made an executive decision and ordered in pizzas, garlic knots and Caesar salad. He even ordered a pizza-size chocolate chip cookie for dessert.

The original activity for Saturday night had been long forgotten, but we needed to come up with something new. Everyone had a lot of pent-up energy that needed to be released. Now that Trent's body was gone, there was no worry about anyone finding the cold room and we went to remove the chairs on the upper floor of Hummingbird Hall and set it up for a dance. We found some colorful lanterns to decorate with and Kevin St. John produced some CDs with dance music.

It was strictly no partners, just wild gyrating to the pulsating beat. Cloris and I offered to fix up the cottage for Madeleine so she could have one night there, but she refused. She gave a sideways glance to Milton, who was in the middle of the dance floor, waving his arms wildly as he circled Bella and Lexie. Whatever plan she'd had for them spending some alone cozy time was kaput.

The dancing ended with a wine toast in the Lodge and they all went off to their rooms.

"We made it," Cloris said as she, Crystal and I hugged each other and prepared to go our separate ways. When I finally left, it felt strange to hear the echo of my footsteps on the dark driveway as I walked to the street. There was still a residue of mud and some puddles, but just like Vista Del Mar, my house was saved by being upslope from the mess.

All was safe and dry inside. Julius gave me an indignant stare, but when I found the note from Dane, I knew Julius's antics were all for show. Dane had listed all the times the black cat had been served his favorite food with a reminder that I was running low.

I wanted to call and thank him, but it was late on a Saturday night and I worried what I would disturb. The events of the weekend had cleared my thoughts and there was something I had to say to him. But not with somebody else listening.

Grateful to be able to sleep in my own bed, I pulled the covers up around me. Julius quit his indifferent act and cuddled next to me, purring loudly. And I drifted into an exhausted sleep.

Chapter 31

I awoke with a start and was half out of bed before I realized where I was and that I did not have to worry about breakfast for a crowd. Even so, the dining hall was my first stop when I went across the street. I arrived to a very different scene in the kitchen. There were bags of groceries on the counter and a bunch of people in white uniforms in the midst of preparing food.

My next stop was the Lodge. The overnight guy had taken over and was manning the registration desk and a couple of housekeepers were moving around the room dusting and vacuuming. The barista was back at the espresso machine in the café. It was a relief to see everything back to normal.

I joined the group for the breakfast glad that I didn't have to prepare it. It seemed as if the dancing the night before had released everyone's tension and they were all subdued. I was surprised to see Tag sitting next to Lucinda, meaning that instead of taking her home he had spent the night. Their shoulders were touching and they seemed in their own little space. Madeleine had a forlorn expression as she looked at the pair's closeness. Milton was having an animated conversation with everyone else at their table. I felt so bad for Madeleine and I wished there was a way I could fix it.

After breakfast, Crystal snagged everyone for the final workshop. She was back in her own clothes, but instead of a bunch of colors showing under her black sweater, there was only an aqua T-shirt. Her makeup seemed more subtle, too. She saw me looking and winced. "I had to do something since Stephanie was so upset with what I considered my look. I don't want to be an embarrassment to my daughter." She shrugged. "I agreed to comprise—to a point. No way am I going all neutrals."

She started them off by handing out pieces of cardboard and showing them how to pin the hearts to it and then spray them with starch. While the hearts were drying, she demonstrated making the length of chain stitches and showed them how to attach the hearts. There were protests all around that they had not made enough hearts. "I said you would all go home with a finished project," she said and turned her tote bag upside down. A cascade of red hearts poured out. "They are even already starched."

While they worked on putting the last part of the project together, the conversation started. The first topic was James, or Wilson. "I didn't even notice him until the whole thing with the cops yesterday," Leon said. "With all that hair and beard, I wouldn't have recognized him anyway." He looked at Lisa. "I didn't recognize you. But then, well, you weren't this hot when I saw you before."

Dorothy scolded him for his comment, but Lisa shrugged it off. "My job was to stay in the background so no one paid much attention to me. It was always all about Trent." She put down her hook before she continued. "I had no idea he was going to be here, though when I saw him, I didn't mind showing off my new look—like to show off what he was missing. He wasn't happy to see me and told me I should leave. I probably would have if there had been a choice.

"I suppose Audrey knew it was me, but she didn't let on and I wasn't about to enlighten her. Though I couldn't help myself and did make the comment about karma. Now I know why she said that she knew what I did, but that it didn't work. She must have thought I was the one who killed Trent and tried to frame her." Lisa turned my way. "You thought I did it, too."

"I'm so sorry, but then you were the one who pointed me toward the real killer," I said.

"She must have recognized Wilson even with all the long hair and beard," Lisa said, looking at Mindy.

"I didn't even really think about it," the artist said. "I just automatically recognized his overall shape being the same as the caricature I did of the guy staying in the cottage."

"As soon as I saw how Mindy had drawn him and Lisa told me who he was, I realized he was the one who had killed Trent and was trying to pin it on Audrey," I said.

Lisa shook her head with regret. "He seemed so mild-mannered at the retreat that I never would have guessed he would be so vengeful."

They wondered what would happen to him now and I said that he would probably be charged with the two murders, but then a jury would decide his fate.

That ended the subject and the topic became more personal. Lisa began to talk about herself. "In a strange way, I got what I wanted out of the weekend. I came here hoping to find a way to deal with my life better, and of course learn about working with yarn. It's been an adjustment to this new look." She patted the white-blond hair. "And to find out if blonds really do have more fun. This look is too extreme and not how I feel inside. But the plain Jane with the honker I used to be wasn't me either. I'm thinking somewhere in between. I want to have my brown hair again and I think a pinky shade of lipstick is less *look at me, look at me*, but I'm keeping the new nose," she said with a chuckle.

"It certainly wasn't the weekend I had planned," Dorothy said. "Everything went wrong. The food didn't arrive. Most of my people didn't arrive. Two people dying and it turning out to be murder. Whew, that was a lot." She patted Mindy's hand. "I'm so sorry that your mother won't be pleased. You can tell her it's my fault."

Mindy had a big smile. "As far as I'm concerned, your retreat worked for me. That epiphany I had when I said no to more cake means everything. When I realized how I honestly felt—" She shook her head is amazement. "I think it's a change that will last too." She stood up and pulled out the loose apricot sweatshirt she was wearing. "You can't tell because it was so baggy to start with, but it's looser." She chuckled. "Who knows, maybe I even lost five pounds." She looked over the group. "And I used my art to help solve a murder." She turned to Dorothy. "So, don't worry about my mother. I've decided not to."

JoJo took the floor next. "I'm not sure if I told all of you what I learned over my many, many wellness retreats," she said, punctuating it with a self-deprecating chuckle. "And it was reconfirmed by this one. It's not what the program promises, it's what you do with it." She gave a meaningful look at Leon.

He let out a heavy sigh. "I get it. Continuing to blame Dr. Nicholson or anyone else for the mess in my life isn't going to make a difference for me. It's up to me to fix it." He had lost the angry scowl as his gaze moved around the group. "I called my wife this morning and told her how much I miss her and what a mistake I made." He stopped and took a deep breath. "I took a shot and asked her for another chance." He appeared hopeful as he said they were going to have dinner to discuss it. There were *aww* sounds all around and then a smattering of applause. That is, except from Evie Delano, who was taping the moment on her phone.

"I'm sorry, I'm sorry," she said. "I was going to ask your permission before I posted it." She shrugged. "It's not like I could do it from here anyway." She gazed at her phone lovingly. "I know what I said about thinking some of my followers might be stalking me and that they were unrelenting in demands for more posts. But I missed their feedback and all that attention. I would lose my sponsors, too." She pushed the brim of her floppy hat up. "I can't help myself, or really, I don't want to." She turned to JoJo. "JoJo's company is going to be one of my sponsors now and I'm going to start mentioning her soap in my posts. You all know firsthand that it really is great." Her glance went to Cloris. "I could certainly mention this place, too. Just tell me how you would like me to present it."

"I'm speaking for Lexie and me," Bella began. "We were thrilled with the weekend, even with being stranded, and of course we're sorry about the two people who died and that James or Wilson ended up being arrested." She let her gaze take in all of them. "Working with yarn in a group was all that we hoped for. We got to know all of you and got to make something to remember this weekend by."

Lexie started unloading all of the little crochet creations they had showed off when they first arrived. "We want you all to have your own support amigurumi," she said. As everyone went to pick one out, JoJo took out handfuls of her business cards attached to small bars of her fragrant soap and handed them out as well.

"I guess I'm next," Milton said, addressing the group. "I got mostly what I came for," he said without giving any details. "Since we're giving out things, I thought I could make you all characters in my next book and give you a signed copy of my current one." They all accepted his offer with smiles. Only Madeleine looked bereft. I was really going to have to fix it.

Tag was sitting next to Lucinda trying to use one of the kits. His row of stitches looked perfect and then one was uneven. Shaking his head with frustration, he ripped everything out and put down the hook and yarn. "I'm glad to be here. I was so worried." He looked at Lucinda. "All I could think about was seeing you again." He took a deep breath. "I didn't even care if the knives were crooked." Lucinda's eyes widened in shock and she leaned over, kissing him on the cheek.

• • •

Lunch was over and everyone gathered in the Lodge to check out and hang out a last time. They all thanked Crystal and showed off their completed garlands. Even Leon, who said he was going to offer his to his wife. "It's kind of mushy," he said. "You know, like I'm offering her my heart."

There was the sharing of emails and promises to subscribe to Evie's YouTube channel. Mindy handed out the caricatures she had done of all of them. I was glad to see she had drawn a new one of Leon that didn't have his head erupting. They were all lingering, not quite ready to say goodbye.

Except for Madeleine. She had gotten her suitcase and told me she was leaving. She seemed in a huff as she went out the door and I knew I had to do something.

I found Milton dropping off signed copies of his book in the gift shop and pulled him aside.

There was no time to be subtle and I went to confront him directly. "What exactly did you come here for?" I began. "You must have known that Madeleine thought it had to do with seeing her." I didn't mention her plan to stay in the cottage, not wanting to completely give away her expectations and disappointment.

He looked down and seemed uncomfortable. "I'm sorry," he began. "I did want to see her, but there's a problem." He heaved a deep breath. "She's wealthy and I'm not even close. I know her sister thinks I'm a fortune hunter. I didn't want to go there for dinner and have Cora put me in a corner when there wasn't anything I could say about my prospects." He looked into the main room at the knot of people getting ready to depart. "I came here this weekend because there were numerous retreats going on and I wanted to study how they were done. I thought if I could put together a business of putting on weekends for mystery writers, I would have something more to offer." He looked up at me. "I have my pride."

I thought about how upset Madeleine was and how rejected she felt. "Why didn't you tell her?" I said, throwing my hands up in frustration. "You should have told her how you feel. All of it. She thinks you don't care and now she's going home." A voice in my head said that I was a fine one to talk.

Milton snapped to attention. "I was waiting until I had something concrete to show her. I had no idea she would take it that way." He looked around hopelessly and said he had to find her.

I thought of the de rigueur scene in every rom-com when someone ends up running to catch up to their beloved before they flew off to Paris or got on a boat. "Then you better hurry. She's parked near the Lodge." He dashed off before I could wish him luck.

There were final hugs and then the ones who had driven went to their cars and those who'd flown got in the van to go to the airport.

Lucinda and Tag were sitting by the fireplace, enjoying each other's company. Kevin St. John was pacing behind the registration counter and seemed frustrated. Crystal was pulling her plastic bin of supplies and heading to the door. She saw me looking at the manager and she chuckled. "He's probably upset that everything worked out without him."

Sammy and Cloris were on their way into the café. They stopped and he brushed his hand against her hair and a glowing butterfly appeared. It felt a little bittersweet, but I was happy that they had found each other.

When I went outside to go home, Madeleine's golf cart was stopped in the middle of the driveway. I chuckled that Milton had caught up with her, but then golf carts only go so fast. He was holding her hand and looking into her eyes. She was absolutely glowing.

• • •

It was a relief to go back to the Blue Door that night. I looked forward to the peace of going into the closed restaurant and baking the desserts and muffins. I turned on the soft jazz and started in on the apple pies.

Dane had agreed to come by and we were finally going to have "the talk." There was something final about it and I was ready to deal with whatever.

The knock came just as I was putting the new version of the pies in the oven. The weekend of cooking for the group had made me want to expand my horizons. I had made them in a rectangle shape with a shortbread crust.

"This is it," I muttered to myself as I went to the door. My mouth felt dry. I was surprised at how nervous I felt, but then this was new territory.

He was wearing jeans and a pocket T-shirt under a hoodie. We said our hellos and then went to the sunporch. Neither of us sat and I avoided looking him in the eye, not sure how he would react to what I was going to say.

"Well, it looks like you survived," he said in a light tone. It seemed like it was going to lead to some small talk and I wanted to get the whole thing over with.

"We might as well cut to the chase," I began.

"Uh-oh," he mumbled. "Look, I'm sorry—" I put my hand up to cut him off before he could say more.

"I have something to say first." I forced myself to stand a little taller, hoping it would make what I was going to say easier. "When I heard about you and Stacy—from virtually everyone in town—I was going to react in my usual way. I would cut my losses and leave Cadbury, my baking jobs, the yarn retreats—all of it. And I would do something else, somewhere else. "But—" I looked in his direction but not at him directly, still not ready to see his reaction. "This has become my home. I have friends, a house, my work and a life. I don't want to leave."

"You don't have to," he started and I cut him off again.

"I'm not finished. All this is very hard for me. So please don't stop me."

He put up his hands in capitulation. "Okay then, go for it," he said, clearly curious.

"I know that I have told everyone that I am okay with you and Stacy having your second chance, but I realized it wasn't fair to not tell you the truth and how I really feel. I am not going to go quietly into the background. Stacy might be part of your past, but I'm the one in your present." I was beginning to falter, but pushed myself to go on. "And, well, you offered your heart to me before and—" I reached in my pocket and took out one of the crocheted hearts I had made. "And now I'm offering you mine."

Now, I finally looked for the reaction in his eyes. "I don't know what to say," he stammered. "It's such a romantic gesture."

"I know and not like me. I get it. You've already moved on." I let out a heavy sigh. "Sorry if I made you uncomfortable, but at least I was honest about how I feel. Go on and be happy. You can keep the heart and give it to Stacy. But I wouldn't tell her where you got it." I tried to sound like I was taking it all so well that I could joke about the heart and started to move him toward the door. But he stopped me and shook his head. "How about you let me have my say."

I didn't want to prolong the misery, but it seemed like I had no choice. "Proceed," I said, preparing for the truth.

"Finally, finally you stopped having one foot out the door," he said. "And admitted that you want to stay here. And you admitted what I knew all along. You love me, you really love me," he said in a singsong tone with a smile. I went back to pushing him to the door.

"I've heard enough." It was my worst nightmare. I had been open and vulnerable and he was teasing me about my feelings. Instead of getting the message and leaving, he planted himself and looked me in the eye.

"If you hadn't insisted on finishing your piece—which, by the way, was great and what I have been waiting to hear—I would have told you that Stacy left. It was a temporary fantasy about a second chance, but as you said, she was part of my past and you are my present and hopefully future. Now, if you'll stop trying to push me out the door." He wrapped his arms around me as it all started to sink in. "We have some catching up to do. I want to hear all about your weekend and how you all managed to survive."

He sealed it all with a kiss that neither of us wanted to end and was only broken when the timer buzzed, notifying me that the pie was ready.

Garland of Hearts

These directions are for a garland for a door or window.

It's a good idea to use a stitch marker for the first and last stitch of each row of the heart, so that stitches are not lost. It's helpful to make a list of rows and check off when completed. It is a good idea to count stitches as each row is completed. The heart shape gets more defined with the two rows of edging and when blocked.

The hearts are approximately 5 inches across. The size of the length of the strand that holds them together depends on where it will be hung.

Stitches used are Chain (ch) and Single Crochet (sc)

Supplies:

1 skein Peaches & Crème Original, red. worsted, 4-ply. 2.5oz/70.9g, 120yds/109m, 100 percent cotton

Size J 6.00 mm hook

Tapestry needle

2 small stitch holders

Piece of cardboard

Pushpins

Spray starch

Hearts (Make 5)

Ch 9

Row 1: Sc in second ch from hook and across, ch 1, turn (8)

Rows 2–5: Sc across, ch 1, turn (8)

Row 6: Sc in 4 stitches, ch 1, turn (4)

Rows 7–8: Sc across, ch 1, turn (4)

Row 9: Sc across, ch 1 (4)

Edging Row 1: Sc around. Mark the first stitch. At the bottom point (where the slipknot is), sc, ch 1, sc in the same stitch. Sl St to the marked first stich, ch 1.

Edging Row 2: Sc around with sc, ch 1, sc in the same stitch at the bottom point. Slp St to first sc, fasten off and weave in ends.

To block heart, shape, and use pushpins to attach to the cardboard. Spray with spray starch until damp and let dry.

Make a strand of chain stitches to fit the space where the garland is to be hung. Finish off and weave in ends. Lay out strand and arrange the hearts. Attach hearts by using a small length of the yarn to tie them through a chain. Trim excess.

Happy Days Retro Cake

2 cups flour
1¼ cups sugar
2 teaspoons baking soda
2 eggs beaten
2 teaspoons vanilla extract
1 15.25-ounce can fruit cocktail in syrup, undrained

Topping
¾ cup brown sugar
¾ cup pecans or walnuts, chopped
4 tablespoons butter cut in small pieces.

Preheat oven to 350 degrees. Prepare a 9 x 13 pan by greasing or lining with parchment paper.

Mix the flour, sugar and baking soda in a medium bowl.

In a small bowl, mix the eggs, vanilla and undrained fruit cocktail.

Pour the liquid mixture over the dry mixture and combine by hand.

Pour the batter into the pan.

Combine the brown sugar and nuts and sprinkle evenly over the batter.

Arrange the butter pieces evenly over the topping.

Bake for 40–45 minutes, until a toothpick comes out clean. Can be served with a dollop of whipped cream. Enjoy!

About the Author

Betty Hechtman is the national bestselling author of the Crochet Mysteries and the Yarn Retreat Mysteries. Handicrafts and writing are her passions and she is thrilled to be able to combine them in both of her series. She also writes the Writer for Hire Mysteries, which are set in her Chicago neighborhood of Hyde Park and have a touch of crochet.

Betty grew up on the South Side of Chicago and has a degree in Fine Art. Since College, she has studied everything from improv comedy to magic. She has had an assortment of professions, including volunteer farm worker picking fruit on a kibbutz tucked between Lebanon and Syria, nanny at a summer resort, waitress at a coffee house, telephone operator, office worker at the Writer's Guild, public relations assistant at a firm with celebrity clients, and newsletter editor at a Waldorf school. She has written newspaper and magazine pieces, short stories, screenplays, and a middle-grade mystery, *Stolen Treasure*. She lives with her family and stash of yarn in Southern California.

See BettyHechtman.com for more information, excerpts from all her books, and photos of all the projects of the patterns included in her books. She blogs on Fridays at Killerhobbies.blogspot.com, and you can join her on Facebook at BettyHechtmanAuthor.

Made in United States
North Haven, CT
25 May 2024

52946677R00143